I can't handle i...

Despite everything he ... uttered those words of ... tough, hard core of him ... *...n take this, dammit.*

But the problem with Pat was that she undermined his toughness. Awoke tender emotions. When he was around her, the only part of him capable of hardness seemed to be his too-easily-aroused body.

He wanted her with a hunger that was more than physical. A selfish hunger.

Pat would be good for him.

But he wasn't good enough for her.

Hell, his struggle to control himself around her was proof in itself of his inadequacy.

It was a bitter pill to swallow. But Clint finally had to admit that battling his desire for Pat might prove to be too much for him.

And that when he reached the breaking point...he would have to go.

Dear Reader,

We hope you will enjoy the many books coming your way from Silhouette Special Edition® this month. We've certainly tried to warm up your winter!

Make sure you don't miss the warm and wonderful story of Steve Anderson from *Room for Annie*. He's looking for love in Montana and meets Myrna Temte's THAT SPECIAL WOMAN! in *A Lawman for Kelly*.

Then for those of you who love a baby story there's Cathy Gillen Thacker's latest, *Matchmaking Baby*, where Joanie's old flame turns up just as someone leaves a baby on her doorstep—and so he thinks he's a dad!

There are two gorgeous lawmen heroes in Cheryl Reavis's *Mother To Be* and Sharon De Vita's *The Lady and the Sheriff*, a burly ex-marine in *The Wrong Man...the Right Time* and a rancher looking for a wife in *Texas Dawn*. So we've given you plenty of strong men to fantasise about this month, that's for sure.

Have fun and come back for more wonderful romantic reading next month.

The Editors

The Wrong Man...
the Right Time

CAROLE HALSTON

SILHOUETTE

SPECIAL EDITION

*Silhouette, Silhouette Special Edition and Colophon are
registered trademarks of Harlequin Books S.A., used under licence.*

*First published in Great Britain 1997
Silhouette Books, Eton House, 18-24 Paradise Road,
Richmond, Surrey TW9 1SR*

© Carole Halston 1997

ISBN 0 373 24089 9

23-9711

*Printed and bound in Great Britain
by Mackays of Chatham PLC, Chatham*

CAROLE HALSTON

is a Louisiana native residing in a rural area north of New Orleans. She enjoys travelling with her husband to research less-familiar locations for settings but is always happy to return home to her own unique region, a rich source in itself for romantic stories about warm, wonderful people.

Other novels by Carole Halston

Silhouette Special Edition®

Chapter One

In Yellville, Arkansas, population 1,181, Clint Adams stopped for gas. He gritted his teeth against the pain as he got out of his Chevy Suburban, which contained his worldly possessions. His bum leg hurt like hell.

Clint could endure the constant throbbing. It was the tremor in his muscles, the physical exhaustion, which made him want to yell out a string of curse words and vent his anger over being turned into a damned weakling. His long stay in the hospital had melted ten pounds off his big-boned frame. Another six weeks of lying around after he'd left the hospital hadn't put the weight back on or given him back his strength.

"Don't rush things, Sergeant. Take it easy for another month or two," the doctor, an orthopedic specialist, had advised a week ago when he'd taken the cast off Clint's leg. *"Let that leg mend and build your stamina back up gradually."*

"Build it for what, Doc?" Clint had answered bitterly.

His career in the marines was over. For Clint, who'd joined at eighteen and finally found a home, that meant his life was over at age thirty-five.

Clint cursed himself under his breath as he hobbled awkwardly to the rear of the Suburban to unscrew the gas cap. Something as easy as gassing up an automobile became an ordeal when you weren't mobile.

Holding the pump nozzle in place with his right hand, Clint braced himself with his left hand against the sturdy black metal of the carryall vehicle he'd bought secondhand up in Chicago, where he'd set out on his trip south to the Ozarks. He was within twenty miles of his destination, the Buffalo National River. It seemed a long way, after pushing himself and traveling hard all day for no good reason. After all, what was the hurry?

At the end of the row of gas pumps was an air hose. Clint noted it, thinking dully, *I should check the pressure in my tires.* He shook his head, knowing that limping the distance around the big vehicle from tire to tire, and bending or squatting, amounted to more punishment than he was up to. "Helpless cripple," he muttered to himself just as an oversize van pulled up smartly alongside the air hose. Lively bluegrass music spilled out the rolled-down windows.

Clint glanced up and read the faded legend stenciled in bold letters on the side of the van: Tyler Canoe & Cabin Rental. In a reflex action, he lifted the hand splayed against the side of the Suburban and touched the pocket of his shirt, feeling the crackle of the folded brochure he'd stuck there. Without thinking, he also shifted his balance, resting his weight on both feet. A stab of pain in his injured leg brought a grimace to his face.

The driver's door of the van swung open and out hopped a slim brunette woman, humming the catchy tune of the bluegrass music. Her ponytail bobbed as she gave the door an energetic slam. Looking over at Clint, she smiled, radiating small-town friendliness.

Clint nodded, feeling at least a hundred years old.

Her eyes were blue, and expressive, like her face. She held his gaze a second or two longer, beaming her vitality at him. Then her smile faltered. Clint realized he was scowling.

"Hi there, Pat." A male voice, hailing someone, drew her attention. She turned her head, as did Clint, toward the gas-station building. A sandy-haired man in neatly-pressed khaki slacks and a red knit sports shirt had emerged and was making a beeline toward her.

"Hi, Jeremy," she hailed him back. By this time she was on her way to the air hose.

"I have a slow leak in this rear tire," she explained, pulling the hose with an efficient movement. In her other hand she held a tire-pressure gauge.

Jeremy had reached her. "Let me do that for you."

"I'm not a paying customer." The protest was slightly embarrassed. She relinquished the hose and gauge without further resistance.

"How's business this spring?" he inquired, squatting in front of the tire. "Lots of canoers?"

"More than I can book trips for, with just this van for shuttle service. Dad's old bus bit the dust last year. The guy I hired up and quit, so I don't have a driver. Homer Perkins, bless his old heart, helps out by minding the store for me while I'm out transporting parties myself." She related her problems so cheerfully they barely sounded like complaints.

"You need someone with a chauffeur's license, don't you?"

"Right. And someone reliable and sober who wants seasonal work with no benefits. It's a tall order," she added.

"I'm shorthanded myself," Jeremy said, rising, having finished using the air hose. "Candy Owens, who's been working for me since she was in high school, got married and moved to Harrison."

"I noticed your Help Wanted sign in the window."

"Hey, Jeremy! Telephone!" A mechanic bawled the message from the large doorway of the garage portion of the gas station, interrupting the conversation Clint couldn't have helped overhearing unless he was deaf. "It's one of your kids calling!"

"Excuse me, Pat," Jeremy said with obvious regret. "It's probably nothing important, but you never know. Say, if you're not in a hurry, come in and have a soft drink," he invited over his shoulder as he trotted away.

"Thank you. I will," she answered after the briefest hesitation.

Clint had finished pumping his gas and was replacing the nozzle, jamming it home. He sensed her glancing toward him as he reached for the cap for his gas tank, which he'd set on the roof of the Suburban. The damned cap seemed to jump out of his fingers, fell to the pavement and rolled several yards toward her van. Clint muttered a profanity low enough that it wouldn't reach her ears.

In the time it took him to cope with his disgust for his clumsiness and take one halting step, she'd reached the cap and picked it up. "Here you go," she said, bringing it to him. "The automakers should attach these things, shouldn't they?"

His hand brushed hers as he took the cap. The accidental touch was like a fleeting connection with her buoyant spirit. Clint was struck by an urge to grasp her hand and hold it, as though he could tap into her zest for life. His own neediness filled him with self-contempt.

"Thank you," he said, not sounding grateful.

"You're welcome."

While he was screwing the cap on, she walked to the driver's side of the van with her springy stride and tossed the tire-pressure gauge inside. Then she headed for the building to take the fellow Jeremy up on his offer of a soft drink. Clint limped along behind her, his jaw clenched against the shooting pains in his injured leg. The jaunty swish of her ponytail made him feel more decrepit.

As they came nearer to the plate-glass door, Clint quickened his gait, wanting to reach it first and hold it open for her. He made no pretense of being a gentleman, but he was used to performing routine courtesies for women. Sweat popped out on his brow, the sheer agony of overexercising his damaged ligaments and tendons slowing him down again.

She swung the door open for herself, but instead of entering, she held it open, looking back at him. Her smile held a hint of self-consciousness that Clint barely registered. He was too stung by the sympathy in her blue eyes. His self-esteem had taken a lot of kicks during the hellish weeks just past. To be seen by her as an object of pity was like a killing blow to his male pride.

"I'm not handicapped," he said harshly.

"Sorry," she apologized and slipped inside ahead of him.

Entering, Clint saw that the guy Jeremy was behind the counter talking on the phone. From his end of the conversation, he was obviously settling a childish dispute. "It's Mandy's day to watch her program, Jerry. You can run next door with a videotape and ask Mrs. Roberts to tape your program. I'm sure she'll be happy to do that for you. Yes, if she invites you, you can stay at her house and watch it. But don't invite yourself. Got that? You two behave yourselves until I get home and don't give Mrs. Grambly any trouble." He rolled his eyes at Pat, grinning good-naturedly as he hung up.

"Big crisis?" she inquired. She was standing at the counter, her hands stuck in her front jeans pockets.

"Major crisis," he replied. "The VCR's on the blink. My son can't tape the daily episode of a situation comedy that he's probably seen four or five times, at least. He tried to bribe his little sister into missing her cartoon show, but she held her ground."

"You don't mean to tell me you're a family with only one TV in the house?"

Jeremy nodded. "My two kids consider themselves deprived."

There'd been no mention of his kids' mother. Clint deduced that she was out of the picture and that Jeremy, who either owned or managed the gas station, was a single man again, interested in dating Pat. She had probably come by the station for the main purpose of seeing him.

The way they were ignoring Clint, he might have to stand there in the background, his damn leg hurting, while they made a date.

"If you don't mind, I'd like to pay for my gas," he said, hauling out his wallet as he limped forward. "Then I'll get out of here and let you two get on with your courting in private." His voice sounded angry and resentful to his own ears, deepening his self-contempt. He was like a wounded dog, snarling at innocent people.

Their heads snapped around toward him. Jeremy's fair-skinned face turned almost as red as his shirt. Pat's cheeks were pink with embarrassment, too, but her blue eyes flashed with indignation.

"You don't have to be *rude!*" she exclaimed. "If you're planning to spend some time here in Arkansas, you'd better work on your attitude!"

"That'll be nineteen dollars and eighty-nine cents," Jeremy said, quickly intervening in a courteous tone. "Is there anything else you need today, sir?"

Clint shook his head rather than risk growling an answer and making more of a sorry spectacle of himself. He slapped a twenty on the counter and hobbled out without waiting for his change, conscious that they were watching him go.

They made a good-looking couple, both of them so wholesome and likable. Clint should wish them well in their budding romance. The fact that he didn't, added to his misery.

"You think he's a disabled veteran?" Pat Tyler broke the awkward silence, her gaze trained on the tall, gaunt stranger headed toward his black automobile. His vehicle was as somber and rugged as he was. "Those are military fatigues he's wearing, aren't they?"

"Yes, and something tells me they were issued to him. He didn't buy them in a store," Jeremy replied. "My bet would be Marine Corps. As for the 'disabled' part, I sure wouldn't care to take him on in a fistfight. He strikes me as a tough customer."

"Me, too." Pat shoved her right hand deeper into her pocket, recalling the brief contact that had occurred when the stranger took the gas cap from her. Touching him had been like touching his pain and raw masculinity. "I shouldn't have been nasty to him. He might have injured his leg in the service of our country."

"You weren't all that nasty." Jeremy grinned sheepishly, transferring his attention to her. "The guy hit the nail on the head, as far as my intentions go. I've been working up my courage to ask you out."

"I've been expecting you to ask me for a date," she admitted. "So has everybody else in Marion County, for that matter." Pat glanced up to see the black Suburban pulling out onto the highway. She watched it drive away. An odd regret tugged at her.

"It's been two years since Susan died," Jeremy said, his voice sober. "I haven't dated anyone up until now. It's been so hard to think of myself as single."

Pat smiled at him with compassion. All the embarrassment had faded from the conversation and, along with it, any element of excitement. "You and Susan were so happily married. The thought of dating probably makes you feel unfaithful to her."

"Exactly."

"But you're lonely and need companionship."

"That's the situation in a nutshell, Pat." He went on. "So how about it? Would you like to have dinner with me tonight at the Front Porch?"

"It'll be the same as making an announcement in the

newspaper that we're going together. People will start asking about the wedding date."

He grinned, shrugging. "I'm ready to face the music. What about you?"

Pat made a rueful face, but her reply was earnest. "I've always liked you, Jeremy, and my evenings get awfully lonely these days, with both my parents gone."

It was his turn to look compassionate. "You lost your dad just a year ago. I know you miss him terribly. You two were very close, weren't you?"

She nodded, swallowing at a lump in her throat.

"If nothing else, we can be good company for each other." Jeremy's words were gentle. "Shall I pick you up out at your place—say, about seven o'clock?"

"That's a long way for you to drive. I live thirteen miles out of town. Why don't I just meet you at the Front Porch?"

He was insistent on picking her up. "This may not be the most romantic first date, but it's still a date," he declared.

Pat didn't argue further.

The gas station suddenly got busy. She said goodbye, mentioning that she had errands to run around town. As she climbed back into her old van, still parked by the air hose, Pat smothered a sigh. *It'll be fun to go out with Jeremy tonight,* she told herself, trying to kindle the anticipation that was lacking.

One of her errands was to drop off a stack of her home-made brochures at the chamber-of-commerce office, which doubled as a tourist welcome center. Her mission accomplished, Pat stepped out onto the sidewalk and saw a black Suburban driving past on the street. It braked, and her heart gave a wild leap. Then she noted that the driver was a woman and she felt a foolish letdown.

It wasn't the gaunt stranger's automobile. He was miles away by now, headed perhaps to Louisiana or Texas. Pat would never see him again. Never know his name or his story. Unless he was featured someday on one of those missing-persons TV shows.

Pat couldn't imagine that she would forget him anytime soon. His fierce dark eyes. His somber face. The tense line of his jaw with a muscle twitching in his hard cheek. His tall, big-boned body and halting gait. She even recalled small details, like the outline of a folded piece of paper in his shirt pocket. A letter from a woman? A sexy blonde or redhead, no doubt. Not a girl-next-door type like herself.

"The guy was a jerk," Pat said aloud to dispel her own wistfulness. She shoved aside thoughts of the man who'd hardly made a good impression on her. He'd been gruff and unfriendly. Five minutes in his company would probably cure her fascination.

Still, she couldn't help wishing that Jeremy, nice guy that he was, had some of the same effect on her. Then she might feel more eagerness about their date tonight.

Clint pulled the brochure for Tyler Canoe & Cabin Rental from his pocket when he was a few miles out of town. He'd picked it up an hour earlier in Mountain Home at a bustling tourist center staffed by helpful elderly women. The plain homemade brochure, probably produced on a copy machine, had caught his eye. It had stuck out among the slick, more professional advertisements of outfitting companies in the vicinity of the Buffalo National River.

He figured the cabins were rustic, but all he required was a roof over his head for a night or two. Then he would be headed back north to Chicago, for want of anywhere else to go.

It had been foolish of him not to call from Mountain Home and make sure he could rent a cabin tonight. But the number on the brochure wasn't a toll-free number, and Clint hadn't had any change in his pocket to use a pay phone at the tourist center. So he'd just stuffed the brochure into his pocket. Seated once again behind the wheel of his automobile, he'd given tired consideration to checking into a motel. Then he'd cursed his weakened condition and kept on driving.

The inside of the brochure was a crudely-drawn map. Clint consulted it and tossed the brochure onto the passenger seat.

The scenery became rugged as the two-lane highway dipped and climbed and crested steep foothills with wooded slopes. The modest homes were spread farther and farther apart, sometimes separated by miles of dense pine and hardwood forests. Clint had to keep both hands on the wheel to execute hairpin curves. His leg throbbed. His head ached. He thought longingly of an ice-cold beer.

I'll buy a six-pack, he promised himself. The brochure made mention of a convenience store, and surely he could buy beer and soft drinks there.

The headache had gotten worse by the time Clint eventually spotted a sign on his left alerting him that Tyler Canoe & Cabin Rental was a mile ahead. The faded block lettering looked familiar. The same amateur sign-painter had probably stenciled the name of the mom-and-pop enterprise on the shuttle van back in Yellville.

Another sign that read Tyler's and featured a long arrow directed Clint onto a gravel road that brought him eventually to a one-story frame building with a large gravel parking lot. In front of the building sat a single gas pump. To the right were several canoe racks, partially filled with canoes, and an old derelict bus set on blocks. On the left a narrow road wound up a hill into a pine thicket. Clint could just barely make out a small log cabin with a front porch.

Not a single person in sight anywhere. No signs of life. The several automobiles had the look of having been parked there for hours. Two bore out-of-state license plates. The third was an ancient pickup. Clint pulled up beside it and killed the engine of the Suburban. Not a sound came to his ears through the open car window. The quiet was like a balm on his raw spirit.

A movement drew his attention. A huge mixed-breed dog had come around the corner of the building, walking with slow dignity. The animal approached the Suburban and stood as though patiently waiting while Clint got out, grunting with the pain.

"Are you planning to bite a hunk out of me, fella?" he asked, holding out his hand. The dog came nearer in response to the invitation. Balancing on his good leg, Clint leaned down to pet him. His coat was short and stiff, dark brown liberally sprinkled with gray. "You're getting up in years, aren't you, old guy?"

His answer was a warm lick on his fingers that held more comfort than any words of commiseration that had been spoken to him during the last nine weeks.

The door to the building was flanked on one side by an oblong plate-glass window and on the other, by a row of windows with panes. A bell tinkled when Clint thrust open the door and stepped inside what was obviously the convenience store mentioned in the brochure. The cheery noise of the bell died away, the last sound waves drowned out by the snores of an old man napping in a rocking chair, one of three mismatched chairs grouped sociably around a table that had been discarded from some kitchen in years past.

Clint cleared his throat loudly, and the old man's eyes popped open.

"Howdy," he said in a rural accent. "Guess mebbe I dozed off and grabbed a few winks. Et too much dinner." He patted a rounded belly loosely covered by a pair of denim overalls worn over a long-sleeve plaid shirt buttoned snugly at the throat. "Turnip greens and corn bread and a poke chop. Ain't nothin' better than a mess of turnip greens out of the garden."

"I'll have to take your word for it," Clint said. "Are you the person I talk to about renting a cabin?"

"I shore am." He heaved himself to his feet, rising to his full height of five feet six or seven. "Name's Homer

Perkins. Me and Pat Tyler grew up together as boys, went squirrel huntin' and fishin'. It's a sad thing to go to the funeral of an old friend like him. He passed away a year ago this month," Homer added. "Heart trouble. His wife, Lorna, a real fine woman, she passed on three years ago. Cancer. Terrible disease." He shook his head. "What was it you was askin' about? Oh, that's right, about rentin' a cabin."

"You have one available?"

"Let me check and see." He made his way unhurriedly toward a counter with a cash register, talking as he went. "I know for sure that two out of the three of 'em is spoken for. Folks usually call up and reserve 'em by the week. The rate's cheaper. Though it ain't cheap, not in my book. Money don't buy what it used to. 'Course them cabins is nice enough to live in, even got a microwave oven. Pat built 'em hisself with his gal's help. She was always a little tomboy, tagged around after him."

Behind the counter now, Homer paused to adjust the straps of his overalls, settling them more comfortably on his shoulders, before he began to rummage in a drawer, continuing to ramble on. "Lorna and Pat had done give up on havin' any young'uns when Lorna got in the family way. Pat was some tickled. They was both sure it was a boy. Took to calling it Little Pat before it was ever born. The name stuck when, lo and behold, Little Pat turned out to be a girl." He chuckled, his expression reminiscent.

Clint hobbled over close to the counter so that he could lean on it and rest his leg. "Having any luck?" he inquired.

Homer looked at him blankly. "Forgot what I was doing for a minute there," he admitted. "Us old geezers get forgetful." He cast a hopeful glance out toward the road before he resumed his rummaging. "That gal of Pat's ought to be back from town soon. She's got her pa's easygoing disposition. Sure would like to see her settle down with a good man before she turns into an old maid. Folks have been kind of hoping her and Jeremy Wells might get together. He owns a gas station in Yellville. Him and his wife moved to Arkansas from Memphis, Tennessee, 'bout eight or ten years ago. Purty black-haired gal. She up and died a couple of years back, without being sick a day. A vein or artery busted in her brain.''

Clint silently supplied the medical term. A brain aneurysm. He straightened from the counter, hit by a wave of fatigue.

"Hold on," Homer said. "I don't see any slip filled out on that cabin up on the hill, overlookin' the holler, so I'll rent it to you, if you want it."

"How much?" Clint pulled out his wallet.

"Fifty dollars. Told you the price was steep," the old man added, making his own interpretation when Clint hesitated, frowning.

"How much for a week?"

"Three hunnerd even."

Clint counted out three one-hundred-dollar bills.

Homer left the money lying on the counter while he found a blank registration card in the drawer. Clint printed the usual information while the old man rattled directions for finding the cabin and located the key. After Clint had pocketed the key, he limped down an aisle to the coolers along the back wall. All he saw was bottled and canned soft drinks. Fruit juice. Mineral water. No beer.

"Dry county," Homer called.

Clint cursed under his breath. He snatched a six-pack of cola, paid for it and left.

The cabin was the same one he'd glimpsed from the parking lot. Clint lugged his duffel bag inside and dropped it on the floor. A weary glance around told him that the cabin interior was clean and comfortable. There were homey touches, like a large, round, hooked rug in the sitting area and a colorful wall decoration over the sofa—a rooster made out of various beans and corn kernels glued onto a painted board.

Through an open doorway into an adjoining room, Clint

could see a double bed. A flight of stairs led up to a loft that would be furnished with more beds. The place was much too big for him. It would accommodate a family. Tomorrow when he was rested up, he would probably regret his impulse to plunk down a week's rent, Clint reflected wearily, yanking a can from the six-pack of colas on his way over to a full-size refrigerator in the kitchen area.

The refrigerator was spotlessly clean inside, empty except for a box of baking soda. He dropped the rest of the six-pack onto a shelf and limped to a back door leading onto a screened porch. Out on the porch, he sank down into a crude homemade chair and straightened his bad leg. It throbbed painfully. His head ached. Fatigue weighed him down. He had to summon the energy to pop open the cola.

"Damned dry county," he muttered, taking a swig. Tipping back his head, he rested it against the rough wall of the porch and closed his eyes, shutting out the tranquil view of a green meadow sloping down into a hollow and in the far distance a valley with foothills forming a backdrop. His stomach growled, and hunger was added to all his other discomforts.

Chapter Two

"Feller rented the cabin overlookin' the holler," Homer said. He was filling Pat in on the business he'd carried out in her absence. "Paid cash. Money's in the register, and the card he filled out is there on the counter. Didn't notice until after he'd done gone that he just wrote in Chicago, Illinois, for his home address and didn't give any telephone number."

"The main information aside from the person's name is the make of automobile and the license number," Pat replied, soothing his concern over the incomplete guest-registry card.

"That's all there. Name's Clint Adams. Wonder if he's kin to them Adamses over in Flippin. Don't reckon he is. They all got that orange-colored hair and blue eyes that bug out."

"How many in the party?" she asked.

"Jest him. Looked all tuckered out. Figured he was travelin' through, on his way to somewhere. Wasn't carryin' no canoe on top of his vehicle. Surprised me when he took the cabin for a week.''

"And he paid cash?''

"Pulled out three hunnerd-dollar-bills and slapped 'em down. Bought a six-pack of cola after he found out he couldn't buy no beer in this neck of the woods. Walked out without waitin' for his change.''

Homer's words tripped a lever in Pat's memory. In her mind's eye she saw the grim stranger paying for his gas earlier at Jeremy's gas station. "What kind of car?'' she inquired, walking over to the counter to read the registry card for herself.

"Big black carryall.''

Pat's heart beat faster as she gazed at the printed information. The lone man who'd rented her cabin drove a Chevy Suburban licensed in Illinois. "Homer, did he walk with a limp?''

"Shore did.''

It *had* to be the same man. "What did he look like?''

"Tall, big feller. Dark hair and dark eyes. Sounds like you know him,'' Homer said.

"No, but I saw him today at Jeremy Wells's gas station.''

"Did you, now?'' The old man wiped a hand across his face, partially concealing his delighted grin at her mention of Jeremy Wells.

"I'd stopped to put air in that rear left tire. Jeremy was there. We're going to supper tonight at the Front Porch.'' Pat felt she owed it to the old dear to give him advance news of tomorrow's hot item on the county social grapevine. Aside from that, she was more comfortable discussing Jeremy than the total stranger who'd rented her cabin. He *hadn't* traveled on to a distant destination. She would see him again, undoubtedly have a conversation with him. The prospect was ridiculously thrilling.

"I hear tell they serve some mighty good food there,''

Homer declared. "Me, I'm gonna have a big helping of warmed-over turnip greens for my supper."

He said goodbye and left, a pleased twinkle in his eyes. Pat heard his vintage pickup driving off faster than usual and knew he was in a hurry to get home and tell his daughter, Ethel, about Pat's date. Ethel, who cleaned the cabins for Pat between tenants, would approve. Everybody would, Pat reflected, feeling even less enthusiasm than before.

Jeremy is a nice guy. You'll enjoy his company, she told herself for the umpteenth time as she gazed at the registry card filled out by Clint Adams. His printing was slanted and legible, suggesting that he was practiced at printing. The letters had been penned rapidly, no doubt impatiently. His signature was scrawled and barely decipherable.

"Clint Adams," Pat said aloud. The syllables were hard on her tongue. Hard and masculine, like he was. What a coincidence that she'd run into him in Yellville and afterward he'd shown up here at her store and rented a cabin for a whole week.

Was it a coincidence?

"Had to be," she said, the down-to-earth Pat answering the foolish romantic who lived on inside her. It was time to face up to reality. Time to stop holding out for that special man to come along and sweep her off her feet. Pat would be thirty years old when her next birthday rolled around. She didn't want to be an old maid. She'd promised her dad before he died that she wouldn't walk through the forest in search of the perfect tree and end up with no firewood for the winter.

Jeremy Wells was a nice man. A good man. He could never adore her the way he'd adored his first wife, but he liked Pat. Pat liked him. Their mutual liking might develop into something deeper, might lead to marriage. Jeremy would make a devoted husband to a second wife. He'd already proved himself to be a wonderful father. All of which had taken Pat to his gas station today to give him the nudge he needed to ask her out.

She put Clint Adams's card away in the drawer where she kept current guest-registry cards for the cabins and shut the drawer with a little push. With thirty minutes to put to good use, she restocked shelves, then locked up and drove to Rush, a popular takeout point on the banks of the Buffalo River. Her party of six, all canoeing novices, had arrived minutes earlier. Their smiling faces told her they'd enjoyed their day's float.

The men helped her load the three canoes, bottoms up, on top of the van, securing them to the rack with elastic cord. They obviously didn't mind giving her a hand, but Pat still thought longingly about hiring a strong, dependable man for the summer season. She needed to mind the store herself, answer the phone and take reservations, handle the cabin rentals and generally run the business. It was too much for Homer to handle. As much as she appreciated his help, she couldn't depend on him to keep things straight.

On the ride back to the store, Pat put aside her worries and joined in the casual conversation and laughter. She genuinely enjoyed socializing with her customers. On arrival, the people in her party helped to carry paddles and life jackets to the storage room before they piled into a late-model sports-utility vehicle. "See you next year!" they sang out in a lighthearted chorus as they drove off.

"Call me when you know your plans, and I'll reserve your canoes," Pat called, waving to them. Much of her business from year to year was with repeat customers.

In addition to her shuttle van, one automobile remained in the parking lot. It was the transportation for a group of four college guys who were taking a two-day trip on the Buffalo, camping out overnight. Pat would pick them up at Rush tomorrow afternoon. Her schedule was jam-packed for the entire day. She sure hoped Homer didn't wake up ailing.

On that thought, she went back inside the storage room to refill the food dish for the stray pregnant cat who'd recently taken up residence. The shy animal had evidently slipped in through the back door, which was frequently left open during the day. "Okay, Mama Cat. You can come out of hiding. The place is all yours for the night."

A plaintive meow sounded from a corner, but the cat didn't appear. There wasn't time to try to coax her out. Pat needed to get ready for her date. She exited through the back door, following her usual habit of walking back and forth between the store and her house, which was located behind the store some hundred-or-so yards.

Her driveway forked off the road leading to the cabins. She'd reached it and was striding along at a brisk pace when she suddenly remembered a conversation she'd had that morning with Ethel. "You better put some candles in that cabin I just finished cleaning," Ethel had said, referring to the one Homer had rented to Clint Adams.

"There should be a whole box of candles there," Pat had replied. "We haven't had a power outage recently. Surely that cute young couple didn't swipe them." The last occupants had been newlyweds from Little Rock.

"Nope. They burned 'em to stubs. Must've ate their dinners by candlelight."

"In that case, I'm glad they enjoyed them. Thanks for telling me, Ethel. I'll take some replacements up later."

But she hadn't. It had slipped her mind.

Should she take some candles up now? No, there wasn't time. And there was certainly no emergency. But the candles would give her an excuse to go to the cabin sometime during the day tomorrow. Preferably when *he* was there.

Silly idiot! Pat scolded herself, walking on to her house with a springier step.

For her date she wore a slim denim skirt, a red cotton blouse made out of a bandanna print, and red flats. For makeup she brushed a powder blush on her cheeks and applied some lip gloss. After a couple of hasty experiments with a different hairstyle, she resorted to her tried-and-trusted ponytail, using a red ruffled elastic band. Primping in front of a mirror had never appealed to Pat—not even when she was a teenager. If it had, maybe she would have developed more skill at applying makeup and fixing her hair. Fortunately, she'd always had lots of fun anyway, without being feminine and pretty.

Dressed with a couple of minutes to spare, she waited for Jeremy out on her front porch, seated in the swing. He arrived promptly in his minivan, the type very popular with young families, and sprang out to open the passenger door for her. He was wearing slacks and a striped shirt. His sandy hair had a healthy sheen. It was neatly combed, and he looked freshly showered and shaved. Pat caught a whiff of his aftershave lotion as he gave her a hand up into the passenger seat.

"You smell nice," she said, realizing that she'd forgotten to spritz on some cologne.

"I hope the scent isn't overpowering," he replied.

His hint of uncertainty took Pat aback. "No, it's a clean, piney scent. Your kids must have bought it for you as a present," she guessed. Obviously he'd used a new men's fragrance.

"No, I bought it myself. I finally used up my supply of the stuff I've been using for years. Decided to get out of the rut," he added.

Suddenly Pat understood the deeper layers of meaning in what had seemed a casual conversation. Sympathetically, she laid her hand on Jeremy's shoulder. "Susan liked the old scent a lot, didn't she?"

He nodded. "She gave me a gift box of it the first Christmas we were married."

"I'll bet she'd like this new scent you picked out yourself. I know I do."

Jeremy put his hand over hers and squeezed it. His voice was gruff with emotion when he answered, "Something tells me she'd approve of my dating you. Sorry, Pat. I didn't mean to start our date out like this, on a down note."

"No apologies. Come on. Let's get going. I'm starving."

"You're a great person." He closed the door and came around to climb in behind the wheel.

"Did you get any responses to your Help Wanted sign today?" she asked, starting them out on a new subject as he backed the van around.

"Several, but none of them very promising." He elaborated with entertaining descriptions of the unlikely job applicants.

Pat was smiling with amusement when they reached the intersection of the driveway and the road leading up to her rental cabins. She wasn't so caught up in the moment, though, that she didn't peer in the direction of the cabin in which Clint Adams was staying. Through the trees she got just a quick glimpse of his black automobile and felt the foolish little thrill of his presence.

The cola had calmed the rumbling of Clint's stomach. He'd summoned the energy to go inside the cabin and stretch out on the bed, fully clothed except for his boots. Hunger pangs eventually awoke him from a deep sleep of exhaustion. He got up, refreshed enough to contemplate driving back to Yellville to get something to eat. There might be a closer restaurant in some small town farther along on Highway 14, but then there might not be.

In the bathroom, he washed his face. A bleary-eyed glance in the mirror told him he didn't look clean-shaven. Maybe a shower and shave and a change of clothes would make him feel more human, he reflected.

The decision made, Clint persevered doggedly, the whole procedure of cleaning up taking twice as long as it once would have and costing him dearly in using up his store of replenished stamina.

By the time he climbed behind the wheel of his heavy-duty vehicle, he would have gladly paid fifty bucks to have a couple of hamburgers delivered to him. Still, it did feel good to have washed the grime away. Clint was slightly more alert to his surroundings than he'd been earlier. On his way out to the highway, he took the trouble to turn his head and glance down the driveway that intersected with the narrow gravel road. The driveway presumably led to another cabin or to the Tyler house. Probably the latter, he concluded, considering the location directly behind the store.

Passing the store, which was closed, as he'd expected, Clint noted the two vehicles in the parking lot, one of them the shuttle van Pat Tyler had been driving today. Three canoes had been loaded on the rack on top of it in the meantime. With no able-bodied man in her employ, had she loaded them herself? he wondered, frowning at the idea.

The distance to Yellville didn't seem quite as long as it had a few hours ago, maybe because Clint occupied his mind with replaying the ten or fifteen minutes he'd spent at Jeremy Wells's gas station that afternoon. Visualizing Pat Tyler awoke the nearest thing to pleasure he'd felt in the last nine weeks.

He'd never met a woman before who'd affected him like sunshine breaking through the clouds after days on end of gloomy weather. Clint wanted to see her again. Even at the risk of having her look at him with pity in her pretty blue eyes.

The parking lot of the Front Porch was almost full. Several motor homes took up more than their share of space. "Good. Lots of out-of-state licenses," Pat remarked.

"I see several familiar cars and pickups," Jeremy replied. His rueful tone told Pat that he wasn't looking forward to making an entrance any more than she was.

As on any night of the week, there were local people eating at the popular restaurant along with tourists. It took Pat and Jeremy a full ten minutes to make their way to an unoccupied table; they had to stop and chat and pretend they were oblivious to the surprised and delighted reactions.

Finally they sank down in chairs. Almost immediately Betty Dunkin, their waitress, bustled up, a coy smile on her face. Betty was Homer's niece and the mother of half-a-dozen children ranging from high-school age to grammar-school age. "My, don't you look pretty tonight, Pat!" she exclaimed, as had several others.

"How's Joe?" Pat and Jeremy both asked in unison. Joe was Betty's husband, who'd been disabled about five years ago in a freak accident that had left him with a serious back injury. She waited tables at the Front Porch to supplement their income.

"He's doing pretty good. Tries to lay off the pain pills as much as he can. A shop over in Eureka Springs is buying his carved walking sticks. The owner says they sell like hotcakes."

During the rest of Betty's answer, Pat sneaked a glance at Jeremy and saw that his color was high, revealing his embarrassment. Her own cheeks felt warm, and she knew she was probably blushing, too. The level of discomfort wasn't nearly as bad for her, though, as it had been at Jeremy's gas station that afternoon when Clint Adams, a total stranger, had bluntly sized them up as a couple who were "courting."

Pat remembered his exact words, spoken in his deep voice. *If you don't mind, I'd like to pay for my gas. Then I'll get out of here and let you two get on with your courting in private.*

"Did you want iced tea, too?" Betty was asking her. Pat had tuned out completely and hadn't heard Jeremy order iced tea.

"Please."

"Would you like the buffet?" Jeremy inquired of her. "Or would you rather order from the menu?"

"I know I can't go wrong with the buffet," Pat replied, conscious of Betty looking on while they conferred with that awkwardness of a first date. "It's always good."

"I've never been disappointed. We'll have the buffet," he told Betty, who urged them to serve themselves and went off to get their iced teas.

"Don't say I didn't warn you it would be bad," Pat said. "At least no one's taken our picture."

Jeremy's grin was strained. "No. Not yet." He glanced at the long line of people at the buffet. "Shall we wait until the crowd thins?"

"By all means."

Betty dropped off the glasses of tea. Pat picked up the caddy of packets of sugar and sweetener and held it toward him. "Sugar?"

"No, thanks. I just use lemon in my tea."

"Do you? I like my tea sweet."

"Susan did, too. Sorry," he said quickly. "That just slipped out."

"It's okay for Susan's name to come up," Pat assured him. "For you not to mention her wouldn't be natural. Especially since I knew and liked her."

"Thank you for being so understanding." His voice was full of his gratitude. "Know what I don't understand?" he said, watching her dump three packets of sugar into her glass.

Pat stirred and sipped. "What don't you understand?"

"The better I get to know you, it makes less and less sense to me that some very lucky man hasn't talked you into marrying him by now."

"I was never in a hurry to get married like a lot of girls are. Probably because I was a spoiled only child and perfectly happy living at home."

"You don't seem spoiled to me."

Betty Dunkin paused on her way by their table. "Now's a good time to get your food. There's more folks coming in the door."

Jeremy thanked her politely. Both he and Pat glanced automatically toward the entryway. Pat was lifting her glass of tea to take another sip. Her arm froze.

"Hey, that's the grouchy fellow in the black Suburban," Jeremy said.

Pat lowered her glass to the table with a little thunk,

sucking in a deep breath to calm her heartbeat down to normal. She certainly didn't need her memory prodded to recognize the lone man making his way toward an empty table near theirs. He'd changed clothes and looked taller and more ruggedly male in jeans and a long-sleeved shirt made of heavyweight cotton. For him to appear here tonight made it all but certain that he and the man named Clint Adams who'd rented her cabin were one and the same.

"He looks like he's in a slightly better mood," Jeremy observed. "Well, shall we take Betty's advice?"

"Sure." As she got up and accompanied him to the buffet, Pat tried not to be conspicuous about watching Clint Adams. Coming to a stop at the empty table, he didn't sit down, but remained standing as Betty sailed up to him. Betty pointed at the buffet in the midst of her exchange with him. His gaze shifted and collided with Pat's.

Feeling color flood her cheeks, Pat smiled and waved a hello. Beside her, Jeremy lifted his hand in a greeting, too, when Clint Adams glanced at him, obviously with recognition. In response to Jeremy's salute, he nodded solemnly.

Reaching the stacks of smaller plates at the salad section of the buffet, Pat took a plate and helped herself to lettuce. She assembled a green salad from the ample fixings and ladled on a dressing, managing not to look over her shoulder. It was probably her imagination, but she could feel Clint Adams's eyes on her.

Back at the table, she noticed that she'd included at least two food items that she didn't particularly like—bell pepper and raw onion. And the salad dressing she'd taken—blue cheese—was probably her least favorite.

It would be interesting to see what ended up on her plate for the main course, Pat thought wryly. Her rattled state, she knew, had nothing to do with being on a date with Jeremy. In fact, she'd lost all sense of awkwardness where he was concerned.

"I didn't think to ask if you like to eat your salad along

with the rest of your meal," she said to him after he'd sat down.

"I can go either way." He smiled. "We might be accused of putting on airs, though, eating in courses."

Pat agreed with him laughingly. Her mind wasn't fully on the conversation, though. She was following Clint Adams's progress through the buffet line.

"More tea?" Betty had come with the tea pitcher. While she was refilling their glasses, she chatted with them. As she was leaving, the pastor of the church they both attended and his wife stopped by their table briefly to say hello and to introduce her mother, who was visiting from Florida.

By the time Pat was able to pick up her fork again, Clint Adams had in the meanwhile sat down at his table. Somehow she would have expected him to sit with his back to her and Jeremy, but he hadn't. He'd picked the chair that gave her a frontal view.

Pat's gaze was drawn to him like steel to a magnet as she tried to uphold her end of the conversation while she demolished her salad, crunching up bits of onion and slivers of bell pepper, too.

"You weren't kidding. You were starving," Jeremy commented.

Actually she'd hardly tasted her food, but she couldn't confide that to him.

They got up and filled dinner plates at the buffet, which featured four or five meat selections and probably a dozen vegetables and side dishes. Pat chose at random, serving herself a slice of ham, candied yams and green beans. Fortunately she had the presence of mind to pass over the turnip greens and also the fried okra—two vegetables she wasn't wild about.

Seated, Pat made a determined effort to divide her attention between her dinner and Jeremy. To her credit she sneaked fewer glances over at Clint Adams, who seemed absorbed in eating his meat loaf and mashed potatoes. He didn't go back for seconds, nor did he get a dessert or order coffee. When he'd finished, he got a bill out of his wallet, dropped it on the table and left, without waiting for Betty to bring him his check.

Pat put down her fork and watched him limp out. Jeremy followed her gaze. "I wonder where that guy's staying," he said curiously.

"I'm not positive, but he may be renting one of my cabins." She went on to explain her statement.

He frowned. "I'm not too keen on the idea of him seeing you here in town and then hotfooting it to your place."

"There's probably no connection."

"You're uneasy, though. I couldn't help but notice the way you kept looking at him."

"Not really 'uneasy,'" she replied. "Certainly I'm not afraid of him, if that's what you mean."

Jeremy gave his head a worried little shake. "You're very vulnerable, a woman living alone and renting to total strangers. It was different when your dad was alive."

"I'm capable of protecting myself, believe me. Don't forget that I got my first hunting gun when I was ten."

He smiled, looking amused. "You've got quite a reputation as a good shot, all right. Most of the men in these parts would like to see you banned from the turkey shoots."

Pat laughed. "Ready to hit the dessert bar?"

They talked of other things, much to her relief. It would hardly be tactful to admit to Jeremy that she'd had trouble keeping her eyes off the stranger from Illinois not because he frightened her, but because he fascinated her. It was moth-and-candle stuff that she would have felt silly putting into words. The whole time he was in the restaurant tonight, she'd been all fluttery with excitement. After he'd gone, she'd experienced a sense of letdown.

If she should turn out to be wrong and her renter, Clint Adams, wasn't the man who'd appeared here tonight, Pat would be greatly disappointed. She wanted to have at least one conversation with him with no one else around. That would probably be enough to snuff out the flame of the candle.

"You don't have to get out."

Jeremy ignored her words, swinging open the driver's door. "I'm old-fashioned enough to walk my date to her door."

His words stilled Pat's hand, which was grasping her door handle. It had never been easy for her to play a feminine, "helpless" role. Her natural impulse was to open doors for herself, pull out her own chair at the dinner table, don her coat with no assistance. Growing up as a tomboy had certain drawbacks. She'd never developed basic female talents like flirting and giving guys the come-on with body language, as some of her girlfriends in high school and in college the one year she'd attended had done with such admirable skill.

The awkwardness was suddenly back as Jeremy gave her a hand down to the ground and escorted her along the walkway to her front porch, where her aging dog, Rowdy, had risen to his feet and awaited them.

"I see you have a watchdog," Jeremy observed. "That makes me feel better." On the porch he snapped his fingers and coaxed, "Come here, big fellow, and make friends." The huge canine ignored the summons and lay back down again, keeping his head raised as though to say he wasn't relaxing his vigilance.

"He's getting up in years," Pat said, to smooth over the rebuff. "Once, he would have knocked you down, trying to lick your face."

"Will he attack me if I kiss you good-night?"

"To make sure he doesn't, why don't I give you a good-night kiss?" she answered lightly.

It was a chaste kiss, and he didn't try to prolong or deepen it. He did put his arms around her when their lips had parted. Pat slipped her arms around his waist and hugged him back, taking comfort in being held close and offering comfort in return.

"I'm glad I asked you out, Pat," he said. "I hope you're not sorry you accepted."

"No, I'm not at all sorry, Jeremy."

"Please don't give me up for a lost cause. This was a big hurdle tonight."

"Don't be silly. I admire you for being the kind of man who doesn't easily get over losing his wife. And yet you've carried on and upheld your responsibilities."

"I'm lonely."

"So am I." She loosened her embrace and he dropped his arms away. "Good night. And thanks for dinner."

"It was my pleasure. Good night." He unlocked the door for her, another of those little niceties that Pat always forgot to expect.

Jeremy's heart was heavy as he drove to the highway and headed back to Yellville. What a dud he was as a date. He wouldn't blame Pat Tyler if she passed on a second date with him. She deserved a guy who would fall head over heels in love with her, the way he had fallen for Susan in about the first thirty minutes he'd known her.

Susan. She'd been the love of his life. As long as he drew breath, he would always miss her, always long to hear her voice, long to touch her and be with her. It was as if a piece of his soul had been ripped out of him.

Jeremy didn't expect ever to be as happy as he'd once been, but he had to try to be a happy person, for his kids' sake, as well as for his own. His best chance for contentment was to remarry. He was convinced of that. And while no woman could ever replace Susan as his children's mother, they would benefit from a step-mother's attention and care—if the stepmother were a loving, kind, sensitive woman who opened her heart to them.

Pat Tyler was certainly a good and caring person. Look how she'd nursed both her parents when their health had gotten bad. And kids loved her. Jeremy had observed her at church socials and school and county events when she would organize games and contests and sports activities. He suspected she was enough of a kid at heart that she enjoyed playing games herself.

Yet she was levelheaded and conscientious and bright. Cute. Brimming with personality. Likable. *Lovable,* if a man was capable of loving.

Jeremy sighed. He wondered if it was fair of him to pursue a relationship with Pat. She might settle for him out of loneliness and always feel cheated.

Such worries were definitely premature. Before things ever got serious between him and Pat, they would know each other very well. Jeremy wouldn't marry her unless he was sure that he could fill her needs.

Chapter Three

It was only nine-thirty, too early for Pat to go to bed. Watching TV all by herself didn't hold much appeal. Nor did reading. "I guess I could go over to the store and do some tidying up," she said to Rowdy, who'd come inside the house with her. "But I know what you're thinking. That I really should catch up with my bookkeeping. Okay, but first I'm going to change out of these clothes."

She patted the old dog on the head and didn't scold him when he followed her through the house to her bedroom. In the past year she'd relaxed the rules. Before then, he'd been restricted to the kitchen and large utility room, both with tiled floors. And only in winter. In the warm weather, he'd slept on the rear screened porch.

Pat had had to coax him at first to come sit with her in the living room, the first infringement. She'd wanted his company. The house had been so quiet and empty after her father had died. She'd never been the kind of person who liked solitude.

"You're sociable, just like your daddy," her mother had remarked fondly more than once.

There were many other similarities in temperament. Patrick Tyler had thrived on being physically active. So did Pat. He'd hated office work, and she did, too. Her least favorite part of being a proprietor of a small business was keeping simple ledgers, paying bills and balancing the separate bank account—chores her mother had done with efficiency and without complaint.

The room that served as a home office located off the kitchen had been Lorna Tyler's turf, just as the kitchen had been. Pat always felt her mother's presence when she worked at the old-fashioned desk with cubbyholes for invoices and receipts and correspondence. Sometimes she could imagine Lorna instructing her and also chiding her in a loving tone when her daughter's thoughts drifted and she was apt to make a careless error. *Pay attention to what you're doing, Pat.*

Pat considered herself one of the more fortunate people in the world to have been born to parents who were hardworking, good people and who loved her as much as a child could possibly be loved. If she could have changed anything, she would have timed her conception and birth earlier in their married years, so she could have had them around longer. She missed them both so much.

"Come on, Rowdy. The least you can do is give me some moral support while I pay bills." Having shed her outfit and pulled on jeans and a T-shirt, Pat roused her elderly pet, who'd settled himself on the carpet at the foot of her bed and fallen asleep.

He obediently got to his feet and accompanied her into the office, where he lay down beside her mother's swivel chair that had been bought secondhand at a flea market. "I need to oil this chair and stop the squeaking, don't I?" Pat said to the dog. She smiled when he raised his massive head and looked at her. "Okay, okay. I'll do it later. I know I shouldn't procrastinate."

With a sigh, she began to organize the clutter she'd allowed to accumulate, placing invoices into a pile. She paused as both the overhead light and gooseneck lamp on the desk flickered. Seconds later the room went pitch-black. She waited a few seconds, but the electricity didn't come back on.

"Must have blown a transformer," she said. "You can't expect me to work by candlelight—" Her voice broke off. *Candles. There weren't any in the cabin Homer had rented to Clint Adams.* "Let's go check the breaker box and make sure it's a power outage."

Her pulse hammering, Pat made her way into the kitchen and got a flashlight, then went to the utility room. All the breakers were in the On position.

By now it was nearly ten o'clock. He might have gone to bed. But what if he hadn't? What if he were stumbling around in the dark cabin, bumping into walls and furniture? Pat cringed at the idea.

"We'd better take him some candles and a box of matches from the store, Rowdy, just in case he needs them." She didn't speak the rest of her train of thought aloud. Delivering candles gave her a legitimate excuse to find out tonight whether Clint Adams was who she thought he was.

Outside it was also pitch-black. Lighting the way with the beam of her flashlight, Pat walked to the store and let herself in through the back door. "You stay out here, so Mama Cat won't get upset," she instructed her faithful canine, whose name was a misnomer at this mature stage of his life.

The candles she supplied to renters were the same ones she sold to campers—stubby white tapers packaged in boxes of four. Easily locating them on a shelf next to the matches, she took a package and a box of matches and rejoined Rowdy for the trek to the cabin. He plodded alongside her.

Pat's own step was light and surefooted. It was ridicu-

lous, but she was almost giddy with suspense and anticipation, as if she were setting out on an adventure. Her shoes
crunched on the gravel of her driveway as she cut across
it and took a path through the woods that was a shorter
route than following the road. She emerged in the clearing
in front of the cabin.

"Almost there, Rowdy." Her voice came out breathless.
She'd kept it low, just in case Clint Adams had turned in
for the night and was asleep. For that same reason she was
careful not to train the beam of the flashlight on the front
porch and risk shining light on the window of the down-
stairs bedroom.

If all was quiet and there was no sign of life, she guessed
she would just leave the candles and matches where he
would find them the next day.

Beside her Rowdy whined deep in his throat, a sound of
friendly greeting. Pat slowed down, but he walked on
ahead. Puzzled by his behavior she lifted the flashlight
enough to illuminate the bottom steps of the porch. Startled
at the sight of a pair of men's boots, she raised the beam
higher in a series of jerky movements. Denim-clad legs
with muscular thighs came into view. A shirt Pat recognized. Broad shoulders. A familiar scowling face partially
shielded by a big hand.

"What the hell!" The deep voice, rough with irritation,
brought a little thrill of certainty. Clint Adams *was* her surly
stranger.

"Sorry," Pat apologized, lowering the flashlight.
"Didn't mean to blind you." She walked closer. "We
haven't been formally introduced. I'm Pat Tyler, your land-
lord." Briefly she trained the beam on herself so that he
could recognize her. "I brought you some candles."

"You're traipsing around in the woods by yourself at
night?" A foolhardy thing to do, his words implied.

"Not by myself. Rowdy came along for protection." Pat
located her dog with the flashlight. He'd gone up to the
steps where he stood, making a dignified bid for attention.

"I think he sized you up immediately as a friend. Here're the candles and a box of matches." Holding out her hand, she took the last few steps.

"You don't know me from Adam and you come here at this hour of the night, a lone woman?" he demanded, taking the two items from her. "Are you crazy?"

"But I do know you're not Adam. According to your registry card, you're Adams. Clint Adams, right?"

"That's me. Are you bringing candles to your other renters, too?"

"No. There should be candles in their cabins. The young couple who stayed in this cabin last liked candlelight and used yours up. I meant to bring some today, but it completely slipped my mind."

"Well, thanks for putting yourself out."

"No problem. Did you enjoy your dinner at the Front Porch?" she ventured, wanting to engage him in conversation.

"The food wasn't bad."

"You should have tried the peach cobbler. I noticed you didn't have dessert," she added.

"Maybe next time." He lowered himself and sat on the top step, stretching out his left leg. Rowdy apparently sensed an invitation and edged closer. Clint stroked him on the head.

"Jeremy Wells, the man who was with me tonight, tried to make friends with him less than an hour ago, and Rowdy gave him the real cold shoulder," Pat commented, wondering if she dared push her luck and sit beside him on the steps. The thought raised a pleasant tingle along her spine.

"I guess maybe dogs can show sympathy, too."

Like their owners. Pat supplied the unspoken part of his reply, hearing some of the same harsh resentment that had been in his voice this afternoon at Jeremy's gas station when he'd informed her, *I'm not handicapped.*

"Probably he just took a liking to you," she suggested. "I raised him from a puppy. We called him Rowdy because he was so rambunctious. I couldn't tell you how many shoes he chewed up and ruined.''

There was no answer from him, but he continued to pet Rowdy, stroking along his broad back, giving Pat the merest excuse to linger a minute longer.

''Aside from no electricity, is everything okay with the cabin?'' she asked.

''So far everything's fine,'' he stated.

''Just let me know if you have any problems or complaints.''

No answer. With zilch success at drawing him out, Pat didn't have much choice but to leave him to his solitude, which he apparently preferred to her company. ''Sorry for the inconvenience of the power outage,'' she said.

''It's no big inconvenience. And it's no fault of yours.''

''When I register guests, I usually mention that we occasionally lose our electricity out here in the country. But I didn't know whether Homer warned you of the possibility.'' She couldn't resist pulling a few more words out of him.

''That was one thing he didn't get around to telling me.'' There was a touch of irony in his deep voice.

''Homer loves to talk. I guess he filled you in on his whole life history.''

''Not his. Yours.''

''Oh. How embarrassing.'' Pat's cheeks were warm in the darkness. ''And how boring for you.''

''He shouldn't be announcing to every Tom, Dick and Harry who stops by your store that your parents are deceased and that you're a single woman. It could put bad ideas into the head of the wrong sort of man.''

''I'll have to make that point to Homer.'' She mustered her nerve. ''No doubt he also told you that Jeremy Wells is currently my main marriage prospect.''

''Homer's counting on an invitation to the wedding.''

''After my showing up with Jeremy tonight at the Front

Porch, everybody else in the county will be watching the mail for their invitation, too.''

"He seems like a nice enough guy," Clint said—his first voluntary comment.

"Jeremy's a terrific person. You'd like him if you got to know him." Pat smothered a sigh. The sense of adventure had fizzled. "Just out of curiosity, was it a spur-of-the-moment thing that you stopped in and rented this cabin? I usually give a discount to customers who are taking the recommendation of friends or family members who've stayed here."

"That's not the case with me. I picked up one of your brochures at a tourist center in Mountain Home."

So seeing her in Yellville hadn't influenced him one whit. Surprise, surprise.

"I just sent another supply off to them this afternoon. Well, I've intruded on your privacy long enough. Good night." Pat's voice came out glum.

"Thanks again for the candles."

"You're welcome. Coming, Rowdy?"

Clint gave her dog a gentle pat on the rump. "Go with her, big fella."

Rowdy obeyed as if he understood the gruff command.

"See you," Pat called over her shoulder as she trudged off. She didn't expect any answer and there wasn't one.

It was stupid of her to be this disappointed at learning that he'd been headed to Tyler's Canoe & Cabin Rental when she saw him at Jeremy's gas station. *You have about as much sex appeal as a turnip, Pat Tyler,* she grumbled to herself, kicking at a root. Quite obviously, Homer hadn't put any "bad ideas" into his head. Clint Adams probably wouldn't have been tempted to ravish her if she'd delivered the darned candles in her birthday suit.

Coming within sight of her house, Pat saw the glow of lights and realized the electricity had already been restored. She felt even more foolish, more disgruntled.

Romance had passed her by. The sooner she accepted

that fact, the better. Then she could put herself more whole-heartedly into dating Jeremy, who had impressed even Clint Adams as a nice guy.

No doubt the man from Illinois, like everyone else, thought Pat should marry Jeremy. As she probably would do, if and when he eventually proposed.

''Back to the bookkeeping, Rowdy.'' Pat's tone was as disheartened as her state of mind.

Clint wouldn't have sat on his rear end and let Pat Tyler walk back to her house unescorted, if he'd had two sound legs. But he didn't have two sound legs—not anymore. He would only have slowed her down. Worse, he could easily have lost his balance along the way and fallen flat on his face.

His pride couldn't take the chance.

She would have stayed and visited, if he'd been friend-lier. It was fairly obvious to Clint that she was curious about him. But what was the point in getting acquainted? The more she knew about him, the more reason she would have to feel sorry for him.

At thirty-five he was a disabled ex-marine with nothing to offer a woman.

Clint had never put women on pedestals, but he knew he wouldn't have been the right kind of man for Pat Tyler when he was able-bodied. Orphaned when he was a kid and raised by relatives who hadn't wanted him, he'd grown up on the streets of Chicago and was much too hardened by his background and by his active duty as a marine. The right kind of man for Pat Tyler would be a guy as whole-some as she was, a guy with solid character who would make her a good husband. A guy like Jeremy Wells.

Clint hoped Wells appreciated her. What a spunky little thing she was, charging through the woods at night with a flashlight. So *alive*. Not a hint of phoniness about her. She was too trusting for her own safety, but even that trait had its appeal.

Her visit had left him feeling more down on himself, but Clint was still glad the electricity had gone off and he'd had the benefit of a few minutes of her company.

Even in the darkness her personality had affected him like sunshine.

Daylight flooded the cabin when Clint awoke the next morning. He reached out an arm and picked up his watch from the nightstand. Seven o'clock. He'd gone to bed at eleven and slept soundly. It was the first normal sleep he'd had since his auto accident. No crazy dreams. No being wakened by his own groans as he tossed and turned.

He felt rested.

The constant aching and throbbing in his bum leg had even quieted until he could almost fool himself into believing a miracle had occurred and he was a whole man again.

Clint moved his leg experimentally and grimaced. No, no miracle. He rose up, his jaw set for the ordeal of getting out of bed. The old Clint had bounded up, full of confidence that he could handle whatever the day brought, whether he'd awakened in a bunk on a marine base or in a tent in the desert. Now it took him a full minute to go from a prone position to a sitting position on the edge of his bed, with both feet on the floor. He needed a rest before he could cope with a trip to the bathroom before getting dressed.

As for his old cocksureness, it had deserted him completely. Sheer grit and stubbornness kept him going, now that life really had very little purpose.

This morning Clint wasn't quite as whipped as he'd come to expect when he'd wrestled on his jeans and slid up the zipper. Maybe the cool, bracing air coming through an open window of the bedroom made a difference, as well as the good night's sleep. He took deep breaths, inhaling the scent of pine, as he limped barefoot into the bathroom to shave.

More than enough time had elapsed for the toilet to fill after it had been flushed earlier on his first trip, but he could hear water running into the tank. He jiggled the handle, reflecting that the shutoff mechanism had probably worn out and needed to be replaced. The lavatory faucets needed new gaskets, too. He'd noticed that yesterday. They both had developed a telltale slow drip. The leak from the cold-water faucet was about twice as fast, as was usually the case, since it had been used more than the other one.

Clint turned the faucets as hard as he dared after he'd finished shaving and brushing his teeth and had rinsed the sink.

In the kitchen he searched through the cabinets and drawers, hoping to find coffee makings. Nothing. Not even a jar of instant coffee.

Disgusted with himself for not having had the presence of mind to buy a few grocery supplies the previous day, Clint pocketed his wallet and got his car keys from the bedside table in the bedroom. He remembered seeing packets of coffee grounds in Pat Tyler's store, but he wasn't counting on its being open this early. It was only seven-thirty. More than likely, he would have to drive thirteen miles to Yellville craving a cup of coffee.

Pulling up in front of the store, Clint saw that the lights were on inside and the Open sign showed through the glass pane of the door. He'd already noted that the shuttle van was still parked in the same place and the ancient pickup, which he assumed was Homer's, wasn't there. Maybe Pat Tyler was tending the store herself. He got out, his mood lightening.

The bell tinkled merrily when he thrust open the door, and the aroma of freshly-brewed coffee hit him. Pat appeared from the back, broom in hand. At the sight of him, her blue eyes widened with surprise and the flush of attractive color in her cheeks deepened. "Why, good morning," she greeted him, sounding both welcoming and slightly flustered. "You're up early. Is everything okay at the cabin?"

She'd rushed past the pause that would have given him a chance to bid her good-morning. "It will be when I can make a pot of coffee," he replied.

"Oh, dear, isn't the coffee maker working? I'll lend you the one I have at my house. Sorry for the inconvenience—" The pealing of the telephone interrupted her flow of words before Clint could break in and correct her error. "There's the phone. Excuse me while I answer it."

She moved with her agile quickness toward the counter at the front of the store. En route she propped the broom against one of the mismatched chairs arranged around the discarded kitchen table. Her mobility stirred pleasure in Clint, but also made him feel even slower and more clumsy.

"Could I buy a cup of your coffee?" he asked.

"It's free. Help yourself to all you want. Have a sausage biscuit, too," she urged, waving with one arm toward the back wall and picking up the phone receiver with her other hand. "Zap it in the microwave for one minute."

Clint located the coffee maker with full carafe next to a microwave oven on a counter along the rear wall. He fitted a disposable plastic cup into a holder and poured himself a cupful of the steaming brew. As he added a packet of sugar, he surveyed a tray of biscuits, each one with a sausage patty between the two halves. The breakfast sandwiches were still frozen, obviously having been taken from the freezer, but they looked homemade.

Giving in to temptation, Clint tore off a piece of paper towel, wrapped up a biscuit and microwaved it according to Pat Tyler's directions. Carrying coffee and steaming-hot biscuit, he made his way to the table and sat down in the chair that allowed him the best view of her.

"Don't you dare let him come to work, Ethel," Pat was saying. Clint had surmised from her end of the conversation that Ethel was a female relative of Homer Perkins who'd phoned to report that the old man wasn't feeling well.

"You tell Homer I said for him to stay in bed today and take care of himself. If I can't find someone to tend the store for me, it won't be the end of the world. His health is far more important."

She hung up and addressed Clint. "Did you find everything okay?"

He had his mouth full. Before he could swallow and answer, the phone rang again. This time it was a stranger calling to book a cabin for the second week in July. Clint finished his coffee and biscuit while Pat took down the reservation and answered questions about the canoeing conditions on the Buffalo River. By the end of the conversation she was on a first-name basis with the stranger, calling him Jim.

"Help yourself to more coffee. And have another biscuit, too," she said to Clint, holding the receiver to her ear after she'd cut the connection. "Homer's under the weather today. I need to drum up somebody to mind the store for me and answer the phone." She was punching out digits.

Clint got up and poured himself a second cup of coffee while she spoke with a woman named Hannah, who was unavailable because evidently she'd already agreed to baby-sit her neighbor's two children. A second call to a boy named Willie also proved unproductive. Willie had started a regular job just the day before.

"That leaves Tracy Wiggins," Pat announced with cheerful resignation. "If I can't get her, I'll just lock up and let the answering machine take messages. It can't be helped."

Clint had picked up a packet of coffee grounds and brought them to the counter. He stood sipping from his cup and looking over an information sheet on the various canoe trips or "floats" on the Buffalo River while she talked with Tracy Wiggins and finally met with success in lining up a substitute for Homer.

"Come right away, Tracy. I should be leaving in fifteen minutes for Maumee." She cradled the phone, glancing out the window. Two automobiles were pulling up. "Here comes my party of eight."

"How much do I owe you?" Clint asked, pushing the packet toward her. "Include the two cups of coffee and a sausage biscuit, too."

"Oh, darn! The coffee maker!" Pat exclaimed, slapping a palm against her head. "Tell you what. Since I'm a little pressed for time, how about just taking the one here in the store?" She was moving from behind the counter as she spoke. "Would you mind? Take the full carafe, too. And no charge for the package of coffee grounds. It's on the house. Okay?" The last was tossed back over her shoulder as she went out the door.

Clint watched her greeting the college-age guys who'd spilled out of the four-wheel-drive vehicles. One of them stayed outside with her while the others came inside and headed back to the coolers. As they uncapped bottles of soda and ripped open bags of chips, grabbing a quick junk-food breakfast, they congratulated themselves for bringing along plenty of beer to enjoy on their float.

They were probably honest kids, but Clint decided to stick around a few minutes longer and keep an eye on them anyway. It obviously hadn't entered Pat's mind that she was leaving the cash register untended, along with small items of merchandise that would fit into pockets.

Under her smiling direction, the fellow who'd stayed outside loaded up a fourth canoe on the rack on top of the van. Meanwhile another car drove up, and a couple in their forties got out and came into the store. They hovered near the counter, eyeing the stack of information sheets in front of Clint, who was standing there with his weight on his good leg. He shoved the stack over closer to them.

"Thank you," the woman said, reaching for the top sheet.

The phone started to ring. He was debating about whether to answer it when Pat breezed in with her brawny helper. She raced behind the counter. The call concerned reserving canoes for a float. She jotted on a calendar. As soon as she'd hung up, the woman who'd been waiting with her male companion, plainly her husband, stepped forward and asked, "Could you tell us a little about these different floats? Which one would you recommend for novices?"

Pat picked up a pen, flipped over one of the information sheets to the map on the back and made two X's. "This one-day float from Buffalo Point to Rush is great fun and not too challenging for first-time canoers. You'll love it."

Her helper and his pals were crowding close, digging into their pockets for money. "How much do we owe you, Pat?" one of them inquired.

They named their purchases, passing her money, and Pat rapidly made change, darting one or two questioning looks at Clint. After she'd given over the final handful of coins, she turned to him, her manner hesitant. "Did you need help with the coffee maker, Clint? I'm sure one of these able-bodied guys would gladly load it up for you."

"No, I don't need help," he refused curtly, stung by her misconception that he was hanging around waiting for assistance. "As far as I know, the other coffee maker works fine, when it has coffee grounds in it. I do need to pay you."

"No, please don't—" She bit her lip, looking as if she would gladly let him walk out with her full stock of merchandise just to make amends for having wounded his pride.

He'd jerked out his wallet. After tossing down several one-dollar bills, he grabbed up his packet of coffee and limped for the door through a path that opened up for him. Outside he almost collided with a sullen-faced teenage girl who'd just arrived in a station wagon that was departing. A gaudy rendition of the name Tracy on the front of her oversize T-shirt identified her as Homer's replacement for the day.

Even with his ego dragging on the ground, Clint was glad that Pat's temporary employee had come to relieve the pressure on her. He hoped he was wrong in his snap judgment of Tracy Wiggins, who struck him as not having much on the ball.

At the cabin he brewed coffee and hauled a chair from the back porch to the front porch, where he sat, mug in hand, gazing at the parking lot of the store. His view was partially obstructed by trees, but he could keep tabs on the activity. He saw the car driven by the fortyish couple leave. Soon afterward a sporty pickup truck pulled up at the gas pump. A dude in a cowboy hat hopped out, pumped gas into his tank, and swaggered inside. Pat Tyler drove away in the shuttle van with her party of eight guys, the four canoes loaded on top.

Feeling more useless than he'd ever felt in his life, Clint pulled out the sheet of paper he'd been studying at the store earlier. He'd folded it and stuck it in his pocket, even though the descriptions of the various floats hadn't jogged his memory. Nor had the map on the back. He still couldn't recall place names from his long-ago experience as a little boy when his old man had taken him on a day's canoe trip on the Buffalo River, their one-and-only father-and-son vacation outing.

Clint had been eight years old. He and Robert Adams had driven from Little Rock, with a borrowed canoe strapped on top of the family car, an old green sedan. They'd arrived somewhere in this general area and parked in a wooded place, where they'd slept overnight in the car. Clint could close his eyes and recapture being wrapped up in a ragged quilt in the back seat.

His dad must have arranged for shuttle transportation. Evidently he'd made some inquiries about put-in and take-out points, but that part was fuzzy in Clint's mind. He'd paid little attention to conversations among adults in those days. He did remember that they'd launched the canoe on a small pebble beach, leaving the car parked there. All day they'd paddled and floated, passing alongside high walls of vivid red limestone. The water had been transparently clear, and fish had darted beneath them, some of them large. Occasionally there had been ripples and the current had become swift, making the trip more adventurous for Clint.

At noon they'd pulled the canoe out on a long stretch of pebbly beach and eaten lunch—sandwiches made with a loaf of white bread and a package of ham and another package of cheese slices. Clint had drunk a soft drink while his father nursed a bottle of beer. Robert Adams had stretched out, cushioning his head on his wadded-up jacket, and taken a nap while Clint explored and climbed a gnarled tree.

His dad had awoken and they'd started out again in the canoe. During the afternoon they spotted a bear at the edge of the woods. Eventually they'd arrived at the takeout point, another pebbly beach where they had to wait awhile before a man came in a van and took them and the canoe back to their car. The drive back to Little Rock had seemed interminable. Clint had slept through much of the journey in the back seat, wrapped in his quilt.

The next year both his parents had been killed when their house in a poor neighborhood burned to the ground. Clint just happened to be spending the night at a buddy's house in the next block. Through blind luck, he'd escaped, but he hadn't felt at all lucky, being put on a bus to Chicago and pawned off on relatives who didn't want him.

Clint hadn't been back to Arkansas since. Not until this trip, which had taken him to Little Rock a couple of days ago. There he'd driven around some crummy residential areas but hadn't stumbled upon his old neighborhood, which undoubtedly didn't exist now. The cheap rental houses hadn't been built to last.

Driving north on the way back to Chicago, he'd decided for no reason at all to make a detour and see the Buffalo River. He'd had no plans whatever for taking another canoe trip. But he had the upper body strength to paddle a canoe. If that couple he'd seen this morning could safely manage the float Pat Tyler had recommended, then he could manage it by himself.

And maybe he would.

Clint refolded the paper and stuck it back into his jeans pocket. Then he levered himself up out of the chair to go to Yellville and get grocery supplies to last him a few days.

The stretch of rural highway was starting to seem familiar. He recognized houses and farms he'd seen in the daylight yesterday afternoon. Reaching town, he drove past Jeremy Wells's gas station and noted how neat and prosperous it looked. The Help Wanted sign was still posted in the plate-glass window.

By the time he'd located the supermarket, Clint had seen all of downtown Yellville, which consisted of a few blocks of businesses clustered around an old-fashioned courthouse. Most of the buildings were one-story, the architecture plain. The more modern commercial development, including the supermarket, was on the outskirts of town, but there were no big-name discount stores, no fast-food franchises.

What Clint found the most odd was the sight of people waving at one another and stopping on the street to chat. He was accustomed to city crowds and hordes of strangers who rubbed elbows and ignored one another. The honking of a horn had never been a sound of friendly greeting as it apparently was here in Yellville.

At least he wasn't the only stranger in town shopping at the local supermarket. In the parking lot, he saw a motor home with a Michigan license plate and a travel trailer hooked to a pickup truck, both with Florida plates. Inside, the husband-and-wife owners of the recreational vehicles were easy to spot and label as retirees. Clint was the only lone male pushing a cart, and he felt conspicuous as hell.

Warding off curious looks in his direction with a frown of concentration, he traveled up and down the aisles, dropping items into his cart. At the meat counter while he was grappling with the packaging system, which wasn't designed with meals for one in mind, he overheard two women with young children riding in their carts discussing Pat Tyler's date the night before.

"Did you hear that Jeremy Wells took Pat Tyler to supper last night at the Front Porch?"

"Yes, I heard! Bob's parents were there, and my mother-in-law called me when she got home. She said they made such a cute couple."

"I hope they get together."

"So do I. Pat's such a great person, and Jeremy would make her a good husband. Poor guy's been through so much, having his wife die young like that. I've never seen a man more broken up than he was at her funeral. And yet he's carried on for the sake of their two children."

"Every Sunday I see them with him at church services. It brings a tear to my eye. He and Pat both deserve the best. I admired her so much for the way she took care of her mother when she got cancer. Then Mr. Tyler developed heart trouble, and Pat nursed him until he died."

"Well, she couldn't do better than Jeremy, not in these parts. Did you know he has a college degree in business administration?"

"I knew he had a degree in something. From a purely practical standpoint, Pat should grab him. She wouldn't have any financial worries. My neighbor's brother is a CPA and does Jeremy's tax returns."

"He has a fine brick house. The inside is beautiful, I hear."

"It would be such a good thing for them to get together."

"Mommy! I need to go potty!"

"Not so loud, Angela," admonished the mother of the child who'd piped up.

Clint could sense the embarrassed glances at him and realized he'd been standing there eavesdropping, holding a package of two steaks in his hands. He dropped it into his cart and moved on to the pork section, where he picked up a pack with four chops and tossed it in.

Over in the produce department he caught snatches of another similar conversation being held by three middle-aged women who expressed the same sentiments. Then at the checkout counter, the female clerk hashed over Pat and Jeremy's date with an overweight woman in line in front of him.

Their budding romance was clearly the talk of the town, and everyone was wholeheartedly in favor of the match. Clint hadn't picked up any snide undertones.

From his sour mood, though, he might have been subjected to malicious gossip. His leg aching from the exercise, he limped out of the store with his bags of groceries. One of them split, spilling the contents on the pavement, when he accidentally bumped it against the door of his automobile. Instead of cursing the flimsy plastic bag, he cursed himself: "Clumsy bastard."

The drive back to the cabin seemed to deplete most of his fast-ebbing energy. It took him two trips to transport his food purchases inside, thanks to the busted bag. He stuck the meat in the refrigerator, left the nonperishables on the counter and hobbled wearily over to the sofa, where he sprawled full length.

It was two hours later when Clint awoke, feeling rested enough to get up and fix himself a sandwich. After he'd eaten, he stowed the rest of his groceries and discovered he'd neglected to buy salt and black pepper. The oversight wasn't a major problem, because Tyler's store probably sold salt and pepper, Clint reflected. He decided to go immediately rather than wait and take a chance on finding the store closed.

The transport van hadn't been parked in front when he returned from town. It was still gone. As Clint pulled up, he could see the teenage girl, Tracy, with the telephone to her ear.

She didn't so much as glance at him when he entered the store. Slouched against the counter, she swiveled her body so that her back was to him. "Did he *really* say that, Ginger! Oh, *no!* You must have *died!*"

Ginger's reply brought a high-pitched giggle. "I can't *believe...* Oh, that's just *too* much! Did you tell Lisa Ann all this?"

Clint had heard more than enough to know that she was visiting with a girlfriend. "Excuse me," he said in a stern voice. "Do you sell salt and black pepper?"

Tracy's head snapped around. "What?"

"I'm a customer, and I want to buy salt and pepper."

"If we sell them, they're probably over there somewhere," she said with a wave of her hand and looked away again. "It's some man that came in the store, Ginger."

She continued her conversation while he found exactly what he needed, salt and pepper in small shakers, packaged together. Nearby were condiments. He picked up a bottle of ketchup and then put it back down again. Buying it would give him a legitimate excuse to return to the store. When Pat was there.

Tracy kept the phone to her ear by contorting her upper body as she rang up Clint's purchase, took his money and made change, all in slow motion and without any show of courtesy. Her whole manner made it plain that she didn't welcome the interruption.

Now he understood why the teenage girl had been third on Pat's list of people to fill in for Homer. Hiring Tracy wasn't much better than locking up the store. It wasn't any of Clint's concern, but Pat was probably losing business if the girl kept the phone tied up and people couldn't get through to make arrangements for canoe rentals or to reserve cabins.

"Aren't you getting paid to work while you're here?" he asked as he took the bills she'd handed him and stuffed them into his wallet. The question had the tone of a reprimand.

She stared at him in surprise. "Wh-what?"

"When you're not busy with customers, shouldn't you

be doing something constructive? Somehow I doubt that Miss Tyler pays you to talk to your friends on the phone.''

Her expression was a mixture of sullenness, resentment and guilt. Still keeping her eyes on him, she mumbled into the phone, ''I gotta hang up now, Ginger.'' After she'd cradled the phone, she sidled from behind the counter with a dust cloth in her hands.

''You have a nice afternoon,'' Clint said. At the door he glanced back over his shoulder. She was dusting merchandise on the shelves.

Her industriousness might not last long, but at least Pat would get some work out of her. And Clint felt surprisingly good about having done what he could on Pat's behalf.

The rest of the afternoon he read a newsmagazine and napped on the sofa. He also kept an eye on the store parking lot. Pat returned in the van with passengers, who reclaimed their automobiles. She left again. Both times Clint was rewarded with glimpses of her slim figure in motion, complete with bouncing ponytail.

The need grew inside him to see her at closer range. To spend a few minutes in her company.

Pat had just sat down in Homer's rocking chair and was taking a big swig from her bottle of root beer when the door to the store was thrust open. She hadn't heard a car, so the tinkling of the bell startled her, and she swallowed wrong as she looked to see who'd entered. The unexpected sight of Clint Adams towering in the doorway set off a bout of strangled coughing.

''Hi,'' she managed to gasp, while pounding her chest. ''I didn't—hear you—drive up.''

''I didn't drive, for a change. I walked,'' he replied.

''Oh,'' she blurted out stupidly. Before she could stop herself, her gaze went to his left leg. His scowl told her he'd noticed her tactless glance. ''I was taking a break. It's been one of those days.'' She gestured with her bottle of root beer, indicating the chair he'd sat in that morning. "Care to take a load off your feet?"

To her pleased astonishment he actually took her up on the offhanded invitation, limping over and lowering his big frame into the chair. His jeans molded his muscular thighs. "Could I get you a soft drink?" Pat asked, her voice strained. She gave her chest a final pat and lowered her hand, his scrutiny making her self-consciously aware of her breasts.

"No, thanks."

"I hope your day went better than mine did."

He shrugged his broad shoulders in partial reply. "You ran into more problems besides Homer's not showing up?"

"That turned out to be minor. On the way back from Maumee, I had a flat tire."

"That rear left tire that was leaking air?"

"The same. I had a devil of a time jacking up the van and loosening the lug nuts."

He was frowning. "I'll bet."

"I finally managed to get the spare on, and I had to run on it part of the day. It was a rough ride, believe me." Pat risked taking a sip of her root beer and swallowed carefully.

"You got the tire repaired?"

"Thanks to Jeremy. In desperation I called him, and he sent a guy to pick up the tire and then had him bring it back and put it on for me. I hated to take advantage of Jeremy like that, but I was in a bind. I had people depending on me."

"I was around all afternoon," Clint said. "I wouldn't have minded bringing the tire to town for you."

"I saw your Suburban parked at the cabin," Pat admitted. "But it would never have entered my mind to intrude on your vacation time."

"This isn't a vacation."

She blinked, taken aback by the sudden harshness of his tone as well as the reply itself. "It isn't?"

"No, it isn't." He pushed himself to his feet abruptly. "I'd better buy a bottle of ketchup before I forget it."

He seemed to be *angry* all of a sudden. Bewildered, Pat rose from her chair, too, and trailed along behind him. "I hope I didn't say something to offend you, Clint."

"No, you didn't. Don't worry about it."

Something *had* triggered anger in him, but what? "I was enjoying our visit," she ventured, stopping at the counter while he clomped down an aisle going straight to the ketchup. "I didn't mean to sound like I was whining and complaining. It wasn't all *that* bad a day. There were some bright spots. For one thing, Tracy actually worked, for a change. She dusted all the shelves and swept the floor and booked some canoe rentals. I don't know what got into her, but I'm grateful for it."

"She's young and needs strict supervision."

"You saw her?" Pat asked with surprise, going behind the counter as he returned.

"This morning when I was leaving I almost ran into her outside. Then I came in during the day to buy something." He set the ketchup down with a little thud.

"You're probably right about the strict supervision. That's where I fall down. I'm not all that comfortable with being a boss. I kind of expect the people I hire to want to do a good job."

"Not everyone is self-motivated." He handed her money.

"It sounds like you *are* comfortable with the role of boss," she said, ringing up the purchase.

"I'm used to giving orders and taking them. Or I was," he added shortly.

"'Orders'?" Pat repeated. "That has the ring of the military." She gave him his change, her fingers touching his large palm. The casual contact sent tingles throughout her body. "Would you like a bag?"

"No, thanks." The refusal was brusque. He'd closed his

hand around the coins and grabbed up the ketchup in his other hand.

"Sometimes they come in handy. I usually offer." She sounded slightly giddy, the way she felt. "What were we talking about? I've completely lost the thread of the conversation."

"It's just as well," he replied and headed for the door. "Take it easy."

"You, too." He was on foot, she remembered. "By the way, you're welcome to go out the back door. It's shorter. There's a path from my driveway to your cabin. The one I took last night." The offer was impulsive.

"I think I can manage the longer walk." He jerked open the door.

"I don't doubt you can. I didn't mean any insult—"

The door pulled closed on her apologetic voice.

Darn! She'd managed to say the wrong thing again! Pat peered out, watching him tromp with his uneven gait in the direction of the road leading up the hill. Her regret gave way to exasperation at herself after he'd disappeared from sight. "You act like such an *idiot* around him!" she exclaimed, clutching her head in both hands. "Why does he have that effect on you! Your silly heart pounds, and your knees get weak. Your brain turns to *mush,* for heaven's sake!"

Still sputtering aloud to herself, she locked up the store, leaving the cash in the register. There was less than a hundred dollars, and so far Tyler's had never been robbed.

By the time she'd walked to her house and taken a long shower, Pat had calmed down. As she microwaved a frozen dinner and ate it, she mulled over her conversation with Clint Adams. What had he meant by his statement that he wasn't on vacation? Why had he come to the Ozarks?

As uncommunicative as he was, Pat might never get answers to those questions and a hundred others she wanted to ask him. And she just couldn't accept the idea of not knowing anything about him. It was more than normal curiosity. Nothing about her reactions and responses to him were "normal" for her.

He'd known exactly where to find the ketchup. Why hadn't he bought it on his earlier trip to the store? Was there the tiniest possibility that he'd postponed buying ketchup until later when *she* was there?

"Naw," Pat said glumly.

The phone rang just as she finished washing her plate and fork and knife. She answered the call, glad to talk to anyone, even a stranger calling to try to sell her something.

"Hi, Pat. It's Jeremy."

"Hi, Jeremy! I was going to call you tonight and thank you for saving my life."

He laughed. "That's overstating matters just a little bit."

They talked for about ten minutes. With a part of her mind Pat was thinking that he had a pleasant, manly voice. Why didn't it cause a shivery sensation to race down her spine, the way Clint Adams's voice did?

Chapter Four

Clint's fingers were clenched tight around the bottle of ketchup as he labored up the road to the cabin, curbing the urge to hurl the ketchup into the woods.

Pathetic bastard. He'd had to clamp his jaws shut after he'd corrected her about being on vacation. He'd wanted to pour out his whole hard-luck story. Then she would really pity him. Maybe she would offer to get a wheelchair instead of kindly recommending a shortcut.

It made him feel so damned worthless to know she'd needed a favor that day and the thought hadn't crossed her mind that maybe he could help her out. He'd been right there at the cabin, lying around and doing nothing, but she'd called Jeremy Wells and let him solve her problem. Wells had undoubtedly jumped at the chance to put himself out for her. The idea shouldn't have been galling. Clint should be glad that Pat had someone ready and willing to come to her rescue.

You should pack up and get the hell out of here. Head back to Chicago, where you belong.

There was nothing for Clint in Arkansas.

At the cabin he got the pack of steaks out of the refrigerator and removed one to cook for his dinner. Whether he had an appetite or not, it was time for him to start eating regular meals.

There was an outdoor grill for his use, but since Clint hadn't bought charcoal, he used the oven broiler. The steak was too well-done, and the potato he baked in the microwave had a marble center, but he doused the steak with ketchup and ate about three-quarters of it and the cooked part of the potato. In the meantime a pot of coffee had brewed. He poured himself a mugful, the aroma tripping his memory of his visit to the store that morning.

Like every encounter with Pat Tyler, it had been a mix of pleasure and humiliation. Before the day was over, he'd gone back for another battering of his pride. Tomorrow would he keep his distance? Clint asked himself the question as he took his coffee onto the front porch and sat down in the chair. *No way.* If he stayed, he would manage to see her and talk to her.

It had gotten dark by now, but the light from inside the cabin spilled softly out onto the porch and beyond it a short distance, illuminating Pat's old dog, Rowdy, as he approached.

"Hi, there, big fella." Clint greeted him with a note of warm welcome. "Did you come to visit the injured?"

The huge dog took his words as an invitation, climbing the steps with his dignified air and coming near to be stroked and petted.

"Where's your owner?" Clint asked. "Did she go out tonight and leave you at home with no company?" Out with Jeremy Wells. Clint's next swallow of coffee was bitter on his tongue.

Rowdy sniffed the air, eyeing the open doorway.

"You smell my dinner, don't you, fella? Well, you're in luck. There're some leftovers for you."

Clint went inside and got his plate and set it down on the porch. With a delicacy that was completely incongruous with his size, Rowdy consumed every morsel and polished the plate clean. Afterward he lay down beside Clint's chair. Clint sipped his coffee and carried on a one-sided conversation with the animal.

"I'll bet Pat talks to you like this," he said, draining his cup. "I can tell you're used to human conversation."

At the mention of her name, the big dog came alert, glancing toward the store and off into the woods, presumably in the direction of her house.

"You'd better go check on her, fella. She's your first responsibility." Clint gave him a gentle pat on the rump. "Tell you what. I'll save you part of my dinner tomorrow night."

Rowdy gave him a goodbye lick on his hand and departed.

The promise obligated Clint to stay at least one more day.

At daybreak Clint awoke, feeling rested as he had the previous morning. With gray light filtering into the cabin, he got up and limped into the kitchen, shivering with the early-morning coolness on his bare skin, to start a pot of coffee brewing. While he was filling the carafe with water, he glanced out the window over the sink and murmured in surprise, "I'll be damned. Look at that." Deer were grazing in the hollow behind the cabin. Among them was a mother deer and a fawn.

The water from the tap overflowed the carafe as Clint gazed at the unexpected sight, filled with a sense of awe and reverence for nature. This was worth a trip to Arkansas, he thought. It was a living picture stuck in his album of special memories, like that glimpse of the bear on the canoeing trip with his old man.

While he was getting dressed, Clint decided that he would rent a canoe from Pat and make the float she'd recommended to the couple. He would see her during the day and try to set up the arrangements for tomorrow. His best bet was to catch her this morning before things got too hectic.

As he set out on the hike to the store, Clint paused, eyeing the path leading through the woods. Pat probably wouldn't mind if he took her offer in reverse and entered through the back of the store. *What the hell. Take the shortcut.* Clint's mood was such this morning that he could follow his own advice.

Birds were flittering in the trees and chirping and singing. The pungent scent of pine was in the air. Sucking in deep breaths as he walked along the path, Clint felt a surge of something similar to optimism.

Maybe his leg would mend and stop hurting so damned bad. Maybe being discharged from the marines wasn't the end of the world. Maybe—

He cut off the wishful speculation, emerging from the woods onto the driveway that split off from the road. Looking in the direction of the highway, he could see the back of the store. Looking in the opposite direction, he could see the front of Pat's house. It was a modest one-story frame structure resting on cement blocks. Painted white with black trim, it had a porch without a railing. At one end of the porch was a swing.

A fragment of one of the conversations Clint had overheard yesterday at the supermarket popped into his mind. *Jeremy has a fine brick house. The inside is beautiful.*

"Damned small-town gossips," he muttered, conscious suddenly of the throbbing in his leg as he continued on his way.

When he'd gotten closer to the store, Clint could see that the back door was ajar, a good sign that Pat was inside. Then a few yards away from the building he was treated to the sound of her voice. "Mama Cat, you must be eating your weight in cat food. Your dish is empty, and I filled it last night. When are those kittens due, anyway? You can come out. No, Rowdy, you stay in the front of the store,'' she scolded. ''You'll scare Mama Cat—''

A loud hiss signaled the cat's reaction to Rowdy's appearance. Seconds later a furry blur streaked out. Clint was in mid-stride, just reaching the door, and the terrified cat hurtled itself straight at his feet. Concerned about not stepping on it, he tried to hop sideways, lost his balance and came down hard on his left foot. Cursing with the pain, he grabbed for the doorframe.

''Clint! Are you okay?'' Pat had thrown the door wide open and stepped out to grasp his arm.

''Of course, I'm okay,'' he growled angrily. ''Just give me room.'' He jerked his elbow.

Immediately she dropped her hands and moved about a foot away, murmuring, ''Sorry.''

In addition to the pain and embarrassment, Clint felt like a total heel. ''Why should you be sorry? You haven't done anything to be sorry about.''

''I know by now that you don't want any sympathy, but I get all flustered....'' Her voice drifted off. She stepped inside the open doorway, where Rowdy stood surveying the two of them. ''See what you caused, Rowdy? You scared Mama Cat and she nearly caused Clint to fall.''

The big dog whined as though in apology.

''When you come in, Clint, leave the door open a few inches, would you, please? Then Mama Cat can sneak back in.'' With no further ado, she left him to collect the tatters of his pride and enter in his own good time.

Clint's gratitude for her kindness and consideration swelled his chest, making room for a fierce, but gentle emotion he'd never felt before. How many other women would have handled him with kid gloves like that? Not many. Probably none. Pat Tyler was one of a kind. Meeting her came in the same category as looking out the cabin window and seeing those wild deer grazing.

Pat rubbed her palms against her jeans, making her skin burn. Clint Adams's forearm had felt like ridged iron pulsing with warm blood. Some Good Samaritan she was. Every pang of very real sympathy on his behalf was edged with excitement.

If Pat had any hope of acting normally around Clint, she needed some warning that he was nearby. All of a sudden he had been there at the back door when she hadn't dreamed he was anywhere close. Like every other time, she'd done or said the wrong thing and made him angry. Not angry at her. Just angry.

Today he was wearing military fatigues like those he'd been wearing day before yesterday when she'd seen him at Jeremy's gas station. Day before yesterday? Had she actually known him less than forty-eight hours?

Just settle down and treat him like you treat men customers and renters, Pat coached herself as she attended to small tasks like replenishing the stack of information sheets on the counter up at the front of the store.

"Help yourself to coffee," she called, hearing his footsteps in the storeroom. "I haven't gotten around to taking anything out of the freezer for a breakfast snack."

"Can I pour you a cup?" he asked.

The gruff offer took her totally by surprise. "Why, sure," she said. "I take a heaping spoon of creamer and two sugars."

He didn't answer, of course. Finding the silence unbearable, Pat made small talk for both of them, chattering about any safe subject that came to mind. "I'm waiting to hear whether Homer's feeling well enough to mind the store today. I would go ahead and have Tracy come again, since she did pretty well yesterday. But I don't dare risk hurting Homer's feelings. He probably mentioned to you that he and my father were bosom buddies. Ethel, Homer's daughter, does cleaning and also some cooking for me. She's a marvelous cook. You sampled her sausage biscuits."

"I thought those looked homemade. They were good,

even frozen and rewarmed,'' Clint said, on his way to the front of the store, carrying two cups of coffee. The plastic holders looked tiny in his big hands. He handed hers to her.

"Thank you.'' Pat immediately took a big swallow. The coffee was too hot and scalded her throat. "What was I saying? Oh, Ethel's sausage biscuits. You'll have to taste her cake doughnuts. I'll get a box of them out of the freezer. She uses my mother's recipe. Mom was a super cook.''

Clint was leaning against the counter, sipping his coffee and probably resting his bad leg. Pat didn't dare suggest that he might want to sit down in a chair. Since he seemed attentive, she kept talking. "Unfortunately, she didn't teach me to be one, though she would have if I'd been more interested. She had tons of patience.''

"You don't cook for yourself?''

"From the way that question's worded, you're expecting a *no* answer,'' Pat said ruefully. "I'll bet it didn't even cross your mind that I might have made those sausage biscuits.'' While he was noticing that she definitely wasn't centerfold material, he probably hadn't sized her up as the homemaker type, either.

He shrugged. "I didn't give any thought to who had made them.''

"To answer your question, I mainly fix myself sandwiches and heat up meals in the microwave. Ethel, bless her, takes pity on me and makes up some frozen dinners with her surplus. One thing I *can* do well is fry fish,'' she declared. "My dad always cooked the fried fish outside. I learned his method.''

"Deep-fried with a cornmeal coating?''

"Right. Cooked crisp and golden brown. Have you had it cooked like that in Illinois?''

"Not in Illinois, but I ate it when I was a kid growing up in Little Rock.''

Pat's mouth dropped open. "You're from Little Rock originally? So you're an Arkansas native?''

He swallowed a gulp of his coffee. "Technically, I suppose I am."

His answer didn't exactly encourage prying for more information, but her curiosity was stronger than her sense of caution. "Do you still have family living there?"

"No."

"When did you move to Illinois?"

"At the age of nine." He straightened, reaching toward the stack of information sheets and taking the top one. Pat blinked in reaction as he slapped it onto the counter. "Sign me up for the float from Buffalo Point to Rush. I'd like to go tomorrow, if possible."

It took a few seconds for his words on a totally different subject to sink in. "You mean you want to join a party who'll be making that float?"

He shook his head. "No, I don't mean that. I'll make it by myself."

"Clint, that's not recommended by the National Park Service. I'd be worried about you. With your leg—"

"I don't plan to paddle the damned canoe with my leg," he interrupted, ripping the empty plastic cup out of his coffee holder. "But if it goes against your policy, just say so. I'll rent a canoe from your competition." He wheeled around to leave. "Thanks for the coffee."

"Just wait a darned minute!" Pat exclaimed. "If you're going to rent a canoe anyway, you can rent it from me, for pete's sake! Why do you have to be so doggone *touchy?*"

She hadn't realized until he turned around to face her again that she'd planted her hands on her hips. Her indignation fizzled and turned into self-consciousness under his dark scrutiny.

"Look, you have enough headaches without me adding to them," he said. "If you're not comfortable with renting me a canoe, then don't."

"You said tomorrow?" she inquired, picking up a pen. "If your idea is to have the river to yourself, you'll want to start out early." Then in the event of a mishap, chances were good that help would come along. He wouldn't be stranded—a thought Pat found somewhat reassuring.

"Going early suits me fine. What time?"

"Six o'clock?"

"Six o'clock," he agreed.

Pat jotted on her desk calendar as if she could possibly forget. She would have trouble *not* thinking about transporting him tomorrow morning and picking him up later in the day.

"Thanks again for the coffee." He hesitated. "I'll be around today. If you have more tire problems—or if anything comes up and you need a hand—just let me know." Not waiting for any reply, he headed toward the back of the store.

"Thanks, Clint. I'll do that," Pat said after she'd recovered from her surprise. "So long. See you tomorrow morning. If not before then," she added.

After he'd gone, she allowed herself half a minute or so to blow out a breath and recover from his early-morning visit. Why did he affect her the way he did? Some kind of physical chemistry? It was a puzzle. The reaction wasn't wearing off with repetition. Pat was just learning what to expect. A speeded-up heartbeat, tingles down her spine, weakness in her knees. An adolescent self-consciousness.

Hope I don't start giggling, she thought half seriously, snapping herself into action and performing tasks around the store. When the phone rang, she raced to answer it, expecting the caller to be Ethel making a report on Homer. Instead, she recognized the nasal voice of Tracy's mother, Melba Wiggins.

"Tried to call you last night, Pat, but your phone was busy. I said to Fred, 'Wonder who she's talking to for so long at this hour.'" Fred was her husband and Tracy's father. "Finally I gave up."

"What was on your mind, Melba?" Pat inquired, cheerfully ignoring both the note of complaint and the unspoken question: Who *were* you talking to?

To tell Melba any item of personal information was the same as sending an announcement to every person in the county. She was a good-hearted woman, but also a big gossip. Her reason for calling, Pat suspected, was to follow up on the news of Pat's date with Jeremy.

"I wanted to tell you that Fred and I have decided it's not safe for a girl Tracy's age to tend your store by herself. We don't like the idea one bit of her having to put up with rude treatment from strange men."

"Rude treatment from strange men? She didn't mention anything like that to me."

"Nor to me. You know how secretive teenage girls are. I happened to hear her on the phone with her girlfriend, Ginger. Later I pulled the story out of her. It seems this man she'd seen leaving the store yesterday morning came back later in the day and ordered her around. A big, tall, dark-haired man who walked with a limp."

Clint.

"What did he say to her?"

"Told her she shouldn't use the phone, for one thing. Asked her if you hadn't given her things to do when she wasn't waiting on customers. Tracy was on pins and needles after he left, afraid he might come in again."

"I was very pleased at the amount of work she accomplished."

Now Pat understood the sudden reform in the lazy teenager. Clint was responsible. He could have explained Tracy's unusual industriousness and taken credit during his and Pat's late-afternoon conversation. But he hadn't.

"Don't you think you should call the sheriff?" demanded Melba. "That man might be an escaped convict. Like I said to Fred, you don't have the fear of a normal woman, Pat, being raised as a tomboy."

"From your description, Melba, I recognize the man, and he isn't a convict. He's staying in one of my cabins. Tracy was in absolutely no danger from him."

It was odd, but Pat couldn't have been surer of the truth

of her own words. For all his seething anger and brusque, unfriendly manner, Clint wouldn't harm a woman.

"Oh. Well, he's still a stranger."

"That's the nature of my business—renting cabins and canoes to people who come to the Ozarks on vacation," Pat replied. "There's a certain amount of risk, but there's risk in everything in life. I'm sorry Tracy got a scare. If you and Fred feel uneasy about her tending the store for me in the future, then certainly I respect your fears as a parent. Thanks for calling and explaining."

"You know me. Always aboveboard," Melba said. "What's this I hear about you being courted by Jeremy Wells?"

"If going on one date is being courted, then I guess it's true, Melba. Say hello to Fred and tell him how much I enjoyed the fish he gave me a couple of weeks ago."

"That husband of mine loves to fish. Our freezer is over-flowing."

Pat responded and ended the conversation on a friendly note before Melba could get in more nosy questions. Minutes later the phone rang again, and this time it was Ethel with the welcome news that Homer was feeling much better and intended to come to work.

So I'm set for today, Pat reflected with relief.

Maybe those Help Wanted notices she'd put up in town along with word-of-mouth advertising would yield some results before the week was over, and she would hire a driver. She certainly hoped so. Then Homer could just come by to visit and occupy his favorite chair.

At seven o'clock her parties started arriving in numbers large enough for a vanload. Homer showed up. Pat was busy getting the correct number of canoes and life jackets and paddles loaded up and just as involved in getting acquainted with first-time customers and reacquainted with several who were repeat clients.

It was such a familiar scene for her—one she'd thrived on her entire life. Her dad had buckled her into a car seat and taken her along with him on shuttle trips before she could walk. Her mom had held Pat in her arms and helped her ring up purchases on the cash register, pressing Pat's small forefinger to the right numbers. This morning in the midst of the relaxed mayhem, Pat found herself wondering, *Could I be happy without this?*

During the rest of the day, she mulled the question over on those stretches of road or highway she drove without passengers. She also mulled over the information Melba Wiggins had divulged about Clint's having scolded Tracy yesterday for being lax in her duties. Had he just gotten annoyed because Tracy wasn't helpful and attentive when he came into the store?

Or had he been looking out for Pat's interests?

On the return trip to the cabin, Clint noticed the ruts in Pat's driveway. It could use a load of gravel spread thinly for top dressing. A second inspection of her house, even from a distance, also revealed signs of neglect. One corner of the porch sagged, and the white paint had a telltale dinginess. Some years had probably passed since the house had been freshly painted.

A single-car garage was located to one side of the house. The double doors, which were closed, hung crookedly. A missing hinge or two had probably caused the irregular crack down the center. More than likely the garage was a storage building for yard tools and a lawn mower, none of which had gotten much use this spring, from the appearance of things. The lawn needed cutting, and some weed-eating and pruning would improve the looks of the place considerably.

Was there a shortage of labor for yard work around here, too? Clint wondered. He couldn't imagine that there were no teenage boys in the area willing to earn some pocket money. Quite possibly Pat was just too busy trying to run her business without adequate help to worry about keeping her yard neat.

As for house maintenance, that could get expensive. Perhaps she couldn't afford to hire carpenters and painters. Her parents' illnesses might have drained their savings, if they'd had savings. Clint didn't see any evidence of wealth. Unless a car was parked in the garage, Pat must not have an automobile to drive other than the Tyler shuttle van.

She needed good help in the worst way. At the rate she was going, she would run herself ragged while home and business went downhill.

Of course, if she married Jeremy Wells, as everyone who knew her seemed to think she should do, she could wash her hands of all her problems, move to Yellville and live in his "fine brick house."

Hell, if Pat were asking Clint for advice—something she wasn't likely to do—he would have to add his favorable vote, based on his own impressions of Jeremy Wells and what other people had said about him. The words wouldn't come out easily, but Clint would get them out. *Sure, you should probably marry Wells, if the guy has as much going for him as he seems to.*

About fifty times more than Clint had going for him. Ex-marine with a high-school education. Useless.

His morale at rock bottom, Clint limped along the path through the woods. All his earlier optimism had fizzled. When he reached the cabin, he had no interest in eating breakfast, but he downed a bowl of cereal with a sliced banana on top.

At midmorning, he went for a drive, turning left onto Highway 14 and following it to a high bridge that spanned the Buffalo National River. Down below, a group of twenty-five or thirty people were launching canoes. In the large gravel parking lot was a bus owned by an outfitting company whose glossy brochure Clint had passed over a couple of days earlier in favor of Pat Tyler's pamphlet.

He remembered hearing her tell Wells at the gas station that her father's old bus was out of commission. Clint assumed she'd been referring to the one that was up on blocks back in the trees near the store. Evidently it had been in use during past years, allowing Tyler's to transport large groups like this one.

What was mechanically wrong with the bus? Clint wondered as he turned around to cross over the bridge again and head back the same way he'd come. At the turnoff to Buffalo Point, he slowed down and speeded up again. He didn't much feel like sight-seeing.

And he'd told Pat he would be around today.

For lunch Clint made himself a couple of sandwiches. During the afternoon he read and napped. With the inactivity his leg bothered him less. The mere fact that he was making his services available to Pat and thus had a reason to kill time and do nothing seemed to ease his irritability.

At sundown he sat on the front porch, watched the western sky turn a delicate pink color and exerted his willpower by not walking to the store on some pretext. Night fell. Clint fixed himself dinner, cooking an extra pork chop for old Rowdy. The giant dog showed up as though keeping a date, politely cleaned up the leftovers, and visited awhile as he had the previous evening.

After old Rowdy had left, dispatched to do his watchdog's duties, Clint washed up the dishes, went to bed and had no trouble falling asleep. *Must be something in the air, maybe the pine sap, acting on me like a damned sleeping pill,* he thought drowsily as he burrowed his head into his pillow.

The next morning at daybreak when he got up, the deer were once again grazing in the hollow. Clint stood at the kitchen sink sipping fresh-brewed coffee and watched them through the window for several minutes. It was a picture of grace and beauty that soothed the rawness inside him.

His stomach growled as he poured cereal into a bowl for his breakfast, and his mouth actually watered when he was slicing up a ripe peach. Sitting on his butt for the past day and a half must have restored the first signs of his old appetite, Clint reflected, pouring milk from a gallon jug.

He ate his breakfast with enjoyment. When he'd finished, he packed a lunch, wishing he had a couple of beers to substitute for the two colas he stuck into the small cooler. Carrying the cooler, he set out on foot for the store, taking the path through the woods.

This was the nearest Clint had felt to being back in control since he'd regained consciousness in a hospital in Chicago nine weeks ago.

Pat was *ready* for Clint to show up at the store this morning, by golly. The back door stood wide open, in case he took the shortcut again. But she was also keeping an eye on the front door, in case he didn't.

The coffee was made. Raisin-and-bran muffins that she'd baked herself, no less, using a boxed mix, were arranged on a plate. They didn't look like the picture on the box, unfortunately. The tops were somewhat malformed, and the sides had little pieces missing that had stuck to the pan, but she'd eaten one muffin and it had tasted rather dry, but was edible.

Last night she'd been bored and lonely and had gone into the kitchen on some strange impulse. But even her mother's kindly ghost looking over her shoulder and giving instructions hadn't turned Pat into Betty Crocker.

"It's your fault, Rowdy," Pat said to him as he came up beside her and seemed to be surveying the plate of muffins with an air of commiseration. "You went out roaming and weren't there to remind me that I can't boil water without burning it."

He pricked his ears, looking toward the storeroom. Pat's heart began to drum in her chest. "Do you hear someone coming?" she asked, tucking her T-shirt into her jeans more neatly.

Normally she just hopped out of bed in the morning and pulled on the T-shirt that was on the top of the stack, but today she'd stood shivering in her bra and panties, picking out a newish red one to wear with a pair of jeans that weren't threadbare. "Red is a peppy color. It makes me feel energetic," she'd explained to Rowdy, who'd yawned and averted his head as though to say, *Tell me another one.* "All right, I've always been told it's my most becoming color. I admit I want to do what I can to boost my confidence around Clint. Okay?"

Now she spoke in a stern tone to her large gentle pet, also grasping his collar when he made a movement toward the door to the storeroom. "Oh, no, you don't. You wait right here with me to welcome Clint. We're not taking any chances on scaring Mama Cat into making a dash for it."

With her other hand Pat was using her palm to iron out any fold creases in the T-shirt. From her jitters, she might have been all dressed and waiting for her date on prom night.

Clint appeared in the back door, pausing on the threshold, tall and ruggedly male in his camouflage military fatigues. The sight of him set off the usual tingles and melting of joints. If she could just gaze long and hard at him for about thirty minutes, maybe that would cure what ailed her, Pat thought.

"Good morning," she called cheerfully to him, noticing that he looked irritated. "All set for your float?"

"Good morning. I see you've turned this door into the handicapped entrance." His brusque note didn't prevent his deep voice from triggering a quiver of response in her midriff. Pat expanded on her cure theory: While she was looking her fill and getting desensitized to him, he should be talking to her.

Cure or no, the idea was wonderfully enticing.

"You mean because I left it wide open? I didn't do that for your sake. Honest." Pat decided to go ahead and explain. "It was my way of being prepared for you to show up this morning."

He crossed the storeroom and passed through the open doorway of the store proper, stopping when he was a couple of yards away from her. Pat sucked in a lungful of air, realizing that she'd been holding her breath, bracing herself to contend with his nearness. Rowdy's welcoming whine also brought her alert to the fact that she still gripped the dog's collar.

"You can let him go now," Clint said with the same repressed anger. "I've managed to get inside safely without falling on my butt."

"I can't win with you, can I?" Pat demanded, welcoming her spurt of indignation. "Is it such a crime to show some consideration for your fellow man? I try to be nice to everybody who walks in here, with or without a limp." She marched over to the coffeepot, stuck a plastic cup in a holder, filled the cup with steaming liquid and added creamer and sugar, conscious that he was watching her every move. "There," she said, moving aside and gesturing broadly with her empty hand. "Help yourself to coffee, if you want some."

"I've already had several cups," he said, but he set down the small cooler he carried and stepped to the counter, where he followed the same procedure she had, but adding only one sugar and omitting the creamer.

They both sipped their coffee, standing there a few feet apart in silence. Pat sensed that his anger had dissipated. So had her own spurt of ill temper.

"Have a muffin," she invited offhandedly, taking one herself.

He glanced at the plate of muffins. "No, thanks."

"They don't taste half bad." Crushed by his refusal, Pat took a big bite.

"I had breakfast."

"A little dry," she admitted after she'd washed down her mouthful with coffee. "I probably should just pitch them in the garbage."

"Maybe muffins don't freeze well," he suggested.

"These haven't been frozen. They were fresh-baked. By me, not Ethel."

He took a swallow of coffee. "You ran out of her baked goods?"

Pat actually considered lying. But truthfulness was too ingrained in her nature. "No, I just took a notion to try my hand at baking. Go ahead and say what you're thinking— that if the way to a man's heart is through his stomach, I'm out of luck."

He downed the rest of his coffee like it was a liquid dose of medicine. "Maybe your next attempt will be better, when it counts."

"When it counts?"

"When you're cooking something for Wells. He's the guy you're out to impress, not me."

Pat stared at him. "I'm not out to impress Jeremy *or* you. I wouldn't know how to go about it. I was always too busy being a tomboy to learn." Having bared her soul, she gulped down the rest of her coffee while he disposed of his plastic cup in the trash can and set his holder on the counter. "What are you doing?" she demanded.

He'd picked up a napkin and was reaching for a muffin. "I'll take one and have it later, if you're going to throw them away."

"Take the whole plateful and feed them to the turtles, for all I care." Pat tossed her cup in the trash can and left him there to do as he pleased. For two cents, she would have made tracks to her house and changed into her oldest T-shirt in some washed-out color.

Chapter Five

Clint stuck the wrapped muffin in the tray in the top of his cooler and walked to the front of the store, where Pat waited for him, keys in hand.

"Hey, I didn't mean to hurt your feelings," he said.

"Don't make things worse by apologizing."

It was so like her not to make any phony denial that her feelings had been hurt. Clint wished like hell he'd eaten one of the damned muffins. "I really did eat breakfast. Otherwise I would have had a muffin."

"Sure you would." She pushed the door open for him. "Ready to go?"

The odd gentleness welled up in Clint's breast. He wanted to mend the injury to her pride enough to persist. "Look, I'm not picky about food, not after eating most of my meals in mess halls for seventeen years."

"Seventeen years?" She'd been avoiding looking at him. Now her blue eyes were fixed on his face, mirroring interest. "You must have enlisted when you were eighteen."

Clint hadn't intended to shift the emphasis to him. It had done the trick, all right, but he'd laid himself open to questions that would encourage him to spill his guts. He cut off further discussion with an abrupt nod toward the rear of the store. "Don't forget that back door's wide open."

She glanced absently toward the storeroom. "I'm coming straight back here after I drop you off. But I guess I should at least close it."

"You should lock it."

His words of advice were directed to her back. She was halfway to the storeroom, walking with her bouncy stride, glossy brown ponytail swishing from side to side. Clint let his gaze settle on her pert rear and felt a stirring in his loins.

Quickly he averted his head and limped outside. His sex drive had returned, along with his appetite. He was still a man. All he needed was to find a woman who got turned on by cripples, Clint reflected with equal amounts of bitterness and disgust with himself for lusting after Pat.

Rowdy had followed after him. When Clint came to a standstill, the big dog gave his hand a warm lick. Clint stroked his head, hearing the store door being closed.

"Normally he's not so quick to make friends," Pat commented. "He took to you right away."

The lilt was back in her voice, the episode with the muffins apparently forgotten. It didn't surprise Clint in the least that she wasn't one of those women who pouted. Jeremy Wells was a lucky son of a gun, whether or not he ever got a decent home-cooked meal after he married her.

When he'd stepped outside, Clint hadn't noticed that a canoe was strapped to the top of the vehicle. His gaze fixed on it as he turned to walk to the van. He'd meant to load up his own canoe. The fact that she'd had someone else load it in advance was like alcohol poured into an open wound. He clamped his jaw shut but he *had* to say something or bust. "Did you arrange to have some guy meet us and unload that damned canoe?'' he asked harshly as he headed toward the passenger side of the van.

"No, I thought the two of us could manage."

"I can manage fine. You just stay out of my way. I'm not a hundred-and-ninety-pound weakling."

"I've never doubted your strength," she protested. "It's your balance."

"If I lose my balance, I deserve to fall on my butt." He jerked open the van door and hoisted himself into the passenger seat, thoroughly humiliated.

With her agile quickness, Pat had covered the longer distance around to the driver's side and hopped up behind the wheel. "I would never intentionally hurt your pride, Clint." Reinforcing the earnestness of her words, she reached over and laid her hand on his forearm.

Clint's entire body reacted to her warm touch. In his state of charged-up emotion, the stir of desire he'd felt minutes earlier burgeoned into a hard, powerful need. "Don't do that," he bit out, tensing to assert control over himself. But she was already drawing her hand back.

With a deep intake of breath, she wiped her palm on her thigh and then continued to rub back and forth. "Now I say I'm sorry, and you get more offended because I apologize. We go through this same routine."

"Let's change it, then. I'll say I'm sorry for being a bad-tempered SOB. Try not to let me ruin your day." His voice was gruff with his sincerity.

"What's more important is *your* day. I have good days all the time."

Clint reached over and gave her hand a squeeze, partly to thank her for being the rare person she was and partly to halt the rubbing that he found highly arousing. "My day will go all right. Hadn't we better shove off so you can get back?"

"Sure thing." She sounded odd, almost dazed, and sucked in another deep breath before she started the engine, reacting in slow motion—for her. He eyed her with concern, wondering what was wrong. She darted a glance at him, seeming embarrassed.

Why embarrassed? All Clint could figure was that she'd noticed the bulging proof that he'd gotten physically aroused. He cupped his hands over his crotch as the van bumped along the gravel road toward the highway.

"Do you like bluegrass music?" she asked, breaking the strained silence. Or strained lack of conversation. The various rattles and engine noise didn't exactly make for a quiet ride. "My tapes are all bluegrass and country-western."

"Play whatever you feel like listening to."

She pushed a tape into the tape-player unit that had been home installed and mounted low under the dashboard. Lively bluegrass music filled the van. The vocal harmony and joyful blend of fiddle and banjo and guitar might have released some of Clint's tension, if he hadn't had to work so hard at closing his mind to Pat's animation as she tapped out the tempo on the steering wheel and hopped her left knee up and down. Soon her shoulders got into the act and her head bobbed from side to side, activating her ponytail.

He managed during the ten-minute ride to look straight ahead or out his window for the most part and not gaze at her like a hungry wolf. But he didn't manage not to visualize her slim form in the red T-shirt and jeans, pulsing with life and energy. This was a different kind of lust than any Clint had experienced with other women. In it was an element of longing that he could only chalk up to his new status as invalid.

"There's the rangers' station." Pat indicated a brown building on their right. They were driving through thickly-forested national parkland by this point. Clint focused on his surroundings as she called his attention to camping areas for tent campers and others for recreational vehicles, to asphalt roads leading to additional park facilities including rustic cabins for rent and a restaurant that operated during peak months.

Few people were up and about, due to the early hour. It

was out of consideration, Clint knew, that Pat had turned down the volume of the music.

"Here we are," she announced, steering the van down a steep paved incline and then onto a graveled beach. "This is Buffalo Point. Isn't it a pretty spot?"

"I'll say." He followed her example and quietly closed the van door after he'd gotten out.

"Pretty" wasn't an adequate description, but Clint doubted anyone but a poet could capture in words the beauty and tranquillity of the scene he gazed upon with her. A sheer limestone wall with vivid strata of red and orange formed a backdrop on the opposite side of the beach. The river itself was narrow—no more than fifty feet across—and over it hung a delicate veil of mist.

"I envy you," Pat said with a wistful sigh. "Would you believe I haven't floated the river in the past three years?" Before Clint could answer, she walked to the side of the van and began tugging at one of the elastic cords holding the canoe in place.

"I'll do that."

He limped over, and she stood aside and watched him unclip the cords. When he moved to the rear of the van to slide the canoe off, she came, too.

"I don't need your help," Clint told her. "Just stand back."

"The ground isn't level—"

"Damn it, I can see the ground isn't level! I'm not blind as well as crippled!"

"You're not crippled...." With obvious reluctance, she retreated eight or ten yards, giving him the room he wanted.

Clint adopted the same technique his father had used so many years ago, holding the canoe aloft over his head, bottom up like a pod-shaped umbrella. Pat followed behind him as he walked down the graveled incline to the water's edge. Once his right foot skidded a few inches, and he heard her suck in her breath sharply.

"Great," she said when he set the canoe down on its keel, angling the bow out into the river.

"There's nothing 'great' about it," he countered, irked that she sounded so hugely relieved. "I can bench-press two hundred and fifty pounds." Or he *could,* before his accident. Clint had never been into muscle building, but he'd worked out regularly, keeping fit.

"Wow, I'm impressed. That's a lot of weight."

"Not really. Three hundred pounds is a lot of weight." He hadn't been trying to impress her, just get across the point that he had the normal strength of a man his size and age.

"Whatever you say. I weigh a hundred and twenty. That means you can lift two of me." Her cheeks turned pink, and she glanced away from him, as though suddenly embarrassed by the conversation. "Here I am holding you up, in a manner of speaking. I'll go get your paddle and life jacket and flotation cushions for you to sit on. And your lunch." She was on her way to the van.

"You can't carry all that by yourself." Clint limped along in her wake, wondering what had caused her embarrassment. He looked down at himself, verifying that his pants fit comfortably now without disguising the fact that he was male.

On the return trip, Clint was conscious of her matching her pace to his. He forced himself to walk faster, although his bad leg ached from the combination of uphill and downhill hikes. When they reached the canoe and she took the cooler and paddle from his hands, he didn't put up any resistance. He was glad to stand there and rest a minute, with his weight on his good leg.

"There," she said, standing back after she'd finished stowing everything and had stacked four or five square cushions to form a seat for him near the middle of the canoe, which had been designed for two people to occupy the seats in the bow and the stern. Clint understood enough about canoeing to know that he couldn't sit at either end and steer. It made him feel stupid not to have given any thought to improvising a seat.

"Thanks to you, I'm all set now," he said. "I can manage from here." He definitely didn't want her as an audience while he got himself into the canoe and got it afloat. Between his lack of mobility and his lack of experience, the whole procedure was guaranteed to be awkward as hell.

"Have you paddled a canoe before?" she asked. "Usually I give novices some simple instruction."

"Yes, I've paddled a canoe. I know the rudiments."

"Then I'll see you at Rush this afternoon about two o'clock. That's allowing plenty of time for you to stop and have lunch and generally not be in any hurry. You'll see the sign on the beach at Rush. Be sure and don't pass it up because the next takeout point is a long way farther."

"I won't pass it up," Clint assured her.

"The river doesn't branch off. It will take you there."

"I know it will. Thanks again. You have a good day yourself."

Still not taking her cue to leave, she went to the stern and shoved the canoe farther into the water. "Why don't you get in and I'll help push you—"

"I don't need you to help push me off."

"But I nearly always—"

"Just go, dammit," he ordered her, flinging out his arm and pointing toward the van.

"Yes, *sir!*" She saluted him and then turned and marched off, muttering to herself. Clint caught the words "proud" and "hardheaded."

He described himself in much more abusive language while he waited until she'd driven away with a spurt of gravel.

Pat watched him in her side mirror as she drove off. He stood with arms akimbo, gazing after the van with a fierce frown on his face. She hoped he fell in the water and got soaking wet! *No, she didn't hope that.*

Her flare of temper faded, leaving her with a letdown feeling. She was like a balloon that hadn't popped but had just gone all limp on the string. The bluegrass music no longer suited her mood. She ejected the tape and slipped in a country-western tape with soulful songs about love and broken hearts.

Usually the lyrics made her wonder longingly whether she'd ever know what it was like to be in love and in danger of heartbreak. But today she sang along in a mournful tone, thinking about Clint. Was she falling for him? *Had* she fallen for him already?

Or did Pat just want so badly to fall hard for a man that she was imagining her reactions to him? The fluttering pulse. The tingling excitement. The awareness of being female. It was ridiculous, she knew, but she felt downright sexy around Clint. And when he'd touched her this morning in the van, giving her hand a squeeze, she'd had a hot, melting sensation inside.

Could the human imagination play those kinds of tricks?

He'd arrived on Monday, so she'd known him only four days, counting today. In three more days he would be gone, and Pat would undoubtedly never see him again. Never hear his voice. The thought brought an ache to her chest in the region of her heart.

It sure felt like a real ache, not an imaginary one.

Clint was wet to his knees by the time he got the damned canoe afloat with him seated in it. He'd come close to tipping it over. His bad leg throbbed from the punishment as he paddled away from the beach, but at least he hadn't worn himself out, as he might have done just a couple of days ago. Apparently he was on the mend.

For the next five or ten minutes, he could glance to his left and see recreational vehicles and tents high on the wooded bluff. After that there were no signs of human habitation. Aside from the cries and twitters of birds, the only sounds were those that his paddle made dipping into the river and the gurgle of water against the bow of the canoe.

The quietness seemed to unknot Clint's tight nerves. Resting the paddle across the gunwales, he drifted along, keeping pace with a twig riding the current. A subdued babble gradually grew louder until up ahead he could see a stretch of churned-up water. A ripple. He supplied the name for himself as the canoe picked up speed on its own.

Clint steered with the paddle and safely navigated the slender craft between two large boulders. Beyond them the river deepened and the current slowed. He drifted along again, a sense of peace replacing his spurt of exhilaration. The water was as clear as he remembered. Gazing down, he saw the darting forms of fish and heard a boy's voice. His own voice.

"Hey, Dad! Did you see that big one? He was a monster fish!"

A man's voice answered. His father's voice. *"Sure, I saw him. He was a big sucker, all right. Probably weighed five pounds."*

"'Five' pounds? I'll bet he weighed fifty pounds!"

Then came his father's chuckle of amusement.

Clint blinked his eyes hard, clearing away a haze of moisture.

Other bits of conversation from that long-ago canoe trip played in his memory as he alternately paddled and floated, the river narrowing and widening, snaking around bends, rippling past outcrops of rock, sometimes cast into shadow by the soaring height of sheer limestone wall, sometimes bathed in sunlight and bordered by little pebble beaches. Several times he came upon flocks of ducks, which took to the air with an energetic flapping of wings. Dozens of turtles sunning themselves on rocks and boulders dived down with great splashes at his approach.

By noon his stomach was rumbling and the idea of standing upright on land and stretching his muscles was definitely appealing. Spotting a pebble beach up ahead, he decided to stop there and have his lunch, the way he and his old man had done.

Clint ran the canoe up onto the bank, got out and pulled it farther out of the water, so that there was no chance it would float off on its own. With an armload of cushions, he carried the cooler to a spot under a small tree and settled himself in a lounging position with his back against the trunk of the tree.

Popping open a soda, he wished it was a beer, but it tasted good when he took a big swallow. His sandwiches tasted good, too. After he'd eaten them, he unwrapped Pat's homemade muffin. It looked no more appetizing than it had this morning at the store, but Clint took a big bite. He intended to eat the muffin no matter what it tasted like so he could say he had if the subject came up. He hated like hell that he'd hurt her feelings, even if she had been practicing her cooking for Wells's benefit.

The muffin was so dry he had to drink the rest of his soda to wash down the mouthful. It took most of his second soda to finish consuming his home-baked dessert.

Thinking about Pat had roused the fierce gentleness that Clint couldn't identify. Lying back, he closed his eyes and let images of her fill his mind, like a slide show produced by his memory for his pleasure and enjoyment.

Relaxation seeped into his muscles and Clint realized he was drifting off to sleep, following his old man's example on that long-ago canoe trip on this same river. He could visualize his father clearly, sprawled on his back with his cap tipped over his eyes. He could see himself, an eight-year-old boy, exploring the terrain.

Distant memory pulled Clint further back in time and into deep restful sleep. An hour later two canoes passed by.

"That would have been a good campsite," said a bearded young man in his twenties to his three contemporaries. His tone expressed regret.

"We'll find another one between here and Rush," one of them answered.

Clint heard the faraway sounds of voices and wove them into his dreams.

Pat had allowed for a leisurely float when she'd scheduled picking Clint up at Rush at two in the afternoon. She fully expected him to be waiting for her. But there was no canoe pulled up on the bank when she arrived at five minutes past two. No Clint.

Oh, dear heaven, had he passed by the takeout point?

Alarmed, she hurried down to the water's edge and peered in the direction from where he should paddle into view. Thirty minutes crawled by as Pat paced up and down. It was plenty of time to imagine all sorts of mishaps. Maybe he'd overturned the canoe and struck his head on a rock. He might have crawled up on the bank where he was lying, unconscious.

The chances were all but certain that a wrecked or abandoned canoe would be spotted by other canoers before the day was over. However, it might have floated for some distance farther downriver from the scene of an accident, in which case Clint could go undiscovered unless he called out for help.

A dozen other scenarios were possible. Perhaps he'd crashed the canoe and hadn't been badly hurt, but it had gotten away from him. He might have gone ashore and begun hiking through the woods, trying to find his way back to civilization. That sort of thing had happened before.

Her one consolation was the knowledge that a fatality on the Buffalo was rare. Wherever he was, Clint was almost certainly alive.

At two forty-five Pat considered leaving and driving back to the store, where she could make some phone calls to other outfitters. Clint might have gotten to Rush early and hitched a ride with one of her competitors who was picking up a party. That wouldn't be unusual.

Normally she wouldn't hang around like this and bite her fingernails to the quick when a scheduled pickup didn't go off like clockwork. She would go about her business and come back later. But Clint was the type of man who would keep to a schedule. Something had gone wrong. Pat just knew it.

So she stayed, growing more and more anxious. Finally at three o'clock he came into view, paddling furiously. Overwhelming relief swept through her. She hurried down to the edge of the water. Cupping her hands, she called out when he was in earshot, ''Boy, am I glad to see you! I was worried when you weren't here! Don't wear yourself out, paddling so hard.''

He continued to paddle as though every second counted, dipping on one side and then on the other and pulling with all his strength. Obviously he'd had problems, judging from his grim expression. It must not have been a good day, Pat reflected with regret.

''What happened?'' she asked when he was near enough that she could speak normally. Her concern was in her voice.

''Nothing happened.''

''But something must have!'' His brow was wet with perspiration and fatigue showed on his face, but his clothing didn't look as if he'd taken a spill in the river. Had the trip just been too much for him physically? Even in her anxious state, Pat knew better that to pop out with that question. ''I'm just glad you made it,'' she said. ''In another hour, I would have gone to the rangers' station.''

''I was afraid of something like that. That's why I've been paddling like hell, making up for lost time.''

''How did you lose time?''

''When I stopped for lunch, I took a nap and turned into damned Rip Van Winkle.'' He sent the canoe straight toward the shore with a powerful pull.

The day's outing *had* been too much for him. Perhaps sitting in the canoe had been excruciatingly painful. Sympathy welled up in Pat. She grasped the bow of the canoe as it slid up the bank and urged, ''Why don't you catch your breath and rest a minute? There's no big hurry.'' His broad chest was rising and falling with the exertion. At closer range, she could see the weariness in his face.

"I don't need to rest. I've already wasted an hour of your time. You can go and start up the van. I won't be long." Contrary to his words, he hadn't made a move.

"Clint, you're whipped! I can see that for myself! Don't be so darned proud!''

"Damn it, I'm *not* whipped.''

"You are, too!''

She stood her ground, hands on hips. Glaring at her, he swung his right leg over the gunwale of the canoe. While he climbed out awkwardly, Pat strained every muscle to help keep the canoe upright so that he could use it for support. Then she pulled while he pushed and together they slid it up on the bank.

He straightened to his full height, flexing muscles. Tired or not, he was all rugged man and the sight of him affected Pat in the same way she'd come to expect. The temptation was strong to stand there and gaze at him with combined sympathy and female appreciation. Instead, she gathered up cushions and the life jacket, giving him a chance to take a breather.

"Be right back,'' she said, heading for the van.

"I'll bring the cooler. No need to come back.''

"I'm going to help load the canoe. Please, don't make a big issue out of nothing." When he didn't answer, Pat glanced over her shoulder and saw him bending to pick up the canoe, his bad leg thrust out at an awkward angle. Bending it obviously caused too much pain. "Clint, don't—'' She dropped her armload and hurried to him. "It's my canoe, darn it! I should have some say!''

"If I do any damage to the damned thing, I'll pay you the full price for it.''

Holding the canoe aloft, he limped toward the van. She walked alongside him, unable to contain her exasperation. "It's not the canoe I'm worried about! It's you! Your leg is hurting you. I can tell because you're limping worse than you were this morning.''

"Yes, my leg hurts like hell," he gritted out. "So what am I supposed to do? Cry about it?"

"No, but you don't have to be so doggone macho!" They were just a yard or two away from the van by now. "Watch your step," she cautioned. "There're deep ruts here."

"I see them. I'm not blind—" He broke off and cursed violently as he lurched to one side.

Pat acted instinctively, grabbing him around the waist. For one frantic second, she was afraid they both would topple to the ground. "Oh, my God, Clint!" she cried out. Then he regained his balance. Taking no chances, she kept her arms around him, steadying him, as he walked the remaining small distance and slid the canoe onto the rack.

The stiffening immediately left Pat's knees. Instead of loosening her embrace, she clung to him for support, her heart thudding in her chest. "I nearly had a heart attack when you stumbled...."

"You should have jumped aside, dammit. You could have gotten badly hurt." His voice grated harshly with anger.

"But I didn't." She drew in a shaky breath, aware that the weakness in her body was undergoing a subtle change. As the aftermath of panic subsided, the pleasure of hugging him was seeping through her, bringing delicious warmth. The thought occurred that he hadn't ordered her to let go of him. Nor was his body putting up any resistance. Did he like having her arms around him?

Most women would know just what to say to find out, but not Pat. Her cheeks burned with advance embarrassment as she blurted, "I wasn't just seizing an opportunity to get familiar."

"You really think it's necessary to tell me that?" He grasped her arms and unwrapped them, his grip hard. Then he turned around abruptly, facing her. "Don't make the mistake, though, of counting me out as a man."

Her mouth gaped open as she stared up at him in wide-eyed bewilderment. Something besides anger burned in his dark eyes. Something that caused a quivering excitement inside her. Hot desire...for *her?* "Wh—what do you mean?" she stuttered.

"I mean I'm not impotent."

Pat shook her head helplessly, feeling her cheeks going from red to crimson. "Gosh, that's the *last* thing that would enter my mind!"

"Well, my mind isn't so clean as yours. It's as dirty as the next man's. Remember that the next time you're about to grab me around the waist."

"Are you saying you reacted...sexually?"

"Bingo."

He stomped off, heading back down toward the water's edge, where his cooler lay on its side. Pat half turned to gaze after him, the corners of her mouth spreading in a goofy smile of pure delight. Briefly she indulged in fantasy, replaying the last thirty seconds. *Instead of freeing himself from her embrace, Clint wheeled around and swept her into his arms, crushed her against him, kissed her with hungry passion....*

In reality he'd reached the cooler and was bending to pick it up. Pat walked in a daze around to the driver's side of the van. Why, oh, why hadn't he taken her into his arms and kissed her if he'd actually wanted to? She just had to know, even though the explanation probably would be a blow to her almost-nonexistent confidence in her womanly allure.

While he was securing the canoe to the rack, Pat fidgeted behind the wheel, her nervousness growing. She had just twisted the rearview mirror to take a peek at her reflection when Clint jerked open the passenger door, catching her in the act of baring her teeth to make sure they weren't caked with peanut butter and grape jelly from her lunch sandwich.

Feeling like an idiot, she readjusted the mirror while he swung up into the seat.

"All set?" she inquired, starting up the engine. As it rumbled to life, the country-western tape she'd been listening to all day began to play full blast right in the middle of a love song. "Sorry!" Pat shouted over the din of engine and music as she reached down to jab the Eject button. "Didn't mean to burst your eardrums."

"Just relax and drive," Clint said, his deep voice gruff. "Everything's under control."

"Of course, it is."

The van jerked forward when she'd put it into gear and pressed on the gas pedal. Pat gripped the wheel, sensing his frowning glance over at her.

She often had a male passenger riding up front with her—sometimes guys as tall and big as Clint, a few of them movie-star handsome. Why was it that not a single one of them had seemed to be sitting so *close?* She felt buffeted by the sheer force of his raw masculinity. Was he aware of the effect he had on her? Pat wanted to know the answer to that question, too.

"Could we pick up the conversation we were having back there?" she asked as they jolted along on the unpaved road, dense forest on either side.

"What 'conversation'?"

"The last one, if you want to divide what I said to you and you said to me from the time you arrived into separate conversations. Rather than just one continuous conversation." When he didn't make use of the pause she allowed him, Pat had little choice but to stumble on, refreshing his memory. "The first topic was your being late and my being worried. The second topic was our arguing over whether we both should load the canoe. The third topic... Well, we barely touched on it."

"There was more than enough discussion." His reply was brusque.

"For you, maybe, but not for me."

"Look, you're not going to have to fend me off during the next three days. I've never forced myself on a woman, and that's not going to change."

Pat might have pursued the meaning of his last words, spoken with fierce emphasis, *That's not going to change.* But she was more interested in following up on his opening statement. "Your male instincts tell you that I would 'fend you off'? Is that why you didn't try to kiss me?" To her mortification, a trace of wistfulness crept in.

"They tell me I could play on your sympathy. Thanks, but no thanks. I haven't sunk that low that I need charity sex."

"A kiss isn't sex!"

"The hell it isn't."

What he wasn't saying in so many words amounted to a very depressing answer for Pat: any urge he'd felt to kiss her hadn't been so strong that he couldn't easily suppress it. The reason being that he wasn't powerfully attracted to her. Surprise, surprise. She undoubtedly wasn't his type at all. Pat smothered a sigh of utter dejection.

"Hey, don't let that kind nature of yours drag you down," he said with a gruff gentleness that brought a big lump to her throat. "You have problems enough of your own without taking on mine. How did things go today, anyway?"

"Great. Just great," she answered glumly.

"Did Homer mind the store for you or was he still under the weather?"

"He came to mind the store."

Clint pulled answers out of her in an obvious effort to get her mind off what had happened—and *hadn't* happened—back at the takeout place. *Who's showing sympathy now?* she thought to herself. Probably it had dawned on him that kissing her and making her feel desirable would have been an act of charity on his part.

They came to the old ghost town of Rush, once a thriving zinc-mining community. The abandoned buildings had never seemed quite so forlorn to Pat.

Chapter Six

"Shall I drop you at your cabin?" Pat inquired when the store came into sight.

"No, I'll get out at the store and walk."

"You sure?"

"Positive," Clint assured her shortly. "I'm going to unload the canoe for you. Without any help. Or supervision."

"Okay."

He looked over at her, almost wishing that she'd argued with him and shown her normal spirit. During the fifteen-minute ride, she'd been far too subdued for his liking. He hated like hell having been a wet blanket. "By the way, thanks for waiting around for me at Rush."

"You're welcome."

"Hey, I'm sorry for being a jackass. Don't take anything I say to heart."

"I'll try not to."

The van jolted to a halt outside the store. Clint made one

last try to fan to life the spark he'd doused. "Oh, I forgot to mention that I ate that muffin I took along with me."

She shot him a glance. "No wonder you got sluggish and took a long nap. You had a rock in your stomach."

"It tasted good—"

"Bull! Don't you dare feel s-sorry for me!" She pressed her lips together, stilling their tremor. "I have some pride, too, darn it!" With a savage twist of the handle, she flung open the van door.

"Wait." Clint grabbed her arm to stop her from sliding down to the ground. "What's the matter?"

"Let me *go!*" She jerked hard to free herself from his hold.

He loosened his grip to keep from hurting her and sat there stupefied while she slammed the door of the van closed and marched inside. What had that been all about? Shaking his head with puzzlement and concern, Clint got out and proceeded to unload the canoe, first dealing with the elastic cords. He was limping around to the rear of the van when a dilapidated old pickup pulled up and an unkempt-looking man in his late twenties got out. He needed a haircut and his jeans and plaid shirt hadn't been put on fresh and clean that morning.

"Afternoon," he said to Clint after wallowing a cud of chewing tobacco around in his cheek and spewing a long stream of brown juice.

Clint nodded in silent greeting.

"Name's Lester Madden. You ain't Pat Tyler, by any chance, are ye?"

"No, I'm not." Clint glanced sharply at the fellow's face, noting the bleariness of his eyes.

"Hope he ain't up and hired you as his driver. I was wanting to get me that job." Lester spat another stream.

"Pat Tyler isn't a he," Clint said flatly.

"You don't say." Lester grinned, combing his hands through his oily blond hair. "That increases my chances about a hundred percent, if the job's open. I got a way with the ladies. But, say, did you just hire on or not?''

Clint came within a hair of lying. He would be doing Pat a favor by getting rid of this shifty character and saving her the trouble, but she might not see it that way. "I'm not her employee," he growled.

"All *right*." Lester's grin became a leer. "Let me go put in my application." He spat out the wad of tobacco and swaggered toward the store.

Did you just hire on or not? The drawled question echoed in Clint's head as he finished unloading the canoe, every step making pains shoot through his bum leg. His military disability pension didn't preclude him from earning additional income. Eventually he would work at some kind of job. Whatever lowly job he could get.

Despite the long nap that day, Clint was weary. The hour or two of steady, vigorous paddling had taken its toll. Faced with the hike up to the cabin, he limped back to the van for his cooler. Any minute he expected Lester to emerge, his tail between his legs. Pat didn't have Clint's experience with sizing up men, but she was shrewd enough to spot a loser. You didn't go hunting a job looking as if you were sobering up from a three-day drunk, which is exactly the way Lester looked.

Clint wouldn't trust Lester as far as he could throw him. Pat was better off with no driver than with a lazy, irresponsible type. She wouldn't hire the fellow out of desperation. Would she? A picture of Tracy Wiggins, sullen-faced and slump-shouldered, flashed before Clint's eyes.

Cooler in hand, he limped toward the door of the store, intending to find out what was going on inside. He wouldn't put it past Lester to be persistent with a woman and not take no for an answer.

The scene he walked into made him clench his jaw harder. Pat and Lester were standing together near the counter at the front, while Homer looked on from his rocking chair. In her hand she was holding a laminated card.

After a startled glance at Clint, she continued to study the card—in all probability Lester's driving license—with an air of indecision. Lester was holding forth in a boastful tone. "Ain't never been in an accident, which speaks for itself about my driving. I don't like to brag on myself, but I can handle an eighteen-wheeler like it was my pickup out there. That little old van of yours won't hardly be no challenge."

"I need someone dependable who'll report for work every day."

"That's me. I'm as dependable and hardworking as they come."

It was all Clint could do to keep his mouth shut. He tromped toward the back of the store, letting his heavy tread convey his skepticism.

"So long, Clint," Pat said.

"I'm not leaving."

"Oh. I thought you were going out the back way."

"Kin I hep ye find something, young feller?" Homer sang out.

"I can find what I need, thanks."

Clint didn't really need the six-pack of soft drinks he yanked out of one of the tall coolers. It was merely an excuse to stick around.

"You ain't got nothin' to lose from hirin' me," Lester continued, getting the job interview back on track. "If you ain't pleased—and you gonna be tickled pink, I can promise you that—it's a simple enough matter to fire me."

"That's true enough," she agreed doubtfully. "I suppose I could hire you on a trial basis, say, a week."

"Wouldn't hurt none to visit a barber, son," Homer piped up.

"You got a point there, grampa. Soon's I get my first paycheck."

Clint returned to the front of the store, carrying his six-pack in his free hand. He came to stand near Pat. Lester cast him an uneasy look as though sensing that Clint wasn't in his camp.

"Pardon me for butting in," Clint said. "But I met Lester outside, and he strikes me as a man who can tell me where I can buy some good home-brewed beer in this dry county. Or better yet, a bottle of hundred-proof whiskey from one of the stills hidden around in these woods. How about it, Lester?"

An expression of cunning flashed in the other man's bleary eyes before he backed off a step, holding up both hands as though warding off an attack. "You barking up the wrong tree, mister. Grampa over there can probably help you. Me, I ain't touched a drop of alcohol in over a year now."

Pat spoke up in a stern voice. "A sure way for you to get fired right off the bat, Lester, would be to drink on the job."

"Honest, ma'am, I ain't touched a drop in—maybe it's a year and a half!" he declared.

Clint set the six-pack down on the counter with a sharp clack to express his opinion of the statement of sobriety. Pat went quickly behind the counter to the cash register. When she handed over his change, she was careful not to let her fingers touch his hand, he noticed. Nor did she make eye contact with him. Whatever had caused her to flare up at him was still bothering her.

"I kin start to work tomorrow," Lester pressed. "What time you want me to show up? 'Bout seven or seven-thirty?"

"Be here at seven. I'll ride with you and show you the ropes."

"What kind of pay we talkin' about?"

Clint made his exit, leaving by the rear door. As he limped along the shortcut to the cabin, his leg throbbing with every step, he seethed with the frustration of standing by while Pat hired the likes of Lester. The man would work a week, maybe two weeks, a month at the outside. Clint would bet a hundred bucks that Lester's first paycheck would finance a binge.

Of course, Clint wouldn't be around to collect his bet. Tomorrow was Friday and come Monday his week's rent was up. Monday, he would pack up and drive away, leaving Pat in the lurch. But what the hell good could he do if he stayed around?

Clint cursed himself all the more violently because the idea had been born that he could stay around, if Pat wanted him to. Not only *could,* but *would.* Nothing—and nobody—was calling him back to Chicago. Or anywhere else.

"Reckon he'll show up tomorrow morning?" Homer asked as Lester's pickup drove off.

"It won't surprise me if he doesn't," Pat admitted. "But I'm desperate enough to give him the benefit of the doubt. He definitely wanted the job."

"Shore seemed to want it bad, didn't he? Never forget when I was about his age and went to the foreman of a logging outfit lookin' for work...."

Pat tuned out the old man's story, which she knew by heart, to think her own thoughts. She'd been in no mental state to make a snap decision about hiring Lester or not hiring him. Her mind had been on Clint while he was outside. Then he'd come into the store, making it impossible for her to concentrate on anything but him.

"I forgot to mention that young Wells feller called up, askin' for ye." Homer's words penetrated her fog just as the phone started ringing. He'd evidently cut his story short, perhaps noticing her lack of attention. Pat picked up the phone.

"Hi, Pat. Jeremy here." Jeremy's friendly greeting in her ear roused an answering friendliness and a comfortable level of gladness.

"Oh, hi, Jeremy. Homer was just this minute telling me you'd phoned."

Glancing over at the old man, Pat noted the smug grin

on his face as he rocked back and forth, cocking his head to listen to her end of the conversation.

"How about supper tonight at my house with my two kids and me? Are you up for that?"

"Tonight?" For him to ask her out on their second date didn't come as a great surprise, but Pat didn't feel prepared.

"I know it's a last-minute invitation. I hoped you might not have plans."

"I don't, actually."

"Do big juicy hamburgers cooked on the grill tempt you?"

"Most food cooked by somebody else tempts me. I'm the world's worst cook myself." Pat visualized her plate of sorry-looking homemade muffins. If she'd been serving them to Jeremy this morning, and not Clint, the whole fiasco would have been comical, she realized. With Clint she seemed to lose her perspective and take everything to heart. Everything *mattered* so darn much.

"I'm sure you're not that bad. So, are we on for supper?"

To accept was to say that she was interested in dating him, and Pat wasn't at all sure she truly was interested. But to refuse meant staying home alone and fixing her own supper, not only tonight but many other nights. "I couldn't make it before seven."

"Seven's fine. The kids and I will come pick you up, if that's okay."

"Sure, it would be okay. But it's not necessary. I'll just drive myself."

"Call me old-fashioned, but I'd feel better about delivering you to your house safely after dark."

"I'm not at all nervous about coming home from Yellville at night by myself," Pat assured him. "I can make that trip back and forth with my eyes shut."

He didn't argue further, but she could sense he would have preferred his plan better. Why did Pat honestly prefer providing her own transportation? To make it less of a real date?

After she'd hung up, Homer eyed her expectantly, scratching his jaw. Pat didn't mind filling him in on the details that he'd missed. Underlying his curiosity were fatherly affection for her and concern for her welfare. "Jeremy invited me to supper at his house with him and his two children."

"That's real nice," he declared, beaming his whole-hearted delight. "I reckon he wants you to get to know them and vice versa."

Homer undoubtedly reckoned correctly. It didn't surprise her—or upset her—that Jeremy would want his children involved in his courtship of Pat, or any other woman. In fact, she admired him for giving such high priority to their feelings and best interests.

As for the date itself, it actually appealed to her more than the first date had. Pat liked kids. Not in an especially maternal way, she just enjoyed their energy and imaginativeness and love of having fun. Probably she would always be an overgrown kid herself who could get into playing games.

Grilled hamburgers at home with Jeremy and his young son and daughter sounded relaxing and fun. In truth, Pat had no great urge to be alone with Jeremy.

Lester's grin of self-congratulation turned into a sneer as he drove away from Tyler's with the job all sewn up. Dumb women. You could put anything over on 'em. They couldn't tell the difference between lies and the gospel truth, like a man could.

"Ain't had a drop of alcohol in a whole year," Lester whined, mimicking himself. He snickered gleefully and then winced at the pounding in his temples. He needed a drink bad. Now that he had a paycheck coming, he could get some whiskey on credit and celebrate tonight with

Pearl. He would have a highball all ready for her when she got home from her job at the old folks' home.

Maybe she would get off his case now and stop harping about him being out of work. Every woman turned into a nag. It was in their nature, no matter how mild-mannered they might seem at first. The best way for a man to deal with the aggravation was to slap 'em around a little and let 'em know who was boss. Lester had learned that from seeing how his pa handled his ma. She'd sported more than one black eye and bruise during the years Lester had been growing up.

Once he'd gotten Pearl to marry him, he would shut her up with a little rough treatment. Until then, he didn't dare because she might kick him out, as she'd been threatening to do lately. Lester was plum comfortable in Pearl's house trailer, if he could just shut her mouth up.

He needed to hang on to this two-bit job long enough to prove to her that he wasn't lazy. After he'd helped out with the bills awhile, she would be ready to get hitched and change her name to Pearl Madden. Suddenly he would have some rights as her husband. The next time she pitched a hissy fit—look out! He would smack her a couple of good ones. *Wham! Bam!* Lester practiced on the steering wheel of his pickup with his fist.

Yeah, the time had come for him to stop living from pillow to post and shacking up with this woman and that woman. He'd sown his wild oats and was ready to settle down and have some security. Pearl would probably want a young 'un or two in the bargain. Lester would go along, with the understanding that she could hatch kids and raise 'em and keep working at her job at the old folks' home. He wasn't changing no dirty diapers or putting up with a lot of squawling.

Lester made plans for his future, little troubled by the fact that those plans all hinged on his new job. He'd landed it by talking a bunch of baloney while he turned on the charm. More baloney and more charm would help him keep the job, thanks to the fact that his new boss was a woman.

It occurred to Lester that he was lucky the big, tall crippled dude named Clint wasn't the owner of Tyler Canoe & Cabin Rental. If he had been, Lester would still be unemployed. Who the hell was that dude, anyway? he wondered, scowling. From his accent, he was a Yankee.

Lester didn't look forward to running into him again. He hoped Clint Whatsisname would be on his way back north by tomorrow morning.

At the cabin Clint stuck the six-pack of cola in the refrigerator, stowed the small cooler where he wouldn't stumble over it and then hobbled to the sofa. After removing his shoes, he stretched out full length. The cushions had a familiar feel as they sank under his weight. He drew in a deep breath and expelled it with a groan of comfort.

The quietness had a soothing quality, like a gentle massage loosening the tension from his body and easing away the fatigue. *This place is so damned peaceful,* he thought, adjusting the throw pillow under his head. An image of the deer in the hollow that morning materialized on the screen of his closed eyes. Like a nature film, other scenes he'd gazed upon during the day came into focus, one blending into the next. Buffalo Point with its wreath of mist suspended over the river. Unfolding vistas of the Buffalo winding between its banks. A flock of ducks taking to the air. Sunlight slanting down through a grove of trees like a golden spotlight aimed from heaven.

In his half-awake state of relaxation, Clint felt the floating motion of the canoe. He was a part of the scenery himself, like the humpbacked turtles on boulders, like the twigs racing along the current, like the pebbles on the banks and the bold bands of red and orange in the sheer limestone cliffs were a part of it. A sense of calm joy gradually eased all the mental torment that plagued him, clearing the way for untroubled dreams. Clint's mouth softened into a smile for the first time in months as he fell asleep with Pat Tyler's voice in his ears....

"*I envy you. Would you believe I haven't floated the river in the past three years?*"

"*Come along with me today. The company would be welcome. Your company, that is,*" he added.

"*I thought you'd never ask!*"

She climbed nimbly into the canoe, taking the seat up front. Clint got them afloat and climbed in himself. With a thrust of the paddle, he sent the canoe skimming forward through the water.

"*You know I'm curious as the dickens about you,*" she said, smiling back at him.

"*Fire away. My life's an open book.*"

She plied Clint with questions about himself as they glided along, alternately floating and paddling. The conversation veered off into other subjects and they both interrupted the flow to draw attention to their surroundings, but Clint would eventually find himself telling her his whole life story again. Her avid interest made him want to share every experience he'd ever had. He told her about life in the marines, about Desert Storm, about rising in the rankings of the enlisted men from private first class to gunnery sergeant.

"*I'm starving! What about you?*" she asked when the sun was shining down on them from almost directly overhead.

"*I could eat a bear,*" he replied.

"*Speaking of which, look! Over there in the trees! See the bear?*"

"*I see him. Actually I've seen him before, in that exact spot. About twenty-seven years back.*"

"*Really! You'll have to tell me about it. Up ahead is a little rocky beach. Let's stop there for lunch, shall we?*"

"*Don't I see a canoe pulled up on the bank? Somebody must have beaten us to it.*"

"*Darn! It looked so perfect.*"

"There'll be another one not too much farther on the opposite side," Clint assured her.

They came abreast of the beach and glanced at a man lying asleep, his cap tipped over his face. A small boy was climbing a tree that grew in the center of the clearing.

"Isn't he a cute, tough-looking little guy?" Pat mused, keeping her voice low. "He could almost be you at that age."

"He *is* me at that age," Clint said. "I was eight. The man's my dad. He died the next year. He and my mom both did."

"How sad. What happened?"

Clint related the details, which were robbed of any painful remembrance by the telling of them to her. Soon the beach he'd described came into view and they headed the canoe straight for it. Pat hopped out as soon as the bow had run up on the bank. Clint got out, carrying the lunch cooler, and pulled the canoe higher on land.

Together they were walking toward a large flat rock to use as a picnic table when his foot slid on loose pebbles. "Careful! You'll fall!" Pat cried, grabbing him around the waist. Clint dropped the cooler and deliberately sank down on the ground, pulling her on top of him. Her moment's panic dissolved into laughter. He laughed, too, his arms around her and hugging her tight, a fierce gentleness swelling his chest.

"I've never met a woman I like as much as I like you," he said, his voice turning husky on him.

She dropped her eyes, her cheeks turning pink, and wriggled. Her movement had an instant effect. Already half-aroused, Clint could feel his body turning rock-hard.

"Be still, baby...." The whispered words coming from his lips awoke Clint from his nap. He'd been dreaming. The realization jolted him with deep disappointment. He unfolded his arms, which hugged air to his chest, and reached one hand down to tug violently at his trousers. He cursed his longing, sitting up and swinging his feet to the floor.

But his desire for Pat Tyler in the dream had been more than plain old lust, and Clint knew it. In reality, he'd never felt the sweet aching need just to hold a woman close and never let her go.

This was no time in his life to go off the deep end and get hung up on Pat or any other woman—not when he had nothing to offer. *Nothing.* All he could expect in return was sympathy. A vision of Pat's face, her expression compassionate, brought Clint to his feet.

The dose of bitter reality hadn't acted on him like a cold shower. His sexual frustration seemed to feed on the pointless anger that ate at him as he limped over to the refrigerator and jerked open the door to get a cola. The sight of the six-pack he'd bought less than an hour earlier oddly had a calming effect. It reminded Clint of Lester Madden and the big mistake Pat was making by hiring the fellow.

He reached for a cola from his previous supply, shut the refrigerator door and popped open the can. After downing a swallow, he took the cola out onto the front porch. It occurred to him as he sat down in the chair that his nap, brief as it was, had refreshed him physically. Then he turned his thoughts back to Pat and Madden. Would she heed Clint's advice if he urged her to back out of the trial employment she'd agreed to? he wondered, keeping a somber watch on the store parking lot as he took swigs of his carbonated soft drink.

He saw Pat leave in the Tyler van and eventually return with a party of people who drove off in several automobiles. He saw Homer depart for home in his aged pickup.

Now was Clint's chance to have a talk with Pat and advise her not to put Lester on her payroll even temporarily. He felt conscience-bound to offer her the benefit of his considerable experience in dealing with men. At least she might be more wary of Lester and keep a closer eye on him.

As he stood, crumpling the empty soda can in his hand, Clint grimly acknowledged the fact that he would have made another trip to the store this afternoon if Lester didn't exist. Lester gave him a legitimate reason so that he didn't have to manufacture one.

The words he'd spoken to Pat in his dream were true: he'd never liked another woman as much as he liked her. Or in the same way.

"So how was your day, Mama Cat? You managed to sneak out of your hiding place and polish off a bowl of cat food, I see. But you're eating for how many these days— four or five or six?" A sorrowful meow came from behind the chest freezer of the storeroom in response to Pat's conversation. "Here's a refill for you. I'm locking up the store in a few minutes, so you'll have the place to yourself."

She was bending over to empty a generous portion of dried cat food into the small mixing bowl that served as a pet dish when the back door of the store opened and a large shadow fell across the linoleum floor. Startled, Pat glanced up and saw Clint framed in the doorway.

"Hi," she blurted in surprise. "Oh, look what I've done! Clumsy me!" About a third of the cat food had landed on the floor. Flustered, she squatted down to scoop up the hard kernels and toss them into the bowl.

"Sorry. Didn't mean to take you by surprise."

His deep voice, gruff and apologetic, set off the by-now-expected prickles of pleasure. Warmth was spreading through her entire body.

"It's okay. I didn't hear your footsteps. If I had—" Pat broke off, thinking she would probably have spilled the cat food anyway in her excitement if she'd been alerted to his presence.

He stepped inside, finishing the sentence for her with a hard, flat note, "You would have known it was me."

"Why, yes, I would. But not just because you walk with a limp. No one else goes and comes through this door now except me. I don't usually—" She stopped herself again. The whole notion of "usual" just didn't apply to him.

"You don't usually feel sorry for your renters and suggest they take a shortcut." His statement was curt.

"Sometimes I've had good reason to feel a lot more sympathy than I feel for you," Pat declared. Darn, why did she always put her foot in her mouth when he showed up? "I have renters in wheelchairs. One of my cabins has a ramp." Rising, she dusted off her hands. "No harm done. Come on into the store."

"I heard you say you were locking up."

"In a little while, I am."

He followed behind her. Pat sneaked a glance at the old-fashioned school clock mounted on a wall of the store. She should be dashing to her house to take a shower and get ready for her date with Jeremy and his kids.

"How about a cola?" she heard herself asking as she paused near the table and chairs.

"I just— Thanks, I'd like one." He amended what had obviously begun as a refusal. *I just had supper* had probably been on the tip of his tongue.

No doubt he was remembering the muffin episode that morning, which still wasn't funny to Pat. Her normal sense of humor seemed to fail her where he was concerned.

"You won't insult me if you refuse," she said. "I didn't make up a batch of colas just before you came."

"I'll take a cola." He sat down in one of the chairs.

"While I'm getting them, I can pick up whatever it is you need," Pat offered, mindful of the time.

"I didn't come to buy anything."

"Oh. I hope nothing's gone wrong at the cabin."

"No. Nothing's wrong at the cabin."

"Then why— I mean…" She stood rooted to the spot, blushing and gazing at him wide-eyed, her unasked question hanging in the air: why *had* he come?

"Don't look at me like that," he said harshly. "You're

not going to have to come up with a nice way to let me down easy.''

''Let you down easy?'' Pat gave her head a little shake that failed to clear away her bewilderment, but it brought her out of her trance. ''I'll get the colas.''

On the way to the coolers, exasperation at herself for her idiotic behavior came to a head. A resolution formed: *I WILL NOT—repeat, WILL NOT—continue to act this way!*

''I just made up my mind about something,'' she announced, plopping two cans of cola on the table and plopping herself down into Homer's rocking chair. ''I'm sick and tired of being so self-conscious around you. I want you to meet the real Pat Tyler, who would have asked you days ago, 'Clint, how did you hurt your leg?' ''

His jaw tightened and a frown cut lines between his eyebrows as he met her questioning gaze. ''Auto accident.'' He bit the words out.

''Was it recent?''

''The end of March.''

It was now the beginning of June. ''Only two months ago?''

''Nine weeks.'' The correction was curt.

''Where, if you don't mind my asking?'' Obviously he did, but any minute now Pat was going to step into her own skin.

''Chicago. On Interstate 55. An eighteen-wheeler plowed into me.''

End of subject, he might as well have added, reaching for one of the cans of cola. After opening it and setting it in front of her, he opened the other for himself. The loud pops seemed to echo in the tense silence. His abrupt movements had set off a whole new series of tingles that started in Pat's midsection. She watched him tilt back his head and take a big swallow of soda, his throat muscles contracting.

''Tell me more about yourself,'' she said, picking up her can. She caught herself before she lifted the chilled aluminum to her flushed cheek and just held it in her hand instead. "What did you mean when you said you weren't on vacation? Are you on medical leave from the military?"

"Permanent leave. Medical discharge."

The clipped answer was toneless, but Pat could sense that he'd had to pull the words out. She hadn't meant to force him to talk about a painful subject, as his discharge obviously was. Her voice gentle with apology, she asked, "What branch? Marines?"

The cola can crackled loudly in his hand, and dark liquid spurted out onto his taut thigh. He cursed violently and, grasping the arm of his chair with his free hand, ejected himself to his feet. "I don't want your goddamned sympathy!"

Pat was on her feet, too, and gazing back at him helplessly. "I know you don't...."

"Let's talk about *your* problems, since something constructive can be done about them. Mine are just another hard-luck story."

"My 'problems'? You mean with you?" she blurted. The use of the plural confused her. "I think of it more as *a* problem, singular. By the way, I've never had it before."

His eyes left her face to travel quickly down her body. Pat's breasts thrust forward on their own, as though trying to attract his attention. "You don't have a problem with me," he said, his voice harsh and impatient. "What do I have to say to convince you?"

It dawned on her that they weren't on the same conversational track. She set down the cola she still held and folded her arms across her chest. "Not 'with' you, Clint. Of course, you're not hot to ravish me. The shoe's on the other foot, so to speak."

He stared at her, frowning. "What the hell are you talking about?"

"You haven't felt like the Hunk of the Month calendar man when I'm around? That's good. I was afraid you could hear my poor heart thumping like a drum and my pulse fluttering." The feeble attempt at a joking explanation fell flat. Pat sighed. Her embarrassment might have been more intense if she hadn't been so totally dejected. He hadn't watched her closely enough to realize how he affected her.

"I hope you don't think I act like such an airhead around all men," she continued when he just kept looking at her. "Because I don't. And I'm just as puzzled over it as you are, from your expression. There. I'm glad we've got it out into the open."

She turned her back to him, unable to withstand his somber inspection a second longer.

"Pat—"

"Don't you dare feel sorry for me," she interrupted before he could say more. The regret he'd managed to convey in speaking her name told her enough. "So what if I never learned to flirt and be feminine or sexy. I wouldn't trade a single minute of tagging around after my father and being a tomboy." She thought about the moment he'd almost kissed her at Rush and added wistfully, "Or not more than, say, fifteen minutes anyway."

"Never put yourself down."

He'd come up behind her. His hands, strong and gentle, closed on her shoulders. Pat shut her eyes against the delicious sensations. "There go my knees," she confided. "They just turned to water."

"Pat, I'm not the right kind of man for you. You deserve a guy like Wells."

He was "letting her down easy." Not saying straight out that she wasn't his type of woman. Pat hugged herself harder to control the misery spreading through her.

"Thanks for putting it like that. Hopefully, this isn't terminal. I'll survive, as the song says." She didn't sound very convincing to herself. "Speaking of Jeremy, I'm having supper at his house tonight. I should think about getting changed."

His hands had tightened at her announcement of her plans, letting her feel his strength for a glorious second.

They dropped away as he demanded, "Why didn't you say so?"

"Because... Can't you figure it out for yourself?" Pat turned around to face him. She was almost relieved to see him scowling fiercely at her. Disapproval was easier to take than pity.

"You don't date one man and tell another one he makes your heart beat fast," he stated.

"I never have before, honest. And there's no harm done to either you or Jeremy. Not under the circumstances."

"How do you figure that?"

Unfolding her arms, Pat stuck her hands into her jeans. "You'll soon be gone, and things will be the same between Jeremy and me. We'll still like and respect each other. And eventually we may get married, since he's lonely and I am, too. It's not as though he's being cheated, because I don't think he'd want me getting all hot and bothered over him."

"What if I'm *not* soon gone?"

Her heart gave a leap of surprise and foolish hope. "Are you considering staying longer?"

"The thought has crossed my mind. I'm my own boss now." His last words were edged with the first bitterness he'd allowed himself to express openly. He went on before she could speak. "That reminds me of what I came here to get off my chest. That fellow Madden who came looking for a job today is a drunk. It's none of my business, but I wish you'd reconsider hiring him. He's going to cause you trouble."

Pat bit her lip to keep from switching back to the subject that seemed much more important at the moment—his decision on whether to stay longer in Arkansas or leave. But she didn't trust herself not to say, *I wish you'd stay.* "I've already hired Lester," she told him. "If he shows up tomorrow morning, I have to give him the benefit of the doubt. But I appreciate the advice."

"Don't mention it. I wish I could help you out myself—" He broke off with a shrug.

They both heard the crunch of gravel outside and turned their heads to see the vehicle approaching the store. "That's Jeremy's van!" Pat exclaimed. "He came to pick me up anyway!"

She dashed to the door to signal him before he drove past on his way to her house. After he'd pulled up and stopped, he and his two passengers, eight-year-old Jerry and five-year-old Mandy, spilled out. Conscious of Clint behind her, Pat glanced around at him. He was looking past her through the open doorway. His bleak expression tugged at her heart.

"I'll see you around tomorrow," he said, turning toward the back door.

"Don't run off," she objected. "You haven't met Jeremy."

"My running days are over." His reply was heavy with self-contempt, but he took several steps toward her, heeding her request to wait and be introduced.

Pat managed a friendly smile for Jeremy and his children. As much as she regretted the intrusion, it was well-intentioned and probably for the best. "Hi. Do I get chauffeur service?" she asked gaily.

Jeremy's smile was sheepish. "Hope you don't mind too much. Guess it's just the gas-station owner in me that undermines my confidence in your van." He came toward her, holding his little girl's hand. His son hung back, kicking at the gravel.

"I'm running a little late," Pat explained.

"No problem," Jeremy assured her.

"We have the hamburger patties all made, don't we, Daddy?" Mandy piped up. She had her mother's black curly hair and big brown eyes.

They'd reached the doorway. Jeremy stopped and looked back at his namesake. "Come and speak to Miss Tyler, Jerry. You remember her from church."

Jerry lifted a hand in a limp wave. "Hi, Miss Tyler."

"Hi, Jerry." Pat was getting the picture that Jeremy's son had joined the expedition with reluctance.

"Hi, Miss Tyler. I'm Mandy, and I'm five years old." Mandy's greeting came without any prompting.

"It's good to see you, Mandy."

"Do you like onions on your hamburger? My daddy does, but he won't eat them on his tonight unless you do because they make his breath smell bad."

"Never tell a child anything that you don't want announced to the world," Jeremy said dryly.

"Actually I don't like raw onions all that much," Pat admitted, answering Mandy's question.

"Don't you?" Jeremy asked. "I could have sworn you ate them in your salad the other night. So much for my powers of observation."

"Actually a few slivers *did* make their way into my salad."

Clint cleared his throat in the background and made a restless movement. Jeremy glanced inside the store with surprise. Recognition showed on his face as he spotted Clint. "Didn't realize you had a customer," he said, looking questioningly at Pat. *This guy giving you any trouble?* he asked her silently.

"Clint is definitely a good customer," she said, careful not to telegraph an answer back to him. She stood out of the way so that he and Mandy could enter. "He was about to leave, but I wanted you to meet him."

Jeremy ushered his daughter in. He and Clint both took several steps toward each other to shake hands in response to Pat's introduction. "Clint Adams. Jeremy Wells."

"Adams."

"Wells."

Mandy observed the handshake from her father's side. Before Clint could step back, she stuck up her hand. "I'm Mandy Wells, his little girl."

Clint gazed down at her. "Hello, Mandy. You're one of the prettiest little girls I've ever seen."

His gruff compliment combined with the sight of his big hand gently engulfing the little girl's did strange things to Pat.

"Don't tell her that," Jeremy protested with a paternal smile. "She's already vain."

"What's 'vain,' Daddy?"

He ruffled her bangs. "It has to do with primping in front of the mirror."

Pat was aware of Clint's eyes on her. She wondered self-consciously if he weren't visualizing her as a pint-size tomboyish version of her grown-up self. It was hard not to feel jealous of Jeremy's adorable little daughter.

"I won't hold you people up any longer," Clint said. "Have a good evening."

"Same to you," Jeremy said in unison with Pat's, "You, too, Clint."

See you tomorrow, she wanted to add as he limped past her, leaving by the front entrance of the store. The fact that he was choosing not to go out the back door had something to do with pride, she was sure.

"Daddy, why does Mr. Adams walk funny?" Mandy inquired just as Clint reached the doorway. "Does he have a boo-boo on his leg?"

Pat cringed at the childish insensitivity while Jeremy scolded in an embarrassed tone, "It's not polite to ask questions like that, Mandy."

"Why not?"

Clint pulled the door closed behind him, setting off the hollow tinkle of the bell.

Chapter Seven

Jeremy Wells's son leaned against the trunk of a hickory tree over to one side of the store, out of sight of the windows. It was obvious to Clint he wasn't a happy camper. Given Clint's own low spirits, he could empathize with the boy's dejected air.

"Hi, kid, how's it going?" Clint greeted him as he neared the tree on his way to the road leading up to the cabin.

Jerry Wells straightened, interest replacing some of the glumness in his downcast expression. He had his dad's fair coloring and blue eyes, and his fine blond hair was as straight as his sister's was curly. "Hi, mister. Are you a soldier?" he asked, eyeing Clint's military fatigues.

"I'm an ex-soldier. U. S. Marine Corps."

"Wow, a marine." He fell in step with Clint. "Were you in Desert Storm? I gave a report about it in school."

"Yes, I was on active duty for that entire operation."

"What did you do? Did you drop bombs?"

"No, my detail was on the ground. Armored tanks."

"Gosh, that's neat. I'd like to drive a tank. My name's Jerry," he added and eased out a sigh. His troubles obviously still weighed on him.

"Nice to meet you, Jerry. I'm Clint Adams." Clint slowed down to make it easier for the kid to keep pace with him.

"Did you get wounded in battle? I notice you're limping."

"I wish it had happened in battle, if it had to happen." The bitter admission was one he hadn't voiced aloud to anyone before. "Busted my leg up in a car accident when I was on leave."

"Does it hurt a lot?"

"Hurts like the dickens," Clint acknowledged. "Shouldn't you be going back? Your dad will be wondering where you went." They were on the road to his cabin by now.

Jerry plunged his hands into his jeans pockets, his shoulders slumping another inch. "I didn't want to come in the first place. Dad made me. We came to pick up Miss Tyler. She's eating supper with us."

"You don't seem too happy about it."

"I don't want any stepmother," Jerry protested, more earnest than defiant. "I like it just fine with Dad and Mandy and me. Mom died two years ago," he explained. "She had a brain aneurysm."

"That's tough losing your mother at your age," Clint said, his heart going out to the little boy. "I've been there, so I know."

"Your mom died when you were six years old, too?"

"Both my parents died in a fire when I was nine. I was packed off to a strange city to live with relatives who didn't want me. They already had enough kids to feed and clothe. So you might count yourself lucky that you have a father to raise you. Things can always be worse."

Jerry nodded and trudged along, not answering right

away. "Yeah," he said finally. "Like you could have busted up both your legs, huh? And maybe not been able to walk at all."

It was Clint's turn to mull over his own wisdom. "Good point, Jerry," he said. "Next time I'm feeling sorry for myself, I'll have to remember that. Now I think you'd better go join your dad and Mandy and Miss Tyler."

"Will I see you again? I'd sure like to hear about being a marine."

Clint came to a stop. "That's probably not in the books. But I'm glad we had this talk. You keep a stiff upper lip." He clasped the boy's shoulder.

"I will. Bye, Mr. Adams." With a wave, he turned and dashed back down the road.

Watching him, Clint fought a battle with himself, and his better instincts won out. "Oh, Jerry!" he called.

Jerry slid to a halt and trotted backwards. "Yes, sir?"

"Give Miss Tyler a chance. If you do, you'll like her."

"Okay." The halfhearted agreement was slow in coming.

Clint continued his hike to the cabin, every step an effort. But his fatigue was a matter of the spirit, not the body. What a neat kid Jerry Wells was—as bright and likable as his little sister was cute and sweet. Throw in the father—a good-looking, successful, decent man. It was a hell of a package deal that Pat Tyler would be crazy to pass on.

He would be the worst kind of bastard to throw a monkey wrench into the works and mess up her future. So help him, he *wouldn't* come between her and Wells. No matter how much he wanted to.

Clint needed to forget that whole conversation Wells had interrupted just in the nick of time. Another few seconds and Clint would have taken Pat into his arms and kissed her. If the reality had been like his dream—

Absolutely nothing would be changed.

He would still be a disabled ex-marine with a high-school education.

* * *

"It's okay to notice things about people, Mandy, but it's better not to make a comment unless it's something nice to say," Jeremy lectured his daughter.

"Like Mr. Adams saying I was a pretty little girl?"

"Exactly." He tapped her nose gently with a forefinger and then looked around at Pat, who'd been grateful for a chance to cope with all her mixed emotions.

A part of her urgently wished that Jeremy hadn't shown up just when he did, and another part—her sensible self—knew he'd rescued both her and Clint from a horribly awkward situation. Clint had probably been greatly relieved by the interruption. For all his outward toughness, he was a nice man underneath and didn't want to hurt her feelings. Otherwise he would have told her in his blunt way that she didn't turn him on.

"Thanks for coming to get me," she was able to say to Jeremy now. "Give me fifteen minutes to shower and change."

"Take longer than that. The kids and I will take a ride to Buffalo Point and be back in about thirty minutes to pick you up at your house."

"I'll be ready and waiting for you on the porch."

Pat locked up, jogged to her house, took a quick shower and changed into jeans and a Western-style blouse in shades of blue. With five minutes to spare, she sat in the porch swing, the scene with Clint still playing in her mind and bringing hot flushes of embarrassment. Every meeting with him got worse! If he steered clear of her altogether tomorrow, she wouldn't blame him.

Jeremy returned right on time. Pat went quickly out to meet the van, glad to escape her own company. Before he could get out, she opened the passenger door for herself and climbed up into the seat.

"Got your house key?" he questioned her hesitantly when she'd fastened her seat belt.

She patted her right jeans pocket. "In my pocket."

"A woman who doesn't lug a purse around?"

"I hate carrying one," Pat admitted. "I much prefer a fanny pack."

"My mom always took her purse with her." Jerry spoke up from behind them. He and Mandy occupied the middle seat, both wearing their seat belts. "It had her checkbook and wallet and comb and lipstick. She had pictures of me and Mandy and Dad in her wallet. Remember that, Dad?"

A forlorn note in the little boy's voice brought a huge lump to Pat's throat. She noticed that Jeremy's knuckles showed white as his hands gripped the wheel. The urge was strong to offer comfort to both father and son.

"I sure do, son. There isn't much I don't remember about your mother." He shifted into reverse. "All set, everybody?"

"I'm all set, Daddy," Mandy offered. "I want to hurry up and get home so I can show Miss Tyler my room. I'll show her Jerry's room, too, since he doesn't want to. And your and Mommy's room—"

Jeremy interrupted her as he stepped on the brake too hard, stopping the van's reverse motion, "You can give Miss Tyler the grand tour of the whole house while your brother and I get the grill going."

"What's a 'grand tour'?"

"It means acting like a guide, dummy," Jerry answered her with the scorn of an older sibling.

"I'm *not* a dummy! Did you hear him call me a name, Daddy?"

"Okay, you two. Mind your manners," Jeremy scolded. Pat could sense that he welcomed the harmless squabbling, as she did. It allowed them to push the tragedy of Susan Wells's death into the background. "Miss Tyler may bail out right here. I wouldn't blame her," he added, looking over at her, his gaze full of apology.

"Not a chance," Pat declared. "I've got my mouth all set for a juicy hamburger." She kept her smile on her lips as she turned her head to include his two children.

"Without onions," Mandy stipulated, innocently triggering the associations that raw onions would forever hold for Pat.

"Without onions, please," she said, shoving away a vision of herself champing on a burger with a thick slice of onion, Clint sitting somewhere nearby.

Jeremy accelerated, sending the van forward along the driveway. "From now on I'll keep an eye on you and stop you when you reach for raw onions," he promised her. "You didn't seem that rattled at the Front Porch, but I guess I was too rattled myself to notice."

"I'm glad it wasn't obvious." Pat felt horribly dishonest about not explaining that her rattled state hadn't had anything to do with him. But how could she with the children in the back seat? How could she if they *weren't* in the back seat? Jeremy didn't deserve that kind of insult, and she hated to expose herself to him as a silly female. Her behavior around Clint *was* silly. Pointless. Whereas dating Jeremy made good sense.

"I like eating at the Front Porch," Mandy volunteered, joining in the adult conversation. "Don't you, Miss Tyler?"

"Very much. How about you, Jerry?"

"He likes it, too," his little sister answered for him. "He loves fried chicken."

"I can talk for myself, squirt."

"Daddy, did you hear—"

"Okay, you two. Act civilized."

Once again Pat welcomed the normal friction between siblings.

Jeremy slowed down at the junction of the driveway with the road and glanced to his right, following her gaze toward the cabin at the top of the hill. Dusk had started to fall, but Clint's black automobile was clearly visible, as was an empty chair on the front porch. *He must have carried it there from the back porch,* Pat reflected, surprised that he didn't prefer the view behind the cabin. A view with no human beings.

"So Adams *is* staying in one of your cabins," Jeremy remarked, pulling out onto the road.

"Didn't I mention that?"

"No, you said on Monday night that you thought he might have rented a cabin. I forgot to ask," he admitted.

"No reason you should have."

His guilty inflection had raised more guilt in Pat, reminding her that she'd let Jeremy wrongly conclude that her close scrutiny of Clint at the Front Porch was the result of uneasiness. Right at this moment she was giving only token attention to Jeremy because she was absorbed in mentally stationing herself in Clint's chair and visualizing what he could see from that vantage point. A good portion of the store parking lot would be visible through the trees.

She'd glanced in the direction of the cabin often enough these past few days, noting whether his automobile was there, but she hadn't strained for a glimpse of him on the porch because it hadn't seemed remotely possible that he would choose to sit there. Not when he seemed so antisocial.

"I was worried for a second there, when we arrived and you were alone at the store with Adams," Jeremy said. "But he seems an all-right guy. Is his bark a lot worse than his bite?"

Before Pat could frame a reply, Jerry spoke out, "Mr. Adams was a marine, and marines are all tough guys."

"How do you know he was a marine?" his father asked.

"I talked to him when he came out of Miss Tyler's store, and he told me. He said his leg hurts him real bad. He hurt it in a car accident. He was in Desert Storm. He drove armored tanks."

"Sounds like you had quite a conversation with Mr. Adams," Jeremy said. "You two must have hit it off."

"We did. Maybe because his mom died when he only a year older than me. I'm eight years old," Jerry added for

Pat's benefit before he continued, "But Mr. Adams was real unlucky. He lost his dad, too. Both his parents burned up in a fire. So he had to go live with relatives who didn't want him. They already had kids to feed and clothe."

"Daddy, you're not going to die, are you?" Mandy asked tearfully.

"No, Dad's not going to die, *stupid!*" Jerry's denial was vicious.

"I'm going to do my best to stay alive, Mandy," Jeremy reassured his daughter. He let his son's show of temper go unreprimanded. Pat knew that he was more fully aware than Mandy was that Jerry had lashed out in fear.

Her heart ached for the little boy and for Mandy and for Jeremy. But it also ached for Clint, who'd been orphaned when he was only nine years old. No wonder he was hard and abrasive. He'd probably needed to build a wall around himself in order to survive life's hurts.

What had caused him to share his background with Jerry when he was so closemouthed about himself? Had Jeremy's son struck a chord? Pat longed to know what else Clint might have revealed, but to question Jerry seemed like an invasion of his and Clint's privacy.

They reached the highway and turned toward Yellville. "Any responses to your Help Wanted notices?" Jeremy asked.

She filled him in on Lester Madden, realizing as she did that her whole account was colored by the reservations Clint had expressed about Lester. "I won't be surprised if he doesn't work out," she concluded. "Any luck with hiring a replacement for Candy Owens?"

"I liked Candy." Mandy inserted herself into the conversation again. "Her name rhymes with mine, Miss Tyler. Candy. Mandy." The little girl giggled.

"Miss Tyler asked Dad a question, and you butted in." Jerry's criticism of his sister indicated that he was paying close attention himself to what was being said by the adults.

"But I like to talk, too!"

"That's an understatement, Little Miss Chatterbox," Jeremy said with fond irony. "Your brother makes a good point about waiting and joining in when the time is right."

He brought Pat up-to-date on his few applicants since their last discussion of the same subject a couple of nights ago on the phone, none of whom had impressed him as a good prospective employee.

When Jeremy had finished, there was a short lull. "Now can I say something, Daddy?" Mandy asked. She'd obviously been waiting patiently.

"You have our complete attention," he replied with fatherly indulgence.

No words were immediately forthcoming. Pat looked back to see the little girl's face comically distorted in intense concentration.

"She's only five years old," Jerry said to Pat. His gruff disclosure of his little sister's age was offered as grounds for making allowances for her. "You can tell Miss Tyler about your dolls, squirt."

The prompting, which brought a happy smile to Mandy's face and unleashed a flood of chatter, finished winning Jerry a place in Pat's heart. Several times during the remainder of the drive to Yellville, she tried to draw him out, but he stubbornly resisted her friendliness. Not because he necessarily disliked her, Pat understood, but because he was asserting loyalty to his mother.

Unlike Mandy, who'd been only three when Susan died, Jerry had a whole host of memories of his parents together as a couple, of himself as a loved child in their close-knit family. It was undoubtedly painful for him to see Pat occupying the front passenger seat, as his dad's "date."

Jeremy was surely aware of his son's difficulties. From time to time he glanced with concern into the rearview mirror.

All in all, it wasn't the most lighthearted of occasions, but Pat still wasn't sorry she'd been included. Jerry had to adjust to the idea of his father needing female companion-

IT'S FUN! IT'S FREE
AND IT COULD MAKE YOU
£600,000 RICHER

If you've ever played scratch off lottery tickets, you should be familiar with how our games work. On each of the first four tickets (numbered 1 to 4) there are Gold strips to scratch off.

Using a coin, do just that - carefully scratch the Gold strips to reveal how much each ticket could be worth if it is a winning ticket. Tickets could be worth from £6 to £600,000 in lifetime money (£20,000 each year for 30 years).

Note, also, that each of your 4 tickets has a unique prize draw Lucky Number... and that's 4 chances for a **BIG WIN!**

FREE BOOKS!

At the same time you play your tickets to qualify for big prizes, you are invited to play Ticket 5 to get specially selected Silhouette Special Edition® novels which are yours to keep absolutely FREE.

There's no catch. You're under no obligation to buy anything. You don't have to make a minimum number of purchases - not even one! The fact is, thousands of readers enjoy receiving books by mail from The Reader Service™. They like the convenience of home delivery... they like getting the best new novels at least a month before they're available in the shops... and they love their subscriber Newsletter packed with author news, competitions, and much more.

We hope that after receiving your free books you'll want to remain a subscriber. But the choice is yours - to continue or cancel, anytime at all! So why not take us up on our invitation, with no risk of any kind. You'll be glad you did!

PLUS A FREE GIFT!

One more thing - when you accept the free books on Ticket 5, you're also entitled to play Ticket 6 which is GOOD FOR A GREAT GIFT! Like the books, this gift is totally **free** and yours to keep as a thank you for giving the Reader Service a try!

So scratch off the GOLD STRIPS on all your BIG WIN tickets and send for everything today! You've got nothing to lose and everything to gain!

OFFICIAL RULES
MILLION DOLLAR SWEEPSTAKES

Here are your BIG WIN Game Tickets potentially worth from £6 to £600,000 each. Scratch off the GOLD STRIP on each of your Prize Draw tickets to see what you could win and post your entry right away.

This could be your lucky day - Good Luck!

TICKET 1
Scratch GOLD STRIP to reveal potential value of cash prize if the Prize Draw number on this ticket is a winning number. Return all game tickets intact.

LUCKY NUMBER

OI 389028

TICKET 2
Scratch GOLD STRIP to reveal potential value of cash prize if the Prize Draw number on this ticket is a winning number. Return all game tickets intact.

LUCKY NUMBER

GK 483858

TICKET 3
Scratch GOLD STRIP to reveal potential value of cash prize if the Prize Draw number on this ticket is a winning number. Return all game tickets intact.

LUCKY NUMBER

FO 462184

TICKET 4
Scratch GOLD STRIP to reveal potential value of cash prize if the Prize Draw number on this ticket is a winning number. Return all game tickets intact.

LUCKY NUMBER

HS 084127

FREE BOOKS

TICKET 5
Scratch GOLD STRIP to reveal number of books you will receive. These books, part of a sampling project to introduce romance readers to the benefits of the Reader Service, are FREE

AUTHORISATION CODE

130107-742

FREE GIFT

TICKET 6
All gifts are free. No purchase required. Scratch GOLD STRIP to reveal free gift, our thanks to readers for trying our books.

AUTHORISATION CODE

130107-742

YES! Enter my Lucky Numbers in the £600,000 Grand Prize Draw and when winners are selected, tell me if I've won any prize. If the GOLD STRIP is scratched off Ticket 5, I will also receive FREE Silhouette Special Edition novels along with the FREE GIFT on Ticket 6. *I am over 18 years of age.*

E7KI

MS/MRS/MISS/MR _____
BLOCK CAPITALS PLEASE

ADDRESS _____

_____

_____ POSTCODE _____

mps MAILING PREFERENCE SERVICE

THE READER SERVICE™: HERE'S HOW IT WORKS

Harlequin Mills & Boon, PO Box 236, Croydon, Surrey, CR9 3RU.

The Reader Service™

FREEPOST

Croydon
Surrey
CR9 3WZ

NO
STAMP
NEEDED

ship. Tonight would ultimately be good for him. It was good for Jeremy, too, because every date with her should make it easier for him to get back into being a single man, whether or not anything serious developed between them. Mandy was enjoying herself immensely, oblivious to the undercurrents. As for Pat, she would always rather be with people she liked than be by herself.

And she liked Jeremy and both his children very much.

On their arrival at his home, he parked the van in the driveway and the four of them trooped together along the paved walkway to the front door.

"We never go inside this way, Daddy," Mandy said. "Can I ring the doorbell?"

"Nobody's home, stupid!" Jerry growled, bringing up the rear.

Jeremy ignored his son's rudeness. "Since this is Miss Tyler's first visit, I thought we'd treat her like company."

"Is she going to visit us lots more times? I hope so." The little girl eased her hand in Pat's. Pat gave it a little squeeze and held it.

"I remember when this house was being built," she said. "I always admired the tall windows."

"Susan's uncle designed it for us. He's an architect back in Memphis, where we were both from."

"Susan was our mommy," Mandy explained.

"She knows that," Jerry informed his sister scornfully.

After they'd entered the foyer, he pushed past his father, saying, "Dad, I'll go take the cover off the grill."

Jeremy sighed. "I hope you'll overlook my son's behavior, Pat. He's normally a pretty nice kid."

"His behavior is completely understandable. I'm not bothered by it other than wishing I could take away his pain."

He squeezed her shoulder. "Somehow I expected you to key right in on the underlying reason."

Mandy was tugging hard at Pat's hand in an effort to lead her forward. "Daddy, you said you and Jerry would cook the hamburgers while I gave Miss Tyler a 'grand tour.' Remember?''

"In other words, get lost." He ruffled his daughter's bangs. "Make it a quick grand tour and then bring Miss Tyler to the patio."

He left them. Some sixth sense told Pat he was glad to turn her over to Mandy rather than show her through his home himself. His and Susan's home.

"This way's the living room," Mandy urged.

The foyer had already given Pat a hint as to what to expect. The living room and dining room each bore further proof that Susan Wells had combined decorating skill with a homemaker's touch. Wallpaper designs and paint colors were coordinated with furniture upholstery and window treatments that weren't your ordinary curtains or draperies. The overall effect was cozy and inviting, but Pat was still as thoroughly intimidated as she was filled with admiration. Give her an unlimited budget, and no way could she achieve anything close.

Would she even want to try? Her parents' house with its odds and ends of furniture, some of it shabby, was such a different living environment. By comparison it was plain, even tacky—definitely not as clean and tidy—and yet it suited her fine. Except for being so quiet and "empty" in a way that had nothing to do with furniture.

"I'll show you my room next. This way, Miss Tyler." All eagerness, Mandy pulled her along a hallway. Her bedroom was pink-and-white and frilly—the setting for a little princess. Jerry's, located across the hall, was all bright primary colors with a baseball motif. Pat complimented both equally while thinking that she would probably have preferred his room when she was Mandy's age.

"Your house is very pretty," she declared, digging her heels into the hall carpet. "Now let's go see how those hamburgers are coming, shall we?"

"But I want you to see my daddy and mommy's room. It's real pretty. *Please.*"

"Just a peek inside the door, then."

Mandy marched ahead and didn't pause at the doorway of the room she entered. Pat followed behind, reluctance slowing her footsteps. She really didn't want to see Jeremy and Susan's bedroom.

A glance inside confirmed that it was much larger than the children's rooms and was decorated in green and apricot. Susan had managed the impossible, bringing together masculine and feminine tastes. The bed was queen-size. And on the double dresser, in front of which Mandy stood, were framed photographs.

"This is a wedding picture of Mommy and Daddy." Rising on tiptoe, she carefully lifted down one of the photographs and held it so that Pat could see it.

"Careful, don't drop it."

"I won't. I promise. If you and Daddy get married, will you wear a long white dress like this, Miss Tyler?"

Pat grabbed the doorframe, glad that she wasn't holding the picture. "What a question to ask, Mandy! Your father and I— We haven't— We don't know—" She stopped and started over. "Your father and I are just friends right now. What put the idea in your head that we might be getting married?" Had Jeremy? Surely not!

"Mrs. Grambly said it would be a wonderful thing if my daddy found himself a nice wife."

Mrs. Grambly was Jeremy's daytime sitter, who also did housecleaning and some cooking. He'd spoken of her in glowing terms.

"You mean she discussed this with you?" Pat's voice revealed her disbelief.

"I heard her talking on the telephone. Jerry got all mad when I told him. He doesn't even want to go to the wedding. But I do."

"When and if your father has another wedding, I'm sure you'll be present. I wouldn't worry about it until then."

Jerry's sullen attitude made even more sense now. *Poor little boy!* He thought Pat was making plans to move into this bedroom with his dad. The idea didn't seem remotely possible. Nor did it raise the first spark of enthusiasm.

Mandy had set the photograph back in place. "I don't want just to go," she explained, obviously having more to say on the subject of a wedding. "I want to be the flower girl and carry a basket of flowers and scatter them down the aisle of the church, like Angela Brunnings did at her big sister's wedding. I don't *have* a big sister."

Oh, dear heaven, how to handle this? Pat closed her eyes a second to combat a sense of helplessness and then opened them again to see Jeremy's adorable daughter gazing at her imploringly. The situation had its comic side, but she didn't dare smile.

"I'll make you a promise, Mandy. If I marry anyone during the next couple of years while you're young enough, you'll be my flower girl. But let's just keep this between the two of us. Okay?"

Big brown eyes lit up and a satisfied smile tilted the corners of Mandy's mouth. "Okay. It'll be our secret."

Not the first hint of objection to Pat's marrying someone other than Jeremy. Any wedding at all would suit the five-year-old girl's purposes.

"Let's go eat supper," Pat said, grinning with amusement.

The grin died as she glanced again at the queen-size bed with its green-and-apricot-print dust ruffle and green comforter and plump pillows encased in the same print fabric and the same solid green. Marriage was more than companionship. Jeremy probably assumed that she had more sexual experience than she actually did. Not many brides her age could legitimately wear white these days, but Pat could.

It seemed just one more cause for feeling inadequate.

"There's another bedroom that Grandma and Grandpa Wells and Grandma and Grandpa Braddington stay in when they visit us." Mandy had resumed her tour-guide role.

"Maybe another time. All I want to see now is the patio."

"We'll have to go through the kitchen, but you don't have to look."

Pat did look. Susan's kitchen was modern and designed for use. It would have made a lot of women drool with envy. Women who could cook.

It had gotten dark by now, but apparently Jeremy intended them to eat on the lighted patio. A round wrought-iron table was set for four. He looked up from transferring cooked hamburger patties from a gas grill to a platter his son held for him.

"I was about to send Jerry to get you two. We're ready to eat."

Pat sniffed. "Smells delicious."

"I cook a mean hamburger, if I do say so."

"Daddy doesn't mean 'mean.' He means—" Mandy broke up into giggles as her statement turned into a tongue twister.

The adults laughed along with her, and even Jerry smiled before he caught himself and scowled, Pat noticed.

"Can I help?" she asked.

"Sure. You can get Mrs. Grambly's potato salad out of the refrigerator. Mandy, you put ice cubes into our glasses." Jeremy issued instructions for last-minute things to be done. The hustle and bustle was like that of a family all pitching in. Pat thought of herself the previous night heating up her frozen supper in the microwave and eating it in the living room in front of the TV. This was so much more enjoyable by comparison.

But if she married Jeremy, they couldn't have grilled hamburgers and salad prepared by his housekeeper for supper every night. Pat would have to prepare some meals herself in Susan's state-of-the-art kitchen. The prospect wasn't one she dared dwell on without spoiling her appetite.

In a short time they were seated at the table. Everyone's

plate was filled and the bottle of ketchup made the rounds, with Jerry not participating in the conversation. Pat caught Jeremy's concerned, but half-impatient glances at his son and came to a decision.

"Why don't we clear the air so that we can all relish our food?" she suggested, after first taking a big bite of her hamburger. She *was* starving. "I think we'll feel better if we each state our position about the four of us having supper together tonight. I'll go first, if that's all right."

"Please do," Jeremy said, laying down his fork. His expression mirrored both relief and admiration.

She addressed her words to his two children. "I accepted your dad's invitation for the same reason that I went to supper with him on Monday night—I like him as a person. But I have *no* plans as of this moment to marry him. I just don't know him that well. I think I do know him well enough, though, to be certain that he wouldn't marry anyone unless that person got along well with both of you and met with your approval." She gestured, turning over the floor to Jeremy.

He followed her example, directing his remarks to Jerry and Mandy. "Miss Tyler pretty well sized the situation up. There's no wedding being planned. The reason I'm dating her is that I like her very much as a person. I don't mind saying in front of her that I do want to remarry eventually because I'm the kind of man who's happy with a wife and family."

"Can I go next?" Mandy asked, wriggling in her seat with eagerness.

Jerry frowned at her fiercely. "I'm older than you."

"Your brother needs to get his feelings off his chest," Jeremy said. He nodded at his son. "Jerry?"

The little boy fixed his eyes on his glass of milk. "Miss Tyler's nice, but I don't want her to be my stepmother. Mandy and I don't need a stepmother. Mrs. Grambly takes good care of us. She cooks almost as good as Mom and does our laundry and keeps the house clean." He raised his gaze to Jeremy's face. "Doesn't she, Dad?"

"Mrs. Grambly was a real godsend, son. But there's more to being happy than having creature comforts provided, and I think you're old enough to realize that." There was no rebuke in the quiet answer.

Jerry sighed and slid an apologetic glance over at Pat. "Miss Tyler, you really are nice. Mr. Adams was right, but..."

Pat had been sitting there, aching with sympathy. Her emotion somehow made her more vulnerable to the unexpected mention of Clint, which called up his presence.

"What was Mr. Adams right about?" Jeremy asked.

"He said I should give Miss Tyler a chance. If I did, I would like her."

"Support from an unexpected quarter." Jeremy's response, reflecting mild surprise, was spoken more to himself than to her.

Pat struggled not to look as miserable as she felt. Clint had played matchmaker not fifteen minutes after she'd told him the way *he* affected her.

"Now is it my turn?" Mandy inquired.

Jeremy smiled at his daughter. "It's your turn."

"I like Miss Tyler this much." She threw her arms wide. "Her and me have a big secret that I can't tell." She screwed up her face wistfully. "Can't we tell Daddy and Jerry?"

Pat hadn't missed Jerry's scowl at the mention of a secret between her and his small sister. "We can share it with them, but no one else."

"No matter who Miss Tyler marries, I'm going to be her flower girl."

Mandy picked up her hamburger and took a bite. The discussion had obviously been satisfactorily concluded for her. Jerry began to attack his food hungrily, indicating that enough had been said for him. Finally Pat and Jeremy resumed eating, too, after a brief silent communication between them with her telling him, *I'll fill you in on the details later.*

The second bite of her hamburger didn't taste nearly as good as the first. Nor was Mrs. Grambly's potato salad as delicious as it looked. Clearing the air had backfired on Pat because she'd gotten a fifth point of view she hadn't bargained on getting: Clint's. He was all in favor of a matchup between her and Jeremy.

Gosh, that *hurt.*

Cleaning up after supper was a group project, with everyone pitching in and helping. They ate dessert—a scoop of ice cream on a homemade brownie—seated on stools at the breakfast bar in the kitchen. Pat made a determined effort to be her usual happy-go-lucky self, but her heart felt like a brick in her chest.

Jeremy had arranged in advance for a teenage girl in the neighborhood to come at nine o'clock and stay with Mandy and Jerry while he drove Pat home. The girl, Becky, showed up promptly. Pat said her goodbyes to the children, relieved that the evening was going to end early.

She wished that she'd driven herself and was saying goodbye to Jeremy, too. This was one of those rare times in her life when Pat would rather be alone.

Chapter Eight

"Jerry will warm up to you gradually," Jeremy said when they were in his van. "Tonight he was already losing the battle with himself because, like everybody else who meets you, he can't help liking you."

"That's me, Miss Likable," Pat said. The words popped out before she could stop them. She added before he could say anything, "Jerry's just too nice a little boy to carry off being rude and unfriendly."

A split second passed before Jeremy started up the engine. Pat breathed easier as he backed out of his driveway, and she sensed that he wouldn't follow up on her first remark. If he had, she might have blurted out her failures as a woman and made him feel bad because *he* hadn't fallen for her. That was hardly fair when Pat's real complaint was Clint's indifference.

"I like both your children," she stated with sincerity. "You have every reason to be a proud father."

"They're normal children and try my patience at times.

Mandy's actually the more manipulative of the two. By the way, how did you and she get into planning your future wedding?''

Pat answered without mentioning Mrs. Grambly and possibly getting her into hot water with Jeremy, if he didn't already know about the phone conversation that had been overheard.

"That little conniver!" he exclaimed. "I suspected something like that. After her friend Angela was a flower girl, Mandy talked about nothing else for weeks. She came up with the idea that I should get married again and give her a chance to be a flower girl herself. I stressed the point that my next wedding, when and if it took place, would be a very quiet affair. So she was tackling the problem from a different angle, hoping you would be an ally.''

"You think she took me to your bedroom, intending to use your and Susan's wedding picture as a lead-in? No. She's only five,'' Pat scoffed.

"Five going on sixteen when it comes to getting her way. You've been had.''

The conversation evoked all the discomfort she'd felt standing in the doorway of his bedroom, admiring the decorating scheme. Looking at his bed. Now was as good a time as any to broach the subject of sex.

"Mandy started me thinking about the whole tradition of brides wearing white. I wondered if *you'd* wondered...'' Her nerve failed her. Surely he could fill in the blanks for himself.

"Good heavens, Pat, of course I'm not assuming you're a virgin. Susan wasn't, for that matter, and she didn't lose her virginity to me. Nor did I lose mine to her. It didn't make a bit of difference in our relationship.''

"That's good.'' Pat's voice came out small.

"Don't get me wrong. I'm not assuming, either, that you've slept around.'' He sighed. "To be honest, the only thing I've 'wondered' in regard to sex between us is how it would be. Right now I can't imagine making love to any woman but Susan. It's a hurdle I've got to get past. The last thing I'd need is the pressure of being a first lover.'' He reached over and squeezed her hands, which were linked tightly together in her lap. ''Enough said for now?''

''Enough said for now.''

Plenty enough had been said for now. There was no pressing need to reveal her lack of experience with men tonight. It would take goodness-knows-how-many other dates to get them to that ''hurdle'' of making love, thanks to the fact that she had the sex appeal of a broomstick.

Pat smothered a sigh and rested her palms on her thighs, still feeling the warmth and strength in Jeremy's fingers. Clint hadn't squeezed her hand any harder today. He'd been just as gentle, just as earnest in his own rough way, offering nothing more than comfort. Why had his touch affected her like a zap of electricity and Jeremy's hadn't?

''How about some music?'' Jeremy suggested.

''That would be nice,'' she replied.

They listened to a station playing bluegrass and lowered the volume every now and then to carry on conversation. During the companionable silences, Pat's thoughts invariably circled back to Clint. He was like an invisible third party along on her date. She might have felt guiltier except for realizing that Susan's ghost was present, too.

''Here we are, at your place already,'' Jeremy said when he turned off the highway. ''This ride is already getting familiar.''

''My old van slows down automatically.''

Soon the beams of the headlights illuminated the store. It looked deserted and slightly run-down. The sight of it was dear to Pat, but after a fond glance she peered into the darkness beyond it and detected a faint glow of light coming from the location of Clint's cabin. He was still awake. What was he doing? Reading? Listening to a radio he'd brought along or trying to watch a small portable TV set? The reception would be poor.

If she only had the nerve, she could invite him to come

over the next few nights and watch her TV, which was hooked up to a satellite dish and got a zillion channels clearly. Pat was imagining Clint seated in her living room when Jeremy pulled up at her house, killed the engine and took the keys out of the ignition. With an effort she came back to the present.

"Are we having a crime wave in Marion County?" she asked with a smile in her voice. "Nobody's going to steal your van while you walk me to the door."

He looked taken aback for a moment. "I guess you're not a mind reader, are you? I hired Becky to stay with the kids until eleven or eleven-thirty so that we could have some time together. Otherwise I wouldn't have brought you home this early."

"Oh. So you want to come in."

"If it's all right."

"Sure. I'm not sleepy."

Pat truly didn't object to his coming inside and staying awhile. He needed to see her in her home setting, and to-night was as good a time as any.

"As my father would say, this is how the other half lives," she said when they stepped through her front door into the living room.

"I can just hear him," Jeremy replied, his tone reminiscent. He'd barely glanced around at the room. "And see him sitting over there in that recliner. I'll bet that was his chair."

"It was. Have a seat and flip on the TV, if you like. I'll make us some coffee."

"That sounds good. I'll take mine black." He headed over toward her brown tweed sofa.

When she returned a few minutes later with two mugs, he was settled back comfortably, watching an old John Wayne western movie that had been one of her dad's fa-vorites. Swamped by pleasant nostalgia, Pat sat on the sofa a comfortable distance away and became engrossed in the action on the screen.

When the film was over, Jeremy got up to leave. She walked out on the front porch with him and returned the gentle pressure of his chaste good-night kiss. As they had on Monday night, they hugged each other, and Pat took comfort in his strong embrace. When he released her, she felt a pang of separation.

"How about Saturday night?" Jeremy asked. "We could drive to Harrison and maybe take in a movie."

"And not run into quite so many people we know."

He chuckled. "Exactly."

At the bottom of the steps, he stopped and turned around. "It just hit me that your big dog isn't around tonight."

"He may have gotten lonely and gone visiting. He took a big liking to Clint Adams. I'll call him home before I go to bed."

"Can you call loud enough for him to hear you?"

"No, but I can whistle loud enough. Another one of my unladylike skills."

Jeremy grinned. "I won't ask you to demonstrate."

He said good-night again and left. Pat gazed off toward the path leading through the woods. Rowdy's absence gave her a good excuse to go to Clint's cabin in search of him. Just considering the idea awoke shameful eagerness. "No, you will *not* go bothering Clint," she said aloud.

If Rowdy were with him, he was probably enjoying the dog's company. He *wouldn't* enjoy Pat's showing up un-invited. That was the deciding and very disheartening factor that kept her from getting her flashlight—not pride.

The earlier urge for solitude was gone. Given her options of staying out on the porch and keeping herself company or going inside and keeping herself company, Pat switched off the overhead light and sat in the swing in the darkness. There was so much to think about and every train of thought revolved around either Clint or Jeremy. But Jeremy was the one she should focus on. He would still be here when Clint was gone, and he might be thinking about her right now.

Closing her eyes, Pat recaptured the warm, secure feeling of being held in Jeremy's arms. It wasn't a thrilling sensation. It didn't satisfy her deep yearning for romance. But it chased away the loneliness.

It might have to be enough.

Clint saw Jeremy's headlights when he brought Pat home. It was earlier than he'd expected her to be returning. When fifteen minutes passed and the van didn't leave, he knew that Wells must have left his kids with a sitter. He'd gone inside with Pat, and the two of them were alone.

Wells was free to kiss her, to touch her, to make love to her—

Clint cursed to relieve the savage jealousy that ripped through him. Rowdy, lying on the hooked rug in the cabin, raised his head and whined.

"I'm not mad at you, fella."

He picked up his magazine and tried to read, and then threw it down in disgust at himself. There was no reason—absolutely *none*—that he should be stewing over what was happening at Pat's house between her and Jeremy Wells. They might be sitting in her living room, talking or watching TV. Whatever they were doing, it was no business of his.

Before tonight, they hadn't slept together. Clint would bet money on that. He could just tell from seeing Wells around her earlier that he wasn't her lover. Not yet. It was only a matter of time. Maybe they would wait until after Clint was gone. He hoped like hell they would.

"Let's go outside, Rowdy, and get some fresh air."

The big dog got up with an air of patience and accompanied him out onto the porch. The minutes dragged by. Clint kept track of the slow passage of time, glancing at the luminous dial of his wristwatch. Finally, at eleven o'clock, he heard an engine start up. A short time later Wells's van turned onto the road.

When the red taillights had disappeared from sight, the

tension in Clint's body eased. "Well, I guess I can turn the night watch over to you now, big fella." His voice reflected the strain he'd been under. "Time for you to go home to Pat."

Rowdy rose and, after a last warm lick, departed.

Clint stayed out on the porch awhile longer, able now to appreciate the pine scent in the crisp night air. He was going to miss breathing this air. Miss the peacefulness of this place that seemed to seep into his soul.

If Wells weren't in the picture—

But he was in the picture. And he was the better man of the two of them.

"Sure. I can baby-sit again Saturday night, Mr. Wells." Becky folded her sitter's pay and stuck it into the pocket of her jeans. "Stay out as late as you want. Mom won't mind, since I'll be right here in the same neighborhood. I'm glad you started dating Miss Tyler," she confided. "I'm saving up money for a trip to Washington, D.C., with my class next year."

"What you're saying is that you're counting on me as major contributor," Jeremy teased.

Becky smiled sheepishly.

"I'll be needing you at least once or twice a week this summer," he told her in a more serious vein.

"Oh, great!"

Judging by her delighted but abstracted expression, the teenage girl was doing rough calculations of her potential earnings as she said good-night and left.

Even making allowances for adolescent mood swings, Becky's level of excitement over his intention to keep dating Pat Tyler made Jeremy that much more aware of his own lukewarm enthusiasm. Pat deserved better. She deserved a guy who couldn't wait until the next date, a guy who couldn't keep his hands off her.

That guy wasn't Jeremy.

He enjoyed her company. He liked her better every time

he was around her. Hugging her and having her hug him was awfully nice, but it didn't turn him on. Or turn her on, for that matter. This just wasn't what he wanted. What he wanted was for Susan to be alive.

Were the deer outside his cabin again this morning? Intent on finding out, Clint got out of bed and hobbled over to the kitchen window, ignoring the stiffness and soreness of his leg.

Sure enough, his early-morning visitors were grazing in the hollow. He watched for a minute or two before he switched on the coffeepot. To the sound of its gurgling, he limped back to the bedroom to get dressed. With the coffee aroma filling the cabin, Clint felt a sense of well-being he hadn't experienced since before his accident.

He postponed shaving and returned to the kitchen to pour himself a mug of coffee. Holding it in his left hand, he eased open the back door, hoping not to spook the deer. But they took flight, bounding gracefully away into the woods. It was an incredible sight to see.

"Damn," Clint muttered, his tone more awed than irritated.

It occurred to him as he sat down in one of the chairs on the screened back porch that he hadn't sat out there since he'd arrived on Monday afternoon. The reason wasn't hard to put his finger on. From the front porch of the cabin, he could catch glimpses of Pat.

As big a kick as he got from seeing the deer, there wouldn't be any contest if Clint woke up and knew he could see her from another window.

After he'd finished his coffee, he went back inside and had his breakfast. While he ate, he mulled over the question of what he would do that day. He still hadn't come up with any good answer by the time he'd rinsed his bowl and spoon and headed for the bathroom to shave.

He'd jiggled the lever of the toilet when he'd flushed it earlier, but water was still running into the tank. The mechanism was definitely shot. With a muffled curse of impatience, Clint lifted off the top and manually raised the float. Meanwhile both sink faucets and the shower head were dripping, each at its own rate.

Suddenly he knew one thing he could do today—some simple plumbing chores.

Clint met his own dark cynical gaze in the mirror over the sink as he lathered up his face with shaving cream. Now he had a good reason to hike to the store and see Pat this morning. He needed to borrow some tools from her and get her okay. Then later in the day he would have to return the tools. Another good excuse to see her.

It was too small a job to get more mileage out of it than that. He would have to come up with something else for tomorrow.

Clint's contempt for his own motives didn't prevent him from hurrying and nicking himself with his razor. "Serves you right," he told himself disgustedly as he stanched the flow of blood.

Nothing had changed. He still meant to keep the promise he'd made to himself not to come between Pat and Wells. But he could do that and not stay away from her.

This morning he drove to the store. Getting in and out of the Suburban didn't seem to be quite as much torture for him as it had only a couple of days ago. Maybe he was just learning to compensate for not having two sound legs, Clint reflected. Or maybe having his mind on other things made the difference.

As he entered the store, setting off the bell, Pat emerged from the back storeroom, carrying a cardboard box. For a second Clint was afraid she was going to drop it.

"Clint!" she exclaimed. "Good morning!"

The note of welcome mixed with her surprise sent warm pleasure through him.

"Good morning," he replied. "Let me get that for you. It looks heavy."

"I lug this much weight around all the time."

But she met him halfway between them and let him take the box from her.

"Where do you want it?" he asked.

"Over here." She led him down an aisle. "Just set it on the floor along here anywhere."

The flaps of the box were folded back so that Clint could see that it contained an assortment of canned goods. "Why don't I hold it for you? Then you don't have to bend over."

"That's not necessary." The protest was feeble. She began to grab cans and put them in place on the shelves, working with her usual quickness and coordination. In a matter of a couple of minutes, she'd emptied the box.

"Damn, you're fast," Clint marveled.

His remark seemed to fluster her. "It all depends," she said. "Sit me down at a desk with bookkeeping to catch up on, and I turn into a snail. I'll take that empty box. Thanks for your help."

"Are you finished?"

"For now. Let's have a cup of coffee. Don't worry, I didn't bake anything last night."

"No, I don't guess you had much of a chance."

Her eyes widened at his hard-edged remark, which had slipped out. Clint shrugged. "I was up and saw Wells's van coming and going."

The pretty color in her cheeks deepened into a blush. Did her embarrassment mean she'd made love with Wells last night? Jealousy snaked through Clint while he waited for her to answer.

"He came in and we watched an old John Wayne movie on TV. He'd hired a sitter to stay with Mandy and...Jerry."

The mention of Wells's son had tripped her memory and brought a troubled expression to her face. "Did the kid make a pain of himself?" Clint asked.

"Not really. He tried to hold himself apart out of loyalty to his mother. I felt so sorry for him. Just like I feel sorry for Jeremy. Susan's death was such a tragic thing for all three of them."

"Tragic things happen." Clint's voice was harsh because he was wondering how she'd expressed that sympathy for Wells last night.

"Yes, like you having your military career cut off all of a sudden."

"That's not quite in the same category. Let's have that coffee." Better to cut the discussion off right there before he told her that she was one hell of a consolation prize for any man who'd had the props knocked out from under him. That included Wells. Included him.

She nodded and headed off down the aisle with her springy stride, carrying the empty box, ponytail swishing. He was reminded of the deer bounding off. Her movements had some of the same energy and beauty.

"I'll bring you a cup if you want to sit down," she offered.

"Thanks."

Clint needed a moment to regroup. It was a whole new experience for him to be eaten up with jealousy over a woman. Just as new was this fierce protectiveness that Pat touched off in him. To have to hide those emotions while he kept them under control wasn't going to be easy.

He'd just made it to the table when she came with the two cups of coffee. "Here we are," she said.

"That was record time, even for you," Clint commented. "You would make a fortune as a waitress."

She smiled a self-conscious smile. "When you show up, I seem to kick into overdrive. My muscles try to keep up with my pulse, I guess. Don't frown. I'm just telling it like it is. I realize the chemistry's one-sided."

"Pat—" He clamped his jaw closed.

"Oh, I know you like me. Jerry passed along some of his conversation with you. He said you vouched for the fact that I was a nice person. He also mentioned that you were orphaned when you were his age. That must have been awfully tough."

"I survived, just like he will. Look, Wells has a lot more

going for him than I ever did. Aside from seeming like a hell of a nice guy.''

"Jeremy is a nice guy."

"You do want to get married, right?"

She shrugged, nodded and sighed in quick succession, each reaction a *yes* answer to his question. "My next birthday I'll be thirty. I've lived by myself a whole year and don't like it at all. But I'm not in love with Jeremy, and he's not in love with me. Otherwise, I'd be more enthusiastic. I've always wanted to fall madly in love and never have," she confessed.

"Love," he scoffed, putting all his cynicism into the one word.

"You've never been in love?"

"I've had the hots for a few women, but it wasn't anything that lasted. I think what people call love is nine-tenths lust."

"Lust," she repeated, her gaze leaving his face and taking in his shoulders, his chest, his hands resting on the table.

Clint shifted in his chair, responding to her inspection. "Yes, lust." He took a gulp of his coffee.

Pat picked hers up and took a sip. "I haven't had much experience with it, either. But Jeremy and I are working with that other one-tenth, so far." Her tone was glum.

Clint's jaw wouldn't stay clamped this time. "Have you been to bed with him?"

She blushed a pretty shade of rose. "No. We haven't even French-kissed."

The information shouldn't have been as welcome as it was. Clint thought about the state he'd gotten himself into last night when Wells was at her house.

"He's not a teenager with raging hormones," he said. "He probably doesn't want to start anything he can't finish." The explanation was the best theory Clint could offer her. He certainly wouldn't have that much self-control in

Wells's shoes. "French-kissing for a man is foreplay," he added.

"I guess for most women, too." Her gaze lingered on his mouth with the same wistfulness in her voice.

Clint felt himself getting hard. He tossed down the rest of his coffee. "This is a hell of a conversation for a guy like me who hasn't had a woman in going on three months. I think we'd better leave the subject right there."

"You mean you're...bothered by our conversation?"

"That's what I mean. If I stood, you'd see for yourself."

She looked perfectly willing for him to rise to his feet and let her see.

"There's none of this—this *tension* in the air when Jeremy and I talk," she mused with a regretful sigh. "Actually I've never felt it with anyone before. Why you? It's not as though I haven't come in contact with plenty of big, rugged, sexy men. The timing was so—" again she searched for a word, twirling her hands, "—so incredible. On the very same day that I make up my mind to give Jeremy the nudge to ask me out on a date, you arrive. And you stop at his gas station minutes before I drive up. It's like...fate. Or was my whole reaction to you just desperation on my part?"

"Beats me." Clint's voice was bleak. What could he say? If she was giving him multiple-choice answers, *B* was obviously the right one. He definitely wasn't the man to fulfill her romantic fantasies, although he would like nothing better.

"I hope you're not sorry you picked up my brochure."

"I'm not. At least not on my account."

"That's good to hear. I would hate to be a bad memory for you." She smiled at him, perking up. True to her nature, she wouldn't mope for long about anything. "More coffee?"

"No, thanks. I came by to borrow some tools to do some plumbing."

"Tools? Plumbing?"

He explained his intention of offering his free services as handyman and added, "It'll be good to make myself useful, for a change."

"In that case, I certainly won't refuse. But I will insist on reimbursing you for the parts you buy." She had just finished directing him to a toolbox in her garage when Lester Madden drove up outside the store.

Clint stuck around a couple of minutes longer, just long enough to confirm that he didn't like the man's looks any better this morning, even though he was wearing cleaner clothes. Madden had evidently switched from chewing tobacco to unfiltered cigarettes for his first day on the job, and his hand shook as he chain-smoked. If he was a reformed drinker, Clint was a star quarterback in the NFL.

"See you later," Clint told Pat, cutting in on Madden's blather.

"Bye, Clint. Be sure to bring me the receipts from the hardware store. Or I can give you money now to cover the expense, so you won't be out of pocket."

"No need."

"I enjoyed our chat." The color rose in her cheeks as she sneaked a glance at his crotch.

"Same here."

As Clint limped out, he could feel her gaze on him, measuring the width of his shoulders, taking note of the fit of his shirt over the muscles in his back. He'd been sized up by women before, but his response to being sized up by Pat, like all his responses to her, was a totally new experience, as frustrating as it was pleasing to his ego.

He wished he were free to encourage her. He would let her practice her feminine wiles on him and develop more confidence in her powers to seduce a man. But she had too much at stake to mess around with him. Wells was the lucky man blessed with the chance to let loose the woman in Pat.

* * *

"Who is that feller, anyway?" Lester inquired. "Does he live around here?"

"No." *I wish,* thought Pat. "He's renting one of my cabins."

"Fer how long?"

"Just through Sunday. You looked relieved," she observed.

"It don't take a genius to notice when somebody's got it in fer ye. I think he musta wanted this job fer hisself."

"I seriously doubt that. Come on outside, Lester. We need to get canoes loaded up for our first shuttle trip."

Even though she'd brushed aside his comment, it stuck in her mind. Was there any slight possibility that Lester had picked up on something Pat had missed? Would Clint consider taking the job as her driver, if she offered it to him? Was he physically able? Did he have a chauffeur's license? Would he be willing to get one? All these questions kept posing themselves throughout the first part of the day, which went fairly well.

Her only two complaints about Lester were his constant stream of bull and his tendency to drive too fast.

The afternoon didn't go nearly as well. At noon he left in his pickup truck and when he returned, he bought a pack of breath mints, but not before Homer and Pat both smelled liquor on his breath. They confronted him on the spot, speaking at the same time.

"You've been drinking, Lester," Pat stated.

"You had you a nip of corn likker, boy," Homer accused him.

"No, sirree, I ain't done nothin' of the kind," Lester denied, popping several mints into his mouth. "Been having a bad cough and took me some cough syrup. I'm eatin' these mints to take the bad taste out of my mouth."

"You'd better change your brand of cough syrup," Pat said, not believing him. "Remember that I warned you I wouldn't put up with any drinking."

Lester looked wounded, but there was a touch of belligerence in his reply. "Are you calling me a liar? I done told you I ain't had a drop to drink."

Homer snorted his skepticism. "Bet you ten bucks you got a bottle in your pickup."

"I don't get paid to stand around and jaw with you, grampa." Lester swaggered outside.

"Might as well fire him now," Homer advised.

"I'll let him finish out the day." Pat sighed. "I like being my own boss, but I hate being the boss when it comes to firing people." She remembered making the same confession to Clint a couple of days ago.

"Your pa was the same way. But he had your ma to stiffen up his backbone. If you was to stay in business, you'd need yourself a partner who could crack the whip."

"A partner. That's an idea, Homer."

His grin was coy. "From the look on your face, you got somebody in mind."

"I do."

He chuckled with approval, assuming wrongly, Pat knew, that she meant Jeremy. Homer didn't have a clue that she was thinking about Clint. Of course, it fell under "wishful thinking." Clint probably wouldn't be interested in settling down in Arkansas and helping to run a small business like hers. Plus he would be suspicious, and rightly so, of Pat's motives if she sounded him out on the idea.

She wanted him to stay. And not just because he would carry his own weight and supply skills she lacked, although on the basis of short acquaintance, Pat was certain he would do both those things. If he did stay, maybe—

"You gonna get that phone, gal?" Homer's voice and the ringing of the telephone penetrated Pat's daze.

"Who was it?" he asked curiously after she'd taken the call and hung up. "Not bad news?"

"Not really bad. Just a cancelation."

"Canoe trip?"

"No, a cabin rental. There was a medical emergency,

and the family vacation had to be postponed." The cabin with a vacancy was Clint's.

He probably wouldn't want to change his plans, but if he decided he wanted to stay another week, he could. Should she bring up the cancelation and let him know the cabin was available?

Pondering that question, Pat went outside and caught Lester coming from his pickup, popping more mints into his mouth.

The people in her party had just driven up and were getting out of their sports-utility vehicle and unloading camping gear for their four-day float. Otherwise Pat might have taken Homer's advice and gone ahead and fired Lester. Instead she stuck with her decision to wait until the day was over.

"I'll drive this trip," she told him. "You did all the driving this morning."

His lips thinned in anger, and his fists clenched. "You're the boss," he snarled.

It occurred to Pat that she wouldn't mind at all having Clint present when she gave Lester the bad news that he'd flunked his trial employment.

After leaving the store, Clint went first to Pat's garage, wanting to make sure he would locate the tools he needed to do the job. After some searching he found them, scattered hither and yon amid the mess. Maybe another worthwhile project for him would be straightening up the garage, he thought, shaking his head.

At a hardware store in Yellville, he bought gaskets and the replacement parts for the toilet. His errand accomplished, he headed out of town, the route taking him past Jeremy Wells's gas station. The needle on Clint's gas gauge pointed to the halfway mark. He would have pulled in and filled up, if Pat didn't sell gas. Since she did, he would buy it from her, not Wells.

This time next year, doing business with Wells would be

the same as doing business with her, after she'd become Mrs. Jeremy Wells. But Clint wouldn't be around to know about it. Nor did he want to think about it today.

His minor repair jobs at the cabin went well. He'd finished them and replaced the tools by eleven o'clock. The question now was how to kill the rest of the day. The nights of restful sleep and napping and taking it easy had restored his energy. Clint was too restless to sit and read for hours, marking time until he paid a visit to Pat late that afternoon when he could catch her alone.

After he ate lunch, he would see some more of the countryside, he decided.

As he got back into his automobile, Clint thought about how road weary and down in the dumps he'd been when he'd parked in this spot late Monday afternoon. He wasn't his old self by a long shot—either physically or mentally— but the tremor in his muscles was gone and his outlook had improved.

As he'd told Wells's kid, things could always be worse.

Sure, he was wounded, but he was able-bodied and healthy other than having a bum leg. He would find a job. He would adjust to civilian life. He would make the best of a stroke of bad luck.

If Pat weren't spoken for, Clint would finish recuperating and coming to grips with being an ex-marine right here in the Ozarks. But he wasn't about to stick around and be invited to her wedding.

Chapter Nine

The gas gauge was almost on empty when Clint turned off the highway at the Tylers' sign with the pointing arrow. He'd covered quite a few miles of rugged mountain terrain during the afternoon without happening upon a single large town. The hilliest stretches of two-lane highway had been in the vicinity of Jasper. Topping the rise of steep climbs, he'd murmured an awed "Damn" more than once at a view of a valley spread out below, each one of them straight out of a travel magazine.

With his window rolled down, he'd breathed the fresh country air that had a zing to it and tuned in several different radio stations playing country and western or blue-grass. The whole time his destination had been right back here, at Tyler's.

When the store came into sight, he felt a sense of home-coming.

The Tyler van was parked out front, which meant Pat was there. Homer hadn't left yet, nor had Lester Madden.

Both their pickups were easily recognizable in the parking lot. For some odd reason he couldn't explain, Clint was struck by a sense of urgency as he pulled up to the gas pump. It was just nosiness, he told himself. Throughout the day he'd wondered how Pat was faring with Lester. Now he would find out.

Filling his gas tank gave him an excuse to stop without sacrificing his visit with Pat later on. He'd left the receipts in the cabin—not an oversight.

Clint had killed the engine and was stepping down to the ground when he heard a man's voice shouting inside the store. For a split second he froze. Madden? Yelling at Pat or Homer? Filled with a murderous rage, Clint took off at a halting run toward the front door, his hands clenched into fists. He would beat Madden to a pulp if the bastard had gotten rough with Pat.

"Come inside, Lester. We need to have a talk."

"I'll be there in a minute, boss lady. Just hold on to your panties." His tone was surly, and he kept walking toward his pickup. With every trip he'd shown more of his ill-natured disposition.

Pat sighed and glanced again at Clint's cabin. He hadn't returned yet from wherever he'd gone today. Just knowing he was nearby would have given her moral support. As it was, she had only Homer to back her up if Lester got nasty.

"That's good money wasted," the old man commented from his rocking chair as Pat counted out a day's pay from the cash register.

"It'll be money well spent just to get rid of Lester," she replied. "I wish I'd given it to him this morning and sent him on his way, before he got drunk on his cough syrup."

"Cough syrup!" Homer snorted. "Shows you what kind of smarts the feller has if that's the best lie he can tell."

Glancing out the window, she saw Lester swaggering toward the store, his gait unsteady. "Here he comes." She closed the register drawer and moved from behind the counter.

Lester eyed the money in Pat's hand as he stepped inside. A grin that was half sneer spread across his face. "I see you and me are on the same wavelength, boss lady. It suits me a whole lot better to take some cash home with me at the end of a hard day's work. That waitin' until the end of the week is bullcrap." He stuck out his hand. "Gimme them greenbacks."

Pat laid the money on his palm. "We're not on the same wavelength, Lester."

"What's that supposed to mean?" he snarled, stuffing the bills into his jeans pocket.

"It means you're fired," Homer spoke up.

"No, I ain't fired, grampa. I hired on for at least a week."

"Homer, let me handle this," Pat said. "I told you yesterday, Lester, that I wouldn't tolerate any drinking on the job. You're half drunk right now."

"So what if I get a little liquored up?" Lester's voice got louder with each word until he was shouting. He took a step toward her. "It don't affect my driving none!"

Pat stood her ground, even though her instinct was to back away. "Of course, it affects your driving. If you won't take my word for it, I'll call the sheriff and we'll get his opinion."

"You think you scare me, witch, threatening to bring the law down on me?" Lester yelled, his face contorted with his anger. He took another step, his right hand upraised. "For two cents, I'd smack you a good one!"

Homer had stood. "You better git out of here, boy, while the gittin's good! Why, if I was younger, I'd throw you out!"

Lester whirled around toward him. "Shut your mouth, grampa! You ain't nothin' but an old coot!"

Out of the corner of her eye Pat caught a movement at the door, but she didn't dare take her eyes off Lester. Then the door burst open and banged against the wall. She looked and saw Clint charging across the threshold, his fist already swinging in a powerful arc. The rest seemed to occur in slow motion while relief flooded through her. *Clint had gotten there just in time.* Lester's head jerked around. A stunned expression on his face changed to fright. Clint's fist connected with his jaw. The hard thud drowned out Lester's grunt. His knees buckled, but before he could fall to the floor, Clint caught him and dragged him bodily to the open doorway, where he heaved him out onto the gravel.

"Get up, you cowardly bastard, and try bullying me!" Clint raged, limping out to stand over him.

Lester made a whimpering sound as he pushed himself up on hands and knees and crawled several yards before he stood. Weaving and stumbling and glancing back at Clint, he managed to get to his pickup truck, climbed in, and drove away.

Pat had gotten enough strength in her knees to walk over to the doorway and watch. Before she could speak to Clint, Homer made a strangled sound behind her. Turning around, she saw that he'd sat down again in his rocking chair and was clutching his chest.

"Homer!" she cried, immediately alarmed, and ran over to him.

"It's my ticker," he gasped, fumbling in his overalls pocket and pulling out a tiny bottle. "Here, gal." He handed it to her, his hand shaking. "Open this and get me one of them little pills to put under my tongue."

Pat didn't waste any time doing his bidding.

Clint had come up beside her. "We'd better get him to a hospital," he said in a concerned tone.

Homer shook his head. "No need to go to a hospital. Soon as that pill takes effect, I'll be fit as a fiddle again."

"Homer has angina," Pat explained. "He got all upset when Lester threatened to hit me—"

"Threatened to hit *you?*" Clint's fists were clenched

again. "He had his arm raised to hit the old man. Why, I would have—" He broke off.

"I was never so glad in my life to see anyone, as I was glad to see you," she told him fervently.

"You was a sight for sore eyes, all right," Homer added, his voice stronger. "That's some punch you pack, son." He sat up straighter, the color back in his face. "Well, that pill's done the trick again. I'll see you folks tomorrow."

"No, you won't. Not unless you're just visiting," Pat informed him. She smiled fondly. "I'm giving you your walking papers, too, Homer. Tending store all day is too much for you at your age."

"How you gonna manage without me, gal?"

"Either I'll manage or I'll close down."

He nodded. "Your ma and your pa wouldn't have wanted you to be saddled with this place. It would be different if you was marrying a man who didn't have his own business. But that ain't the case."

"Jeremy hasn't asked me to marry him, Homer."

"He will in his own good time."

Clint turned away abruptly.

"Don't leave," Pat said, putting out her hand and touching his arm. It felt like warm iron. "Stay and talk awhile."

"I'm not leaving yet. I'm going out to fill up my gas tank." The reply was curt.

"I'm leavin'," Homer said, rising. "Young feller, you have a safe trip back to Illinois, if I don't see you again before you take off. Come back next year."

"Thanks, Homer, but I doubt I'll be coming back. You take care of yourself."

"I'll shore do that."

They shook hands and then Clint limped out, without a glance at her. Pat had to tear her gaze away from his tall, broad-shouldered form.

"Are you sure you're up to driving?" she asked the old man worriedly.

He grinned, dangling his right hand. "Soon as I git some

feeling back in this paw, I kin drive as good as ever. That young feller's got a powerful grip. Be seein' you. Don't take any wooden nickels, Little Pat.''

Her emotions were already churned up enough. His affectionate use of her parents' nickname for her brought a giant lump to her throat. It was all Pat could do to muster a smile for his benefit. ''Don't worry, Homer. I won't. Bye, now.''

She clapped him on the shoulder and walked to the doorway with him. His steps were sprightly as he took a direct path to his old pickup.

Pat tried to make herself turn around and go back inside the store, but her body wouldn't cooperate. Instead she headed out toward the gas pump, her heart thumping heavily in her chest. Clint was standing beside his carryall, holding the nozzle inserted into his tank and balancing on his good leg, a frown of concentration on his face. Change the location, and it might have been Pat's first glimpse of him on Monday afternoon at Jeremy's gas station.

He looked up, and the sense of déjà vu vanished. Monday was then and today was now. The strange regret she'd felt watching him pull out onto the highway in Yellville welled up a thousand times stronger as she thought of him driving away this coming Monday with no intentions of ever coming back.

''You okay?'' he asked when she came to a stop a couple of yards away from him.

She nodded and then shrugged. ''I've been in happier moods. You were right about Lester. He started drinking at noon. And he's not one of those life-of-the-party drunks. He got more and more ticked off with me because I insisted on being the driver this afternoon.''

''Even if he'd stayed off the booze, you'd have had problems with Lester taking orders from you.''

''Because he's a macho type, you mean. And I'm a woman. Even though I'm not exactly feminine.''

"Because you're a woman." His gaze was fixed on the pump nozzle.

Pat's spirits sank lower. "Homer's right. My parents wouldn't have wanted me to run their business out of some sense of responsibility to them. It's such a hassle getting reliable help. Maybe I should sell off the canoes and just run the store and rent the cabins. But without canoe rentals, I probably wouldn't do enough business to justify keeping the store open, since I'm not located on the highway. What would you do in my place?"

"Shouldn't you be asking Wells that question? He's the guy who should be helping you with tough decisions. Not me."

"Sorry, I didn't mean to unload on you." She turned to go, stung by his harsh tone.

"Damn it! I don't mind answering you. It's just—" He broke off. "In your place I would try not to downsize your operation so that when you sell out, you'll get a good price. Or get a good deal if you lease. I'm assuming you'll either sell or lease, if you marry Wells. You're not going to drive back and forth from Yellville and run a seven-day-a-week business, are you?"

Pat still had her back to him. "I haven't made any plans to move to Yellville. Everybody, including you, is marrying me off, but Jeremy may have different ideas."

"Wells is no fool."

"I guess I'll take that as a compliment." She started back toward the store, her sense of dejection almost over-whelming.

"Hold on a minute." His rough voice held a resigned note that struck her as odd. Pat halted and turned around. "Hell, I have a chauffeur's license. I can fill in as a driver for you for a week or two. You wouldn't have to pay me. Just deduct that amount from my cabin rent."

"That's very kind of you, but—"

"It's *not* kind of me," he contradicted, jamming the noz-zle in place on the pump.

"Yes, it is. Underneath that hard act you're a nice guy, Clint. You feel sorry for me because I'm having a struggle. I wasn't playing on your sympathy just now. Honest."

"Well, how about it? Do you want to hire me or not?"

"Yes, of course, I want to hire you." Pat bit her lip, working up her courage to be honest with him. "But I have real mixed feelings about why I want to. I'd like you to stay another week or two. And not just because I'm desperate for help, but because— Well, you can figure it out for yourself. Aside from that, are you physically able to work? What about your leg?"

His expression wouldn't have looked any different if she'd slapped him hard in the face. "My leg's my problem."

"Now I've hurt your pride, darn it. But knowing you, you would be too stubborn to admit the job was too much once you took it on. Think how awful I'd feel if you pushed yourself and did further damage to your bad leg."

"Forget I offered." He strode toward her, jerking out his wallet. "Here's money for the gas."

Pat took the two twenties he thrust at her. "Clint, please don't be offended." She was talking to his back. "What about your change? This is way too much money."

"I'll get it another time."

He drove off toward his cabin, leaving her standing there.

"Darn. Darn. *Darn,*" she muttered, kicking at the gravel. Why did he have to be so sensitive? Her qualms were perfectly reasonable.

Had he overreacted in order to back out of his offer? It had been halfhearted to start with. Then she'd confessed that she wanted him to stay, under any circumstances. He'd probably had immediate second thoughts about sticking around and having her salivate over him.

The best thing for her was to let him leave and try to forget him. Maybe after he was gone, she could put herself more wholeheartedly into dating Jeremy.

Kicking the gravel every few steps, Pat trudged inside

the store. She was counting out Clint's change when she remembered the receipts from the hardware store he was supposed to bring her. Had he done the repairs? She hadn't even thought to ask him, and he hadn't had a chance to tell her. He'd driven up just in the nick of time and thrown Lester out on his ear.

Pat hugged herself, reliving the scene of Clint entering the store and coming to her and Homer's rescue. Memory aroused the same fervent relief she'd experienced at the time, but it also aroused a thrill of female pleasure. John Wayne couldn't have socked Lester any harder on the jaw or dealt with him any more forcefully, she mused with a dreamy sigh.

Her worries about Clint's fitness struck her as foolish. He was the best judge of whether he was physically able to fill in as her driver. If he felt up to the job and wasn't in a hurry to return to Illinois, shouldn't she hire him temporarily? She was in a terrible bind without Homer to tend the store.

Realistically, it wasn't going to be any easier to forget Clint after just a week than it would be two weeks from now. Knowing that he was soon leaving, she could continue dating Jeremy. Based on the two dates they'd had, Jeremy's courtship had all the signs of being a long, drawn-out affair anyway.

Pat stuffed the change from Clint's gas money into her pocket and wasted no time locking up the store. If she left the matter hanging until tomorrow, she wouldn't be able to think about anything else and probably wouldn't get a wink of sleep tonight. So she would take Clint his change now and ask him about reconsidering his offer to fill in.

In addition she would thank him again. Apologize for insulting him. Inquire about the repairs and the receipts. There was quite a lot of fuel for conversation. With any cooperation on his part, her visit might last a little while.

"Calm down," Pat chided herself on the walk through

the woods to his cabin. It wouldn't do to arrive, bubbling over with eagerness to see him.

He wasn't out on the front porch. The single chair was empty, and the door to the cabin stood open. She should call out and alert him to her presence, Pat realized, reaching the steps.

"Clint. It's Pat."

Silence. Heart thudding in her chest, she climbed the steps and crossed the porch to the open doorway. The back door stood open, too. "Are you decent?" she called out. "Can I barge in on you for a minute? I brought your change."

"Just leave it." His voice came from the screened back porch.

"But I wanted to talk to you. Do you mind?"

No answer.

"I'm interpreting that as a no." With that warning, Pat brazenly entered and passed quickly through the cabin.

Clint was seated in the chair just to the left of the doorway, a can of cola in one hand. "If you came to apologize, don't," he said.

"Okay." She hesitated. "Would it be too pushy of me to ask if I could get myself a cola from your refrigerator? My throat's dry as a bone." It was true that her throat was dry from nerves. And drinking a cola would buy her a few minutes.

"Help yourself."

"Thanks. Be right back." On her way to the refrigerator she glanced around the cabin, noting how clean and orderly everything was. "You sure are neat," she commented.

"You learn neatness in the military." His reply was terse, but at least it was a reply.

"Do you miss the military life a lot?"

"Yes."

She popped open the can and ventured out onto the porch where she sat down in the chair on the opposite side of the door. "How long a career in the marines were you planning on?"

"Twenty-five or thirty years." He took a swig from his cola.

"So when you got out, you would have been forty-five or fifty years old, depending on which time span. If you were going to marry and have a family, I guess you meant to do that while you were still in uniform."

"A wife and kids didn't figure into my plans then, either," he said flatly.

"That's some woman's real loss."

She sighed when he didn't answer, obviously not wanting to continue the conversation. "I should say what I came here to say and not wear your patience thin. First, I know you withdrew your offer, but I'd like to hire you on your terms. Your salary would take care of your rent." He hadn't looked directly at her before now, and his dark gaze was boring into her. "It would be understood that you were leaving at the end of the two weeks you mentioned, whether or not I'd hired someone in the meanwhile. So, how about it?"

He took a gulp of cola. "As much as I would like to help you out, I don't think it's a good idea for me to stay around."

"Why? Because it makes you uncomfortable when I look at you with goo-goo eyes?" Pat's cheeks were hot with her embarrassment. "I promise I'll try to control myself. Maybe familiarity will breed contempt, as the saying goes."

"It's myself I don't trust. I don't want any part of coming between you and Wells."

The statement about not trusting himself had roused a little spurt of hope that he'd immediately doused. "Lord knows, nobody wants that," she said gloomily. "Poor Jeremy and I might be stuck with each other since we don't seem to have many options. You'll be glad to know he asked me out on our third date, and I've accepted. Well?"

His indrawn breath was audible. "Against my better judgment, yes, I'll pinch-hit as your driver."

From his tone he was being persuaded against his inclination as well as his judgment, but Pat was filled with gladness anyway. He would stay. "Great." She managed not to put an exclamation mark in her voice. "I'll see you in the morning, then. Tonight I'll try to round up somebody to tend the store tomorrow so that I can ride with you."

"That won't be necessary. I know the routine of unloading and loading canoes and equipment. You can give any instructions to your customers at the store before we leave."

"But you don't know the location of all the put-in and takeout places."

"Yes, I do. I did some sight-seeing today and went to all of them, using a map."

"Oh." The one syllable conveyed her crushing disappointment that he didn't want her to accompany him tomorrow. She got to her feet and dug into her jeans pocket. "Here's your change."

A quarter spurted from the wad of bills and coins, made a small plunking sound on the wooden floor and rolled underneath his chair. "I'll get it," Pat said and went quickly to kneel down beside him.

"Leave it." His command was brusque.

"I'm already here." She bent lower to see under the chair and retrieved the quarter. Rising up again, she bumped into his hand. Startled, she looked at him. Her heart stopped beating as he looked back at her, his hand still hovering in the air near her face. Gently he grazed her cheek with his knuckles. Pat's whole body went weak at his touch. "Clint?" she whispered.

"Don't, Pat."

"Don't what?" Her eyes closed and she shivered as he stroked along the curve of her jaw.

"You're not that innocent."

Pat opened her eyes. "I didn't come near you just now

with any ideas of…of tempting you, Clint. Honest.'' She made a little face. ''Not that I wouldn't have, if I had more confidence.''

''There's no reason you shouldn't be confident around men.''

''No, no reason at all. Just little experiences like this one. It says a lot about my sex appeal that we're having this discussion.'' Her sigh was wistful. ''This is the second time you almost kissed me and then obviously thought better of it.''

He grasped her wrist and stopped her as she started to rise. ''You want to know why I stopped myself? Because just wanting to kiss you turned me on. You didn't come here prepared to go bed with me, did you?''

''N-no, not r-really,'' she stammered, dropping her gaze to his groin and seeing the bulging evidence of his arousal. ''What are you going to do? Take a cold shower?''

''Just put the money on the table on your way out.'' And let him deal with his physical frustration, his impatient tone added.

With the utmost reluctance, she did as she was told.

More than anything in the world, Pat longed to ask him whether he was attracted to her personally. But she really couldn't bear having him tell her what was probably the truth—that he would have reacted the same way to any woman who came close, because he hadn't had sex in a while.

Other questions crowded her head on the walk to her house. Why had he gone to all the access locations on the Buffalo River today? Had he just been sight-seeing? Or was it advance preparation in the event he went to work for her?

If it was the latter, Pat didn't find Clint's actions at all heartening because he would have been avoiding the necessity for her to show him the ropes as she had done with Lester today. Clint liked her. He felt sorry for her. He wanted to help her out.

But he didn't particularly want her company for any extended time.

Clint uncurled the fingers of his right hand after the sound of Pat's quick, light tread had died away into empty silence. Liar. He'd started getting aroused when he touched her ponytail, before the urge to kiss her was born. The strands of her glossy, dark brown hair had felt like silk and yet crackled with electricity.

Then he'd aroused himself more by touching her face. Her skin was soft and warm, but it burned his knuckles, delivering its own electrical jolt. She pulsed with life. He wanted to wrap his arms around her and trap all that vitality and sweetness and good humor that made up her personality.

Wanting Pat was more complicated than wanting a woman had ever been for Clint. It was combined with yearning and tenderness.

The next two weeks were going to be hell. With a little bit of heaven mixed in.

He shook his head, a grin tugging at his lips at the memory of her asking him with fascinated concern, *What are you going to do? Take a cold shower?*

Clint could have told her that pain was going to be a big help. The whole time she was there, his leg had been throbbing and hurting from the punishment it had taken during his sprint to the store in response to Lester's shouts.

Tonight and probably tomorrow, too, he was going to pay for ignoring the fact that his running days were over.

The flash of amusement killed by grim reality, Clint levered himself out of his chair, stifling a groan, and limped inside the cabin that would be his quarters for another week or two. *Quarters.* Not home.

Pat awoke the next morning with the feeling that something good was happening that day. What? Immediately she remembered. Clint was coming to work for her as her driver. He would show up early and be at the store off and on between shuttle trips. She would get to see him numerous times and talk to him.

And not just today, but tomorrow and the next day and the next!

The arrangement was only temporary, Pat reminded herself, but happiness bubbled up as she bounded out of bed to get dressed. Her hand hovered over her stack of T-shirts while she eyed the blouses hanging in her closet. There wasn't a law that read *Pat Tyler must wear old jeans and a T-shirt for her working uniform.*

"Silly goose!" she chided herself aloud, startling Rowdy. He whined at the foot of her bed. "Everything's okay," Pat assured her pet, shaking out a bright blue T-shirt with a motor-oil emblem decorating the back.

Clint would know she'd dressed differently because of him and wouldn't like it. She would only end up acting more self-conscious around him. So she should wear her usual clothes.

Today was just another working day, not a date. Tonight was the time for her to try to look pretty. For Jeremy.

Her enthusiasm dampened slightly, Pat followed her regular morning routine and was at the store by six-thirty. Since Clint had been making the trip to the store on foot for several days, she assumed he would do so today and was surprised when he pulled up in his Suburban a few minutes before seven.

She'd been sweeping the floor and had reached the front door and was sweeping the dust and bits of gravel out. Holding the broom in hand after she'd finished, she waited for Clint to get out of his automobile. It seemed to take him quite a while. She winced in sympathy when she caught sight of his face. His jaw was set, and he was gritting his teeth. Manipulating his injured leg was obviously causing him considerable pain.

With a frowning glance in her direction, he slammed the

car door and sucked in a breath before he limped toward her. It occurred to Pat that she probably shouldn't stand there and watch him, but she couldn't seem to help herself. Nor could she keep from blurting out in a voice full of her dismay, "You're limping as bad as the first day I saw you in Yellville. Your leg is hurting a lot, isn't it?"

"It hurts," he said tersely. "But it'll loosen up."

"Do you take any painkillers? I'll bet you don't."

"I took a couple of aspirin. Look, I'm okay. Just go about your business."

"But are you able—"

"Yes, I'm *able*. Except for my leg, the rest of my body is too damned able for me to sit around and do nothing." He'd reached her in the doorway. Before Pat could step back, he put out both hands, grasped her at the waist and lifted her off the floor.

"*Clint!* I'm too heavy!" she gasped, letting go of the broom and grabbing his arms.

He set her down inside the store so that she was no longer blocking his way. For just a few seconds longer than necessary, his hands stayed at her waist. Pat's heart was pounding with the pure thrill of being manhandled by him. It nearly leaped out of her chest at the possibility that he might put his arms around her, draw her close to him. How she wished that he would.

Disappointingly, he loosened his hold and pulled his hands away, giving her little choice but to drop hers and balance herself on legs of jelly. "You proved your point," she said with a sigh of regret. "I guess you are able-bodied, all right."

"In some ways, I'm a weak SOB." His words were heavy with disgust. Before Pat could reply, he'd turned abruptly and was limping toward the back of the store. "You want a cup of coffee?" he asked.

"Yes, please."

When he brought the two cups of coffee to the table, she was perched on the edge of a chair, still mulling over his contemptuous remark about himself. It could mean only one thing: he'd wanted to take her in his arms. But the urge, like his urge to kiss her yesterday, hadn't been so strong that he couldn't easily suppress it.

"I'd like to ask you something," she blurted when he'd lowered himself into a chair across from her. "I wanted to ask you yesterday afternoon at your cabin, and I just didn't have the nerve. Are you attracted to me?"

"What difference does it make if I am?"

"Is that a yes? And I want the truth."

"It's a yes," he said flatly and took a swallow of his coffee.

"But I'm not the type of woman you're usually attracted to, am I? You usually like women with good figures who dress in sexy clothes and wear eye shadow and lipstick." When he didn't answer immediately, her heart sank to the level of her toes. "It's not very fair of me, putting you on the spot like this. And maybe I'm not up to hearing the truth, after all."

"It shouldn't be too hard on your ego," he replied, his voice gruff. "As far as liking a woman, I like you better than any of the women I've known who've worn low-cut blouses and short, tight skirts and used a lot of makeup."

"That makes up the majority of the women you have known well." Substitute *intimately* for *well*.

He shrugged. "I met most of them in bars and night-clubs. All I was ever looking for was company and sex, so I picked women who'd been around the block, just like I had."

"That lets me out."

The expression on his rugged face gentled as he looked at her—silently agreeing, she could only assume. Pat welcomed the ringing of the telephone. Anything to end the demoralizing conversation. "Excuse me," she said, hopping up and racing to pick up the receiver before the answering machine kicked on. Clint's gaze had followed her. "Tyler's."

"Hi," Jeremy said. "You sound glum."

"Oh, hi, Jeremy. No, I'm not glum, even though my new driver didn't work out. I had to fire him. But Clint Adams has offered to help me out for a couple of weeks."

"No kidding."

Clint had gotten up from his chair and was heading for the door. Pat held her hand over the mouthpiece and spoke to him, "Have some more coffee."

"I've had enough," he answered.

Was it her imagination or did he sound disheartened?

"Wanted to touch base with you about tonight," Jeremy was saying. "Shall I pick you up about seven-thirty? Does that give you enough time?"

"Seven-thirty's fine."

"Are you sure you're okay with Adams working for you? You're not your usual chipper self this morning."

"I'm okay. Honest. See you tonight, Jeremy."

"I'm looking forward to it. Hope you have a good day."

Pat breathed out a troubled sigh as she hung up. Was it fair to Jeremy to go out with him when she could barely concentrate on talking to him on the phone while Clint was near? Yet she could hardly put Jeremy on hold for a couple of weeks until Clint had gone.

Aside from considering Jeremy's feelings in the matter, she'd led Clint to believe she intended to keep dating Jeremy.

What a mess. But only a temporary one. Two weeks would fly by. Clint would leave. Jeremy would remain and still be Pat's best marriage prospect.

The present complications in her life didn't change the fact that Pat wasn't suited to being an old maid.

Chapter Ten

Her first party of the day was a family of six with four boys ranging in age from eleven to seventeen. They drove up promptly at seven-thirty and spilled out of a carryall vehicle just as Clint was loading up the third canoe and Pat was making her final trip from the storeroom with a pile of floatation cushions.

Partly she'd brought out the required number of paddles, life jackets, and cushions herself to spare Mama Cat the trauma of strangers trooping into her territory. Partly she'd just wanted an excuse to go out near Clint.

Her spirits had already lifted, and she was able to greet her customers with her usual friendliness. During the round of introductions, she presented Clint as their driver. He was reserved and not exactly cordial, but neither was he brusque or unfriendly. Pat noted that both the two adults and their offspring looked to him for supervision, not her, during the hustle and bustle of loading up and getting under way.

She didn't mind in the least. It was like old times when her dad was alive, to step back and share the responsibility.

"Have a great day, guys!" she called, waving goodbye when the van pulled away.

Considering that this was Clint's first time behind the wheel of her van, not just his first shuttle trip as her driver, she should be experiencing some qualms. Instead she felt nothing but confidence that he could handle whatever situation arose.

The phone's ringing drew Pat back inside to begin a busy morning of booking canoe trips and cabin rentals, waiting on customers, and visiting with several local people who dropped in. She was conscious of how much she was enjoying being able to tend the store and answer the phone and accept deliveries herself. It had been more of a strain than she'd realized to have to leave someone less capable in charge.

Clint returned and left again on his second trip. Then his third trip, transporting three couples who vacationed together in the Ozarks every year and were repeat customers. By the time he returned from the next trip, it was noon, and he had a two-and-a-half-hour break before heading to Rush to pick up the first party, the family of six.

Pat had harbored the hope that she and Clint might eat lunch together, but as luck would have it, the store was full of people. He didn't even come inside, but drove off to his cabin.

Her afternoon was relatively quiet, compared to the morning, but Homer came to occupy his rocking chair and was joined by another old crony of her father's, Shortie Upton. They swapped stories and reminisced about the old days. Pat enjoyed their company, but she regretted the lack of any opportunity to talk privately with Clint when he came into the store, especially since she couldn't hang around at closing time. She had to lock up and get ready for her date with Jeremy.

Maybe tomorrow, she thought longingly.

* * *

"Sign right here in the usual spot, if you don't mind." The truck driver who'd just filled Jeremy's below-ground gasoline storage tanks handed him a clipboard.

Jeremy was scrawling his signature when the driver whistled. He glanced up and followed the man's gaze out toward the pumps, where a white car had pulled up and a curvaceous redhead had gotten out.

"If I didn't have this gold band on my finger, I'd sure go out and offer to pump her gas for her," the driver said jokingly, taking the clipboard.

"She's probably wearing a set of wedding rings herself." Jeremy's thumb worried his own broad gold band, which he hadn't been able to bring himself to take off during the past two years.

"Guess I'd better stop drooling and get on the road. Have a good one."

"You, too."

Jeremy busied himself unpacking a carton of quart-size containers of motor oil. When the redheaded woman entered, he smiled and went behind the counter, greeting her pleasantly as he would any customer, male or female, who was a stranger.

"Hi. How're you doing today?"

"I'm doing just fine," she replied in a husky, attractive voice, not smiling back at him.

It was hard for Jeremy not to stare at her. She was flat gorgeous, with jade green eyes and the creamy complexion of a genuine redhead. Her hair was a glorious tangle of red-gold curls. Surely that color didn't come in a bottle, but wasn't it too vivid to be natural? The same was true for the color of her eyes. Did she wear tinted contact lenses?

"That'll be fourteen dollars and forty cents," he said as she dug into her purse. Her left hand steadied it, giving him ample chance to observe the absence of a wedding or engagement ring. "I take all major credit cards."

"Doesn't everyone?" She placed a credit card on the counter and partially turned away from him.

Jeremy wished she hadn't done the latter. It made checking out her figure too easy. She was slender and yet lush in jeans and a simple white knit blouse. Guilt knifed through him as he processed the charge, after first glancing at the name, Terri Sommers. He was gawking at this woman as if she were a centerfold in a men's magazine.

"Here you go," he said briskly, placing a pen beside the charge slip and duplicate.

She stepped up and bent over to sign her name. Even though her scoop neck blouse wasn't low-cut, Jeremy got a glimpse of lace bra and cleavage before he averted his head. Sucking in a breath, he caught just a whiff of her perfume. The scent triggered a reaction much lower in his body than his lungs.

"Is this top copy mine?" she asked in her husky voice.

"Yes, it is."

She stuffed her slip along with the credit card into her purse while Jeremy picked up his slip and automatically checked the signature.

"Come back and see us," he said, opening the cash-register drawer.

"How much does the attendant's job pay?"

The piece of paper slipped from his lax fingers and fluttered down to the floor. "I beg your pardon."

"Your sign in the window says Help Wanted—Attendant. How much does the job pay?"

Jeremy cleared his throat, which had gone dry on him. "Are you interested for yourself?"

"Is there some reason I shouldn't be? You don't specify male or female."

"No, but, er—excuse me." He bent over and picked up the charge slip, straightened and put it in the cash drawer. "The hourly pay will depend somewhat on the prior experience and maturity of the person I hire. For someone I have to train and supervise, I'll start them off at five dollars.''

''That's more than minimum wage.'' She turned to leave.

''Do you live in the vicinity of Yellville?'' he heard himself asking. ''I don't recall seeing you before.''

''I just moved back. I grew up here.''

''Sommers doesn't ring a bell.''

''Sommers isn't my maiden name.'' The conversation hadn't slowed her departure. She'd reached the door and opened it. ''If I don't find a better-paying job, I may be back to apply for this one.''

Jeremy opened his mouth, but no words came out. His brain was sending out conflicting messages. He wanted to say, *Wait, don't run off so fast! How about filling out an application while you're here?* But he knew what he should say was, *Good luck in your job search. Quite honestly, I'm hoping to hire someone who's going to stay with me awhile.*

He said nothing, not even a lame *Have a good day.* She hadn't paused for a response anyway. His lapse in business courtesy obviously didn't concern her as she headed for her car. Jeremy doubted she'd even been aware of how she'd bowled him over with her beauty and mesmerized him with her husky, sexy voice. She was probably used to men reacting the same way he had. Men who wore wedding rings as well as those who didn't.

Jeremy slipped his gold band up and down his finger. Would Terri Sommers have been friendlier toward him if he hadn't been wearing it? The mere fact that he wondered made him feel guilty, as though he were being unfaithful to Susan.

And to Pat, for that matter. She was unofficially his girlfriend. He owed her fidelity of a sort. To experience the kind of male interest Terri Sommers had stirred in him when he was dating Pat wasn't right.

Pat probably even knew Terri. They were about the same age and must have gone to the county school together. Tonight, if he thought about it, he would mention Terri to Pat. She might be able to tell him Terri's maiden name and supply some background information about her to satisfy his curiosity.

Jeremy's guilt deepened as he realized he'd suddenly gotten a lot more eager about his date with Pat tonight.

It was six forty-five when Clint pulled up with his final passengers of the day, the three couples who vacationed together annually. In the meanwhile the two old men had finally left. Pat walked outside to visit for a couple of minutes. That was all the time she could really spare.

As the doors of the van opened, she could hear the laughter and conversation. She knew all six people well enough to put individuals together with voices.

"That's no fair, Clint!" protested Jenny Smith.

"Typical man," Linda Jones jeered. "He sides with the guys."

Trish Reilly, the third woman, added her words of objection to something Clint had apparently said in support of the husbands.

"Damned right, he sides with the guys," Carl Smith declared. "We men have to stick together."

Bill Jones and Kevin Reilly added their comments to the good-natured battle of the sexes.

There were smiles on all the faces. Including Clint's. Pat's heart gave a leap of pleasure at the sight of him smiling and amused. But she also felt a little stab of hurt that he'd never relaxed in her presence and smiled with her. Or at her.

"How was the float?" she asked gaily and got a chorus of enthusiastic answers.

"Here. Have a cold beer, Clint." Bill Jones had fished two cans out of a cooler and held out one of them as he spoke.

"Thanks. Don't mind if I do."

"Pat? How about you?"

She was watching Clint, who hadn't wasted any time popping the can open and was taking a big swig with obvious enjoyment. "No, thanks," she refused.

"There's enough to go around," Bill said.

Carl was in the process of handing cans to the others. Pat really didn't have time to be sociable, but she found herself saying anyway, "Then maybe I will have one."

The beer was ice cold and tasted good. It was fun standing there and talking and laughing and being part of a group of people that included Clint.

Kevin Reilly brought up the subject of dinner. "Hey, the six of us are going out to eat tonight at a restaurant in Bull Shoals. Pat and Clint, why don't you guys join us, if you don't have plans already?"

Clint looked at her, letting her answer first. Or was he letting her answer for both of them? Pat wasn't sure. Never in her life had she been sorrier to have plans.

"I'm afraid I can't. I'm going to the movies in Harrison with a friend. In fact, I really need to run."

She said her goodbyes and made a quick getaway, not wanting to hear Clint's decision. Tomorrow would be soon enough to know whether he'd gone. It was going to be hard enough as it was to try to have a good time with Jeremy without thinking about being out at a restaurant with Clint.

"How about you, Clint?" Kevin Reilly asked.

"I pass, but thanks for the invite." Clint downed the last swallow of his beer and crushed the can.

"You sure?"

"Positive. I'm kind of bushed." *Disappointed* and *jealous* would have been more honest. He wasn't as tired as he would have expected after his first day on the job. The nap after lunch had undoubtedly helped to prevent fatigue.

"Say, there's a couple more beers in this cooler. Why don't you take them?" Carl suggested. "Unless you have your own supply."

"I don't. Let me pay you for them."

His offer was vigorously refused. The couple of beers turned out to be three, and he accepted them without making a big production. In his present mood, he might sit out on his back porch and drink them one after another while he tried to block out the picture of Pat and Wells sitting next to each other in a darkened movie theater, holding hands.

At his cabin Clint drank only one of the beers and put the other two in his refrigerator. Three beers weren't nearly enough to make him drunk. Nor were they a substitute for a square meal. He was out of food to prepare for his supper and needed to shower and change and drive into Yellville to get something to eat. Tomorrow was a workday.

Aside from all those factors, Pat wouldn't be out with Wells every night. It would be damned nice to drink a beer with her one late afternoon.

Lester downed the liquor in his glass and hurriedly hid it on the floor beside the sofa. He'd heard Pearl's car drive up outside the house trailer. She was working the weekend shift at the old folks' home and was bound to be nasty when she walked in the door.

Sure enough, her lips were thinned and her expression was sour. What she needed was a good hard slap, but Lester smiled a rubbery smile and tried to look as if Dolly Parton had entered the living room. He flattered Pearl by telling her she was Dolly Parton's spitting image when actually she was a bleached blonde carrying around thirty extra pounds.

"Ain't you a sight for sore eyes, sugar," he greeted her, his words slurring. "Come give me a big kiss and then fix you a highball and take a load off your feet."

"You're drunk," she said disgustedly.

"I ain't drunk. No such thing! When I came in from work, I had me a couple shots of whiskey 'cause I was dead tired."

"Liar! You haven't left this trailer park today! Lena

Hudgins next door came to visit her mother-in-law around five o'clock. I asked her whether your truck had been parked at my trailer, and she said it had. Did you get fired after one day on the job, Lester?''

"No, indeed, I ain't been fired!" he denied. "I woulda told you I wasn't workin' this weekend, but I knew you'd have a hissy fit.''

"You'd better be telling the truth. Monday morning, bright and early, I'm expecting you to be up and gone.''

"You won't be disappointed, sugar. Now, come on and be nice to me.''

She sighed, undoing the top button of her uniform. "Let me change into some more comfortable clothes. I think I will have a whiskey and soda.''

"Make me one, too, while you're at it. And stick a couple of frozen dinners in the oven, will you, sugar? All I've had to eat today is a sandwich.''

"Next weekend I'm expecting you to take me out to a nice restaurant," she said over her shoulder as she disappeared into the hallway.

"I'll sure do that, sugar.''

Lester's features contorted into a sneer. He balled up his right hand into a fist and smacked it soundlessly into his left palm. "One of these days," he muttered.

Monday he would have to hightail it over to Tyler's, eat some humble pie and get his job back. He could sweet-talk any stupid woman into giving him one more chance.

"Any luck in hiring an attendant?" Pat asked Jeremy on the drive to Harrison.

"Nope. My sign's still in the window." She waited, sensing he was about to add something. When he finally spoke, it was almost with an air of reluctance. "I did have an unlikely inquiry today."

"Oh?''

"A woman named Terri Sommers. She said she used to live in the Yellville area.''

"Sommers?"

"I gathered she's divorced."

"Describe her."

"Red hair, green eyes, attractive. About your age."

"I wonder if that was Terri Baker!" Pat exclaimed. "By 'attractive,' you don't mean drop-dead beautiful, do you?"

"She's a knockout," he admitted.

"Then I'll bet it was her. She was Miss Arkansas and competed in the Miss America contest. It was a big thrill for everybody in Marion County to see her on TV that year. So Terri has moved back to Yellville?"

"Evidently."

"I'll have to call her and say hi." But not for the next couple of weeks. Terri might show up at the store to visit. Pat would have to watch Clint looking her over admiringly, as Jeremy had obviously done today. No, thanks. Pat's female ego didn't need that kind of beating.

"So how are Jerry and Mandy?"

"What? Oh, they're Jerry and Mandy."

It was the first time she'd ever brought up the subject of his children and gotten a distracted reply. Either his mind had drifted to some other subject or else he'd still been thinking about Terri.

If the latter was true, he and Pat might just be in the same boat, dating each other and wishing they were dating someone else they'd fallen for at first sight.

"Mama Cat, you must have given birth by now. Otherwise, you're going to have a litter of kitty elephants." Pat peered into the gap between the chest freezer and storeroom wall. "You have had your babies!" she crooned.

The shy stray cat lay on her side, grooming four tiny kittens while they nursed.

From out in the store came the tinkling of the bell on the door. Pat's delight in her discovery was heightened by a sense of gladness at the sound of Clint's footsteps. He' arrived for work, and she would see him again throughout the day.

"Clint, come and see something wonderful," she said when he'd reached the back of the store, his destination probably the coffeepot. She'd waited because she didn't want to raise her voice and alarm Mama Cat.

Almost immediately Clint appeared in the storeroom doorway. She beckoned to him. He came toward her without saying a word.

"Look between the freezer and the wall." With him standing close behind her, Pat gazed down, too. "Aren't they sweet?"

"When did she have them?"

The deep timbre of his voice caused shivers of pleasure down her spine.

"Last night, maybe. Or yesterday. They're tiny."

"In a few days they'll be underfoot."

"I'll have to get a big cardboard box." She turned her head to smile up at him. His expression gentled as he looked back at her, an indulgent smile tugging at the corners of his mouth. "It's about time!" she exclaimed, feeling a bursting happiness inside her.

"About time for what?" His voice was gruff.

"For you to crack a smile at me. I was so envious yesterday that you'd been joking with the Smiths and the Joneses and the Reillys."

The humor in his face faded, leaving it grim and hard. "It's hard to smile when you don't feel very cheerful about life in general. I don't like being the odd man out." He stepped back from her, turned and headed toward the door. "So how was your movie last night?"

Pat ignored the brusque question, which provided her with her only clue to his "odd man out" comment. "What does that mean, you don't like being the 'odd man out'?" she asked, following behind him. "You're not talking about yourself and Jeremy?"

"What else? Don't you think I was envious, knowing he

was out with you last night while I was eating supper by myself at the Front Porch?''

''You didn't go to Bull Shoals with the others, then?''

''No.'' He'd passed through the door and hadn't slowed down at the coffeepot.

''Don't you want a cup of coffee?''

''I want a lot of things.''

''Like what?'' Pat caught up with him and grasped his arm. ''Could we please just stand here a minute and have a conversation?''

''If I stop, it won't be to have a conversation.''

''Stop anyway—'' She gasped as he halted and put his arms around her, all in one abrupt motion. He lowered his head much more slowly. There was all the time in the world for delicious anticipation to spread through her. ''You're finally going to kiss me...'' she whispered.

I've waited forever for this, Pat thought as Clint's mouth took possession of hers. He kissed her with a tender hunger, his arms tightening around her and conveying the urgency he was restraining. Awash in pleasure, she laid her palms on his chest, feeling the heat of his body and the jolting of his rapid heartbeat. To be free to touch him added to her joy. When she slid her hands up around his neck and hugged him, he groaned in his throat and kissed her harder, moving his head as though seeking to discover completely the softness of her lips.

''So damned sweet,'' he said against her mouth.

''Don't talk, Clint. Kiss me some more.'' *Please.* The last word didn't get spoken because his parted lips were already devouring hers, and his tongue was in her mouth, finding and arching around her tongue. Pat's entire body melted like wax at the hot, sexual mating. Melted and took the form of Clint's hardened contours, his muscular chest and iron thighs and the protruding bulge at his groin.

As though the contact weren't intimate and thrilling enough, he gathered her even closer with one arm, slid the other hand down to her buttocks and lifted her against him

"Hi. I'm almost finished cooking. Come and sample a piece."

He came up to the picnic table that served as her outdoor cooking station in the backyard. The electric skillet she was using was plugged into a heavy-duty extension cord that snaked to an outlet.

"I thought this wasn't a date," he said, his eyes taking in her bright pink blouse. Made of a puckered knit, it came to the waistband of her jeans.

Pat glanced down at herself, flooded with the new pleasurable self-consciousness. "Edna gave me this blouse for Christmas," she explained. "I hardly ever wear it out anywhere because of the color, and the style, well, is kind of clingy."

"You should wear it for Wells."

Not for him. Because he found it becoming and sexy. The unstated messages in his terse recommendation fed the womanly self-confidence Pat had developed in his arms. *Thank you, Edna!*

"Maybe I will," she said, picking up the platter and holding it out, but not so far that he didn't have to step closer to her. "Here. Try a piece of fish." When he took a piece and crunched into it, she inquired, "Taste good?"

"Tastes great."

"Now aren't you glad you didn't turn down supper?" She transferred the last of the fish and half-a-dozen hush puppies from the skillet to the platter and led him to the back door. He stopped and petted Old Rowdy on the screened porch before he followed her into the kitchen.

Pat was envious of her dog. For the few seconds before he joined her, she let herself imagine a friendly Clint who let down his guard with her. The reason he didn't was that he didn't dare because he *was* attracted to her. The knowledge was incredibly thrilling.

"You can have both beers," she told him when he put a can at each place setting at the kitchen table. The brand was the same that Bill Jones had handed her yesterday. She assumed that Clint had been made a gift of a couple of leftovers, and he was generously sharing with her.

"No, you drink one," he insisted.

Pat didn't argue, but she poured only a third of her can into a glass and halfway through the meal emptied the rest of the can's contents into his glass. In her state of mind, tap water would have tasted like champagne, which she'd drunk only a few times in her life.

Happiness was serving him a delicious meal that she'd prepared and downing ample portions herself while he ate twice as much, relishing his food. Their conversation centered around the day's events, except for the all-important happening—his kissing her.

"I have ice cream for dessert," she said when he pushed back from the table.

"Thanks, but I couldn't hold any."

"Later, then. We'll go into the living room and watch TV until our food settles."

He stood and carried his plate over to the sink. "I'll help you clean up and then I'll head back to my cabin."

"I wish you wouldn't. Go back to your cabin, I mean. As for the dishes, I'll just leave them to soak." She brought her plate over and he moved aside while she squirted detergent and ran hot water.

"The deal was that we would have supper and I wouldn't stay."

"Okay. If you'd rather leave. But I get over a hundred channels. All sorts of sports stations and news stations and movie stations."

"Damn it, Pat. Nobody's going to drive up tonight and interrupt if I start kissing you. And you're no help."

"We can bring Rowdy in to chaperon. Clint, we're both too stuffed to get romantic," she said.

"Romance has nothing to do with it. I'm talking sex."

"Too stuffed to get all hot and bothered, then. You can sit at one end of the sofa, and I'll sit at the other end."

"I'll stay for an hour."

Her smile spread over her face. "Good."

In the living room instead of sitting down, he walked over to a wall plastered with photographs. "My mother's gallery," Pat said ruefully, going with reluctance to stand beside him. There were pictures of her at every stage of her growing-up years. "I told her that my home-ec teacher in high school said the bedroom, not the living room was the place to display family photos. Mom's answer was that my teacher could decorate her home as she pleased, and Mom would do the same."

"Good for your mom."

"As you can see, I didn't dress in ruffles and wears bows in my hair when I was a little girl. Jeans and a baseball cap were more my style then, too."

"I like your pigtails. And your smile hasn't changed a whole lot."

He probably was thinking she hadn't changed a whole lot, period, but had simply become a grown-up version of the tomboy who'd climbed trees and gone squirrel hunting with her dad. "This fall after business slows down, I'm going to paint this living room and pack all these pictures away," she announced, her voice glum. "It's silly of me not to change things to suit myself now that my mother and father are gone." She went over and sat down on the end of the sofa, her wonderful confidence fast oozing away.

"Have you thought about whether you'll sell your house or rent it? If and when you do marry Wells?" The questions were terse.

"That could be a bigger if than everyone seems to think. Jeremy might not be desperate enough to marry me. I'll bet you he would jump at the chance to date Terri Baker, if the redheaded knockout who came by his gas station *was* her. What man wouldn't?"

"What?" A puzzled frown on his face, he came over and sat down on the sofa, too.

"Terri Baker. She was Miss Arkansas. She started winning pageants when she was five years old. Her hair is

naturally curly. It was a mass of ringlets. Shirley Temple
would have had to take a back seat to her."

"I doubt she was any cuter than you were."

"She wasn't cute. She was pretty. And in the sixth grade,
she started wearing a bra because she already had breasts.
And hips. From that year on, all the boys' tongues would
hang out when they looked at her."

"That must have been kind of a comical sight," Clint
said with a gruff gentleness that made a big lump form in
her throat. He slid over closer and reached out a hand to
touch her ponytail.

"Be careful," Pat warned with choked sarcasm. "If you
get too close, you'll be overwhelmed by my sex appeal."

"You're damned sexy."

"Oh, sure."

"I wouldn't like anything better than to skin off that
blouse you're wearing."

"There's nothing stopping you. I'm single and eight
years past twenty-one."

"There's a lot stopping me. I have a busted-up leg. I'm
an ex-marine with a high-school education and no profes-
sion. You shouldn't mess around with me and spoil your
chances with Wells."

"Here we are, back to Jeremy. Why don't we just call
it a night, Clint?" Pat blinked hard at a glaze of tears and
bit down on her bottom lip to stop its quivering. "I think
I'll wash up those dishes and go to bed early."

"Come here."

He reached out and pulled her into his arms. Overcome
with her misery, she went willingly and nestled against him,
her cheek pressed into his shoulder. "I wish I hadn't gone
to Jeremy's gas station last Monday. I wish I'd waited. A
week wouldn't have mattered and you wouldn't have seen
my pitiful version of giving him the come-on. Then you
wouldn't have paired me up with him."

"You forget about Homer. He still would have clued me
in."

His hard cheekbone was rubbing her forehead. Pat was cocooned in his strength and masculinity. Comfort was already giving way to pleasure.

"That's right. He bored you with my whole life story, including my limited marriage prospects."

"As much pain as I was suffering with my leg that day and as down in the dumps as I was, I let him rattle on. That should tell you something."

"What?"

"I was interested in hearing about you. Seeing you was like having the sun pop out. You were so full of life. When you picked up my gas cap and gave it to me and your hand touched mine, it was like sticking a finger into a light socket."

"Really?"

He didn't answer, but one of his hands slipped under the edge of her blouse and caressed her bare back above the waistline of her jeans. Pat shivered with delight.

"When I saw you, I thought you were one of the most masculine men I'd ever seen," she confided. "It was hard to focus my attention on Jeremy. I watched you drive away and felt this terrible regret that our paths would never cross again. Then I got back to the store and read your registry card and Homer described you. That night you showed up at the Front Porch, making me almost certain you were renting my cabin. After I'd gotten home and the electricity went off, I didn't waste a second bringing you candles because I just *had* to know. The moment you spoke, there was no doubt. Your voice set off goose bumps the way it always does."

She paused because his hand had caressed its way higher up her back and encountered her bra. The suspense made her catch her breath as his fingers stroked the back fastening. But they slid underneath. Easing out a sigh, she finished up her story. "You weren't very friendly, so I gave you the candles and trekked back home, wishing I'd learned how to flirt."

"I've known my share of women who were experts at flirting, and I like you better than all of them put together."

"You're very sweet, but if I were any one of those women, you would have unfastened my bra by now, wouldn't you?" Pat raised her head and mustered a smile. "I'm okay now. Thanks for the hug." She framed his face with both hands and brought her lips to his, intending to kiss him lightly.

Instead her mouth clung to his when he made a sound deep in his throat. Suddenly he was kissing her with tenderness and hunger, and his touch took on urgency as he caressed her bare skin beneath her blouse. His fingers found her bra fastening again. This time there was no hesitation. With an ease that had to have been born of practice, he unhooked her bra. Pat felt it go slack, felt his hand stroking a path along her side as he moved to the front of her body.

She waited in limbo for him to find her breasts. They had grown rounder and heavier in anticipation. The delicious suspense heightened almost unbearably before he tugged the left cup free, shoved it up out of his way and closed his hand around the lucky breast. Pat moaned with pleasure when he gently squeezed, his palm warm and rough against the hardening peak of her nipple. She reached around behind her and got his other hand and carried it to the neglected side of her chest.

He found his way unerringly beneath the stretchy knit of her blouse and soon she was immersed in double pleasure, in addition to the delight of kissing him. Pulsing waves of warmth traveled all the way to her fingertips and her toes. Pat wanted to stay right there on the sofa forever and ever, with his hands in total possession of her breasts, his mouth in possession of her mouth.

The blissful contentment shattered when he squeezed harder and began to kiss her harder, too. She suddenly needed more oxygen in her lungs. Then his thumbs circled her nipples, going round and round and finally touching them and flicking them. Pat arched her back and gasped unprepared for the rockets of sensation that shot through her and awoke an ache down between her thighs. The waves of delicious warmth grew hotter.

"Oh, my, Clint," she murmured, resting her cheek against his.

"Does that feel good, baby?" His voice was gruff with a protective note.

"I'm not sure there's a way to describe how it feels. Except that my bra might not ever fit again."

He'd released her and was withdrawing his hands.

"Don't stop," she protested.

"I have to stop to take off your blouse."

"Oh…"

Pat was stricken with shyness, helping him peel off the blouse. He tossed it and her bra aside, and she was naked to the waist. The shyness quickly faded under his gaze, which paid her compliments that made her feel seductive for the first time in her life.

"Sit on my lap." He grasped her by the waist. She went willingly and settled on his thighs, her hands on his shoulders. "Your breasts are so pretty." As he spoke, he was bringing his face to her chest.

"Flattery will get you anywh—" The erotic joy of his mouth taking the peak of her breast cut her off midword. Her fingers sank into the hard muscles of his shoulder and her head tipped back as she endured the exquisite sensations his warm, rough tongue raised. "Oh, my, Clint!" she gasped out. "I had no idea…"

"Of what, baby?" He was en route to the other breast, and his hot breath on her cleavage sent another wave of weakness through her. His calling her *baby* a second time was a whole separate thrill.

"That getting sexually turned on could be like *this*…." He had reached his destination and was using his lips, his tongue. Just when Pat thought she might be able to weather the delicious torture, he used his teeth, gently biting her rock-hard peak and reducing her to helplessness all over again. "That's *too* good!" She hugged his head with both arms and he nestled his face in her cleavage.

His hands had been clasping her waist. Now one of them slid down to caress her bottom while the other stroked along her thigh to her knee. During its journey back up, the ache between Pat's legs sharpened and drew her attention away from her tingling breasts. She shifted position and moved her thighs apart for him as his hand reached the crease between her pelvis and upper thigh. He read the invitation and laid claim to her womanhood. Pat writhed against his palm.

"Let's go to my bedroom, Clint," she urged.

"We shouldn't. I can satisfy you without making love."

"Aren't you aroused?" She was seeking the answer for herself.

Clint had raised his head. He groaned, closing his eyes, when her hand pressed against the hard, swollen proof that he wanted her. "Oh, *yes,* baby." It wasn't a reply, but a pained statement of need.

Pat's desire took on a whole different dimension as a longing to give him pleasure and satisfy him flooded her heart.

Chapter Eleven

"In here." Pat led him by the hand into her bedroom. "And don't look at the mess."

Despite her words, he was glancing around, taking in her open closet and pile of dirty clothes on the carpet, her red-and-white candy-striped bedspread and curtains, her dresser top with the lone bottle of cologne and no other feminine touches among the clutter.

Suddenly she was shy and uncertain. "I shouldn't have twisted your arm, Clint," she said, dropping his hand and crossing her arms over her bare breasts. "It's a carryover from grammar school when I threatened to give Tommy Hollins a black eye if he didn't come to my birthday party."

"Did he come?" His tone was gruff and gentle.

"Yes, and he brought me baseball cards for a present. Terri Baker came, too, and all the boys including Tommy fell over themselves trying to impress her." Pat turned her back to him. "No hard feelings, if you want to say good-night and go. I imagine you've cooled off by now, too."

There was no answer, but his arms came around her waist and hugged her tight against his big, rugged body. Pat leaned against him, thrilled by his strength and comforted by his warmth and the regular thud of his heartbeat. If only he would *never* let her go, she thought, the same blissful contentment she'd felt in the living room welling up. "Thanks for coming to supper. And sharing your beers with me. That was very generous...."

He'd planted a tender kiss in the curve of her neck and shoulder and was nuzzling the spot with his lips, sending shivers of delight through her. "You don't want to do that. I'll be locking my bedroom door so you can't leave. *Clint*—" He was kissing a trail along her shoulder, his breath hot on her skin. Pat hurriedly blurted out her fears and insecurities before they dissolved along with the rest of her. "I'm afraid this won't be very good for you. Actually, I've never, well, technically gone to bed with a man, and you're used to women with experience...."

While she talked, he'd unsnapped her jeans and lowered the zipper. Now he was caressing her stomach, sliding his hand down, dipping beneath the elastic of her hip-hugger panties. Pat's whole lower torso ached with delicious anticipation as he shoved his fingers through her thatch of curls. Her thighs relaxed and widened of their own accord, allowing plenty of space for him to rub a finger lightly along her wet crevice. Pat gasped at the intimate pleasure and went limp.

"I thought you said you'd cooled off, baby." His low voice vibrated with a fierce male satisfaction. "I could drown when I kiss you down here."

"It was more cold feet than cooling off. My confidence comes and goes." *Kiss her where he was touching?* Embarrassment added to the heat pulsing through her body.

"You're woman enough for me, or any man."

"I hope you're right."

He was tugging down her jeans, taking her panties with them. To accommodate him, Pat separated her hips from his. Once he'd bared her bottom, he used both hands to caress and squeeze it.

"You have a sexy little rear. Did you know that?"

"No." Were they continuing the conversation about her getting cold feet? For a second, doubt snaked through Pat's sensual haze. "Clint, you're not making love to me to build up my confidence, are you?"

"It would be a hell of a lot better for me if I were."

"What does that mean?"

"You figure it out for yourself. But not now." He turned her around in his arms and bent his head to take her lips in a hard, passionate kiss.

Pat wound her arms around his neck and kissed him back, coupling her tongue with his and tasting his hot, urgent need. For *her.* Figuring out the meaning of anything was unimportant, with time stopping and the world outside her bedroom ceasing to exist.

He was unbuttoning his shirt with impatient, fumbling movements. When he jerked and sent a button flying, Pat pushed away his hands and took over the task herself with some of the same efficiency he'd shown in undressing her. Reaching the bottom button, she tugged his shirttail out of his jeans. After the shirt was open, he shrugged out of it. With her mouth and tongue still engaged in hard, hungry kisses, she explored his chest, plunging her fingers through a furry growth of body hair covering its muscular contours.

Next she treated herself to smoothing her palms over his broad shoulders and from there progressed to his back, caressing the ridged definition and sending tremors through his whole powerful upper body.

At this point Pat felt enough like Delilah with Samson in her power to unsnap Clint's jeans, slide down the zipper, and thrust her hand inside. She didn't quite have the courage to delve beneath the elastic band of his cotton briefs, but instead stroked the heavy, throbbing length of his

aroused manhood with the separating layer of cloth be
tween her hand and his flesh.

"Oh, *baby*," he murmured against her mouth.

Pat's erotic excitement at touching him was mixed with
a vague worry. Would his body fit into hers? "I guess big
men are big...everywhere."

"I won't hurt you. I'll go inside you slow and easy."
He withdrew her hand, kissing her tenderly on the mouth.
Then he picked her up, carried her the few steps to her bed
and laid her on her back. Pat had kicked off her flats earlier
so that all he had to do was finish stripping off her jeans
and panties, and she was naked.

Fortunately the fact that he was also naked to the waist
saved her from feeling as shy as she might have otherwise.
She was busy looking at him and admiring his brawny phy
sique and absorbing his raw masculinity into her pores.

After bending down to kiss her breasts, making them
come tingling to life, he lowered his jeans and briefs and
sat down on the edge of the bed to finish removing them
and his shoes and socks. Pat scooted over to make more
room for him and held out her arms as he joined her.

"I made myself a promise this wouldn't happen," he
said, gathering her close in a wonderful, tight embrace.

"I'm so glad it is happening. I was about to give up on
the whole notion of a rugged John Wayne type coming
along and sweeping me off my feet. I gave you a chance
to escape tonight, and you didn't take it. Now you have to
follow through because I haven't cooled off and neither
have you." She moved her hips, calling attention to the
obstruction his arousal formed between them. "Let's make
love and afterward we'll worry about whether we should
have."

His reply was to loosen his embrace and begin kissing
and caressing every inch of her, making his way without
haste from her breasts to her stomach to her hips and lower
still. The delicious pleasure grew more and more intense
as he neared the hub of her womanhood, parted her thighs

nd kissed her with an intimacy that shocked and excited
er almost more than she could bear. The erotic delight
ecame truly unendurable and then exploded like brilliant
reworks at the warm, rough invasion of his tongue. Pat
ried out with ecstatic release, weathered several more
pasms and finally went limp.

"I'm sorry," she murmured. "I went ahead and cli-
axed."

"No kidding. You're sure you weren't faking that?" His
oice held male satisfaction along with the wry humor.

"But I should have waited. I'm like a cooked noodle,
nd I did so want the sex to be good for you, too."

"It couldn't be much better."

"Not just the foreplay, but the actual lovemaking."

"I'm too turned on, baby, to last long once I'm inside
ou."

"Oh. So you wanted to make sure I was satisfied."

The conversation alone was enough to revive Pat, but
roughout it, he'd been kissing his way up her body, nuz-
ing with his mouth and licking with his tongue, while his
ands worked their magic, stroking her hips and thighs and
awakening the sharp ache of desire. His touch conveyed
s own growing urgency.

"Now, Clint," she said, grasping his head after he'd lav-
hed attention on her breasts.

The short interval during which he sheathed himself was
me enough for Pat's anticipation to build and time
ough, too, for a slight nervousness to flicker to life. It
ave way to hot excitement when he was in position be-
ween her legs and gently eased inside her, filling the hol-
w ache.

"That feels so *wonderful!*" she murmured, stroking his
oulders.

He pushed farther and encountered the membrane that
d apparently survived climbing trees and other rough-
d-tumble tomboy activities. Pat watched the surprise on

his face change to puzzlement, which gave way to stunne
comprehension.

"You're a virgin?" He stared down at her.

"Not for long. Hopefully."

"When you said you hadn't 'technically' been to be
with a man, I didn't realize—"

"It's nothing I want to preserve. Unless you're com
pletely turned off by the idea, please, let's not stop an
discuss it."

He waged a brief battle with himself and the part of hi
won that wanted to continue making love or didn't want
disappoint her. After partially withdrawing, he entered h
again with a hard thrust and broke through the barrier
her maidenhead. The force carried him deep inside her. P
cried out his name—not with pain but with the sheer jo
of the close union.

"I'm okay," she said when moments went by, and h
didn't move or relax his rigid muscles or open his tight
closed eyes. "It just hurt for a second."

"I'm not okay, baby." His voice was pained.

"What's wrong?" She caressed his face and neck an
shoulders with tender concern.

"Nothing's wrong. Everything's just too right. You'
wrapped around me like velvet."

"Oh. Then it is good for you." Happiness floode
through her.

He opened his eyes and bent his head to kiss her on th
mouth. After a while he slowly withdrew a few inches an
just as slowly pushed deeper than before until he couldn
go any farther.

"That's just *incredible*," Pat breathed. "I neve
dreamed…"

"I did."

She wanted to question him about his strained reply, b
the sensations and the emotions crowded out cohere
thought as he guided her to hug his body with her legs an
move her hips in rhythm with his. The climb toward ecstas

was a glorious partnership. Nearing the peak, he urged her to keep pace with him. Pat's physical pleasure when she climaxed mere seconds before he did was enhanced by the joy of sharing his explosive climax and knowing she'd enhanced his satisfaction by sharing it.

After collapsing on top of her, he gathered his strength and rolled over onto his side, bringing her with him and then holding her close as they lay with their bodies still joined. The deepest happiness Pat had ever known flooded her heart and soul. It needed to be expressed, but how? By saying, *I love you?*

"You think it's possible to fall in love in a week's time?" she blurted out shyly, her voice muffled against his shoulder. Immediately she could have bitten her tongue when she tensed at her question.

"I wouldn't know," he said, his tone brusque.

"Forget I asked."

But the damage was done. He released her, eased free and got out of bed. "Is your bathroom close by?"

"Down the hall on the left," she replied miserably.

After gathering up his clothes and shoes, he left the room. Watching him go, Pat realized that she hadn't given a single thought to whether his leg was hurting him while he made love to her.

She got up, too, and donned a fresh pair of panties and a T-shirt. When Clint appeared in the doorway, dressed, she was perched on the side of the bed. Her heart sank at his expression.

"You look angry," she said. "I can't blame you. First I play on your sympathy and get you into bed with me without telling you plainly enough that I'm a virgin. Then I bring up the *L* word."

"Dammit, Pat, I'm mad as hell at *me*, not you! It just didn't dawn on me that you were that innocent!" He struck the doorjamb with his fist. "The signs were all there. I was just too dumb to read them."

Pat swallowed hard at his use of her name. She was no

longer *baby,* but Pat, the grown-up tomboy again. "Don't be mad at yourself. I'm way too old to be innocent."

"At this stage of the game, I shouldn't have been the man who made love to you for the first time."

"Oh, I see where this is headed." She sighed. "Jeremy, right? Well, maybe it'll make you feel better to know that he isn't any more excited about breaking in a virgin than you are."

He frowned. "Wells told you that?"

"In so many words. He was assuring me that he expected me to have had some lovers by my age and he preferred it that way."

"You didn't set him straight that you hadn't had any lovers?"

"No. And now I've had one wonderful lover, and I refuse to be sorry."

"Pat, you don't know men at all if you think Wells isn't going to mind."

"Things will work out the way they should between Jeremy and me, Clint." She stood and took a tentative step toward him. He stepped back out of the doorway, and she stopped, getting his clear message to keep her distance from him. When her misery was manageable enough for words, she inquired, "Did you need to borrow a flashlight?"

"I brought mine and left it on your front porch."

"That was good thinking. Well, good night. See you tomorrow."

He cursed under his breath as he looked at her, regret and frustration written on his face. Then he dealt the doorjamb another punishing blow and departed abruptly without saying good-night. Pat stood in the same spot until the front door closed with a bang. The sound cracked open her numbness. She backed up and sank down on her bed, completely at the mercy of conflicting emotions.

She wanted to cry with utter despair over the way tonight had ended. But she also wanted to hug herself and smile a dreamy smile and relive the wonderful parts of tonight. Did every woman feel like this when she lost her virginity?

Or was this combination of being sunk in misery and floating on a cloud what it was like to be in love with a man who liked you and cared about you, but didn't love you in return?

Throwing her arms wide, Pat flopped backward on her rumpled bedspread. "I love you, Clint," she said out loud, the declaration joyous.

The next minute she was whispering the same words sadly.

In both moods, they rang true.

Walking out of Pat's house and leaving her without a hug, without a kiss, tested all of the self-discipline Clint had developed in seventeen years as a soldier.

He retrieved his flashlight and limped as fast as his injured leg would allow across the overgrown lawn to the driveway, trying to block out the picture of her standing in her bedroom in her T-shirt and looking wistful. He hadn't dared touch her or let her come close enough for him to reach for her because once he had her in his arms, he might have told her everything he was holding in. *You're mine,* he might have said. *Wells can't have you now.*

The words, coming from her "rugged John Wayne type" who had finally shown up, would have put stars in her eyes and pleased her craving for romance. But a few months down the road, she would blink away those stars and wake up to reality too late. She would be sorry she'd screwed up her future by messing around with Clint.

What had happened tonight didn't change a damned thing. He still had a crippled leg and wasn't in the same ballpark with Jeremy Wells as a husband and provider. And probably not as a man. Clint's opinion of himself had gone down several more notches because his conscience had been overruled by his lust for Pat. The fact that she brought out a weak, softhearted side of himself that he hadn't known existed was no excuse. He couldn't live with himself if he hurt her.

He had two options: pack up and leave, or stay and help her out for the two weeks he'd agreed to with the understanding that there would be no repeat of tonight's lapse.

Tomorrow he would give her the choice.

Clint had reached the path through the woods and paused long enough to consider taking the longer route following the driveway to the road and the road to his cabin. It would be safer footing, but he decided in favor of the path. It cut off half the distance and he'd walked it several times in daylight without mishap.

Less than three months ago he wouldn't have debated hiking through the woods at night without a path to follow, Clint reflected with a kind of resigned bitterness as he tramped cautiously over the carpet of leaves and twigs illuminated by the beam of his flashlight. A glow of light winking through the trees pinpointed his cabin when he got close to the clearing. Evidently he'd left a light burning in his eagerness to get to Pat's house for their supper date that wasn't supposed to be a "date."

A picture of her in her jeans and bright pink blouse flashed in his mind and roused a tide of warm pleasure that tightened his groin and tightened a band around his heart, too. God, how he was going to miss her when he left the Ozarks in a couple of weeks. If for any reason at all, the matchup between her and Wells didn't pan out—say, within a year's time—Clint would come back. Maybe by then he would have made his adjustment to civilian life. There would be no holds barred. If she wanted romance, he would give her romance—

"Dammit!" Clint's alarmed curse didn't help him in his desperate attempt to regain his abruptly lost balance. Caught up in the hopeful train of thought, he'd forgotten all about the need to walk carefully and had stepped into a low spot. He pitched forward and sideways, slamming his shoulder hard into a tree as he hit the ground in a belly buster that knocked the air out of his lungs.

Shaking his head to clear it, he pushed himself up into a sitting position and flexed the shoulder and rotated the joint. "On your feet, Romeo," he said with weary cynicism.

To get himself upright, he knelt on his good leg and grasped the tree trunk, using his upper-body strength. It was an humbling procedure, but Clint was too grateful he hadn't seriously injured himself to complain. A dislocated shoulder would have narrowed his options down to one. He couldn't justify staying if he weren't physically able to work as Pat's driver.

And he wanted to stay, just to be around her a little longer.

"What time do you want the alarm set for?" Pearl asked, pulling her nightgown back on. "Five-thirty?"

"Seven-thirty will be early enough, sugar," Lester replied, punching his pillow. Five minutes ago she'd been panting and moaning and calling him her stud and now she was already nagging him.

"You wouldn't get to work before nine o'clock. Friday you needed to be there for seven."

"That was Friday. Mondays are slow."

She eyed him narrowly. "Lester, you're not lying to me about going to work tomorrow, are you? Because if you are—"

"Set the friggin' clock for six-thirty, if it'll make you happy. I'll go early and twiddle my thumbs." He rolled over onto his side with his back to her.

Moments later the click of the wall switch plunged the bedroom into darkness. The bed gave under Pearl's weight as she climbed in.

"If you can stick with this job a couple of months, we'll get married, sweetie pie. I don't mean to be hard on you, but I have this fear of falling into the same trap my mama

did—marrying a lazy drunk and never having anything,''
she explained for at least the hundredth time in that whee-
dling voice, which irritated Lester about as much as her
witchy tone.

He punched his pillow again. ''I better get some sleep
since I gotta get up and go to work tomorrow.''

His words had the desired effect and shut her up. Soon
she was sound asleep. Lester lay there awake another five
or ten minutes, mapping out the next day. He would have
to haul his butt out of bed early even though he could get
himself rehired just as easily in the afternoon. Day after
tomorrow was soon enough to start back to work, but Lester
didn't dare return to the trailer park before five or six. He
would have to kill time somewhere else.

There was only one worrisome factor in going back to
Tyler's store—that big, crippled SOB named Clint. Lester
didn't want to tie in with him again if he could help it. The
mean dude must have driven up Friday in that black carryall parked at the gas pump. Lester would keep an eye out
for it and pick a time when things were quiet at the store.
He didn't want nosy old ''grampa'' giving his two cents'
worth, either, if he was there. This time Lester would insist
on a private interview with Pat Tyler, the woman owner.

She would re-hire him. Lester would mind his p's and
q's and collect a salary for a month or so. He and Pearl
would get hitched, and he could start wearing the pants.

Clint drove up just as Pat was unlocking the front door
of the store. She opened it and waited for him to get out,
trying not to appear flustered and eager and anxious.
''Good morning. I'm running late,'' she greeted him. ''The
coffee hasn't even finished making yet. I didn't oversleep.
It was just one of those mornings when I was slow about
doing everything.''

Slow about getting out of bed because she lay there
thinking about him. Slow about getting dressed because she
had to do battle with the urge to make herself pretty for

him. Slow about her whole routine because she lapsed into dreamy trances, woke from them and sank into bouts of despair. The darkest of the latter centered on the possibility that Clint might show up this morning and announce he was leaving immediately.

"I've had a whole pot of coffee anyway," he said, walking toward her. His voice was as sober as his expression. "I was up early."

Up early doing what? Packing his things? Fear clutched at Pat. "I hope you didn't toss and turn all night, wrestling with your conscience."

"No. I'd made a deal with my conscience before I ever went to bed."

He *was* leaving. She turned and walked toward the storeroom, needing a private place to huddle into a corner and cry her heart out.

"Hold on," Clint said sternly from the doorway.

"I need to check on Mama Cat and the kittens."

"They can wait a minute. We need to talk and come to a decision about something before the phone starts ringing and people begin to show up."

Pat came to a stop, his words sparking hope to life. "A decision?"

"On whether or not I'm going to stick with my offer to stay around here another couple of weeks. It's up to you."

Slowly she faced him, enormous relief washing through her. "Then there's nothing to discuss. Of course, I want you to stay."

"All right, I will stay, with the agreement between us that there won't be a repeat of last night. By 'agreement between us,' I mean a team effort. I can't be fighting myself and you."

"You make it sound like a real battle with yourself, as though you'd be tempted more now than before."

"Damn right, I'll be tempted more. That's why I need your cooperation."

"And if I don't go along?"

"I'll be packed and on the road in an hour."

Pat sighed. "Some decision I get to make. What can I do but agree to your terms? Okay, I'll try my best to block out last night and *not* let myself think about it happening again. It won't be easy, though, since tempting you is about the biggest thrill of my life." Not to mention the fact that she was head over heels in love with him. She didn't dare make that confession.

"One of these days you'll look back and thank me."

"When I'm happily married to Jeremy, right?"

He started to say something and clamped his jaw shut. When he did speak, he'd switched to a different subject. "Are you okay—physically, I mean?"

The gruff question conveyed concern. Embarrassment heated Pat's cheeks. "I'm fine. Thanks for asking."

"I hated like hell hurting you."

"On a scale of one to ten, it was no more than a one, if that."

"In an ideal situation, the guy who made love to you the first time wouldn't roll out of bed and leave. I felt pretty rotten about that, too."

Pat remembered those wonderful minutes when he'd held her close. "You didn't leave immediately. After you'd gone, I let Rowdy in. He sleeps at the foot of my bed. By the time you got to your cabin, I was probably dead to the world."

For a moment she thought he would continue the conversation, but he sucked in a breath and said abruptly, "Well, I'd better gas up the van and check the air pressure in the tires."

"And I'd better make up for lost time."

Contrary to her statement of intention, she stood there seconds longer, feasting her eyes on him as he exited the store. The back view of his tall, broad-shouldered body pleased her even more today with the images of it unclothed fresh in her mind. She could mentally strip off his shirt and enjoy the sight of his powerful upper torso naked to the waist.

Could, but *shouldn't,* not according to the pact she'd made with him in good faith.

Pat sighed and called glumly in response to meows from the storeroom, "Coming, Mama Cat."

At noon Clint stuck his head in the door to tell her that he was driving into Yellville. "Need anything from town?" he asked.

"Just frozen dinners," she replied. "My supply is running low. I may make a run to the supermarket in Yellville myself after I close up today. But thanks, anyway."

"I'm going to the supermarket."

"You are?"

"If you give me a list, I'll do your grocery shopping, too."

"For that matter, I could take your list with me and do yours," Pat suggested. "Better still—" She broke off without finishing the sentence in her wishful tone of voice, but from his expression, he was able to finish it for himself: *Better still, we could go together.*

"I was also planning to get a haircut," he said. "And buy some motor oil for the van."

"In that case, I can't save you a trip. And I guess I'd better pick up my own dinners since I just choose at random. If you like, I'll buy the motor oil, too, when I stop to say hi to Jeremy at his gas station."

"As long as one of us gets it. I'll be back by two-thirty."

Before Pat could recover from her surprise over his sudden curtness, he pulled the door closed with a force that set the bell jangling wildly. What had she said to rub him the wrong way? Everything had been fine until she'd offered to get the motor oil...and had mentioned stopping in to visit Jeremy.

She'd been completely innocent of trying to make Clint jealous, but he'd probably interpreted her words as a clumsy attempt to do just that. And he'd gotten annoyed and angry.

Outside, the door of the Suburban slammed hard, and its wheels spurted gravel as Clint backed up and drove off toward the highway. After the somber black automobile had disappeared from sight, Pat gazed at the empty road, engulfed by loneliness. In a couple of weeks, he would drive away and not return.

Ever.

But today he would be back.

Pat was replenishing the supply of soft drinks in the coolers when Lester Madden arrived in his battered old pickup. A glance at the clock told her what she already knew, since she'd been keeping close track of the time. It was a quarter past two.

"What does he want?" Her question posed aloud to herself was uneasy rather than curious. She watched as Lester got out and smoothed his blond hair before he swaggered toward the door.

Walking much more swiftly, Pat went into the storeroom and got a paddle to use as a weapon if she needed to defend herself. Gripping it in one hand, she came back out just as he was entering.

"Hello, Lester. What can I do for you?"

The sheepish grin plastered across his face faltered as he eyed the paddle and then her. "Howdy, Pat. I come to eat me a big piece of humble pie and try to get back in your good graces." He shook his head solemnly. "Don't know what got into me Friday, actin' that way. Must've been the strain of wantin' to keep my job. There ain't no way it would happen again."

"You're right about that. If you have some idea about getting rehired, Lester, forget it. You blew your chance big time."

"Aw, don't be hard on me, Patty. Put down that paddle

and let's you and me sit down and talk, friendly like." He pulled out a chair at the table with a flourish.

"My name isn't Patty, and I'm not interested in talking to you, period. If you know what's good for you, you'll hurry up and get out of here because any minute now, Clint Adams will be back from Yellville. Remember Clint? He's the big man who socked you on the jaw Friday and tossed you out the door."

Lester scowled, clenching his hands into fists, but his glance out the store windows was nervous. "He snuck up on me Friday. In a fair fight, I'd lay him out on the floor if I had to kick that crippled leg out from under him."

"Is that your idea of a fair fight? Kicking your opponent's crippled leg?"

"Witch, don't you talk to me in that tone!" He took a threatening step toward her.

Pat held her ground, raising the paddle with both hands. "If you come close, I'll bean you, Lester! Then I'll call the sheriff and have you hauled off to jail!"

The mention of the sheriff gave him pause. He glanced uneasily out toward the road again and did a double take, blurting out a foul curse word. Pat followed his gaze and reacted with equal parts of relief and dismay to the sight of Clint's automobile. Her fear for herself was swallowed up in fear for Clint. Lester was no match for him in strength, but he was a cowardly bully who would fight dirty. His plan of attack would be to hurt Clint's injured leg.

"You'd better get out of here fast, Lester," she urged. "That's Clint's automobile."

"Don't you tell me what to do!" he yelled at her, but there was panic in his voice. Apparently he was going to take her advice because he made a dash for the door. Pat dropped the paddle and followed behind him. She was right on his heels as he rushed outside.

Clint's Suburban was roaring fast into the parking lot. He'd undoubtedly recognized Lester's pickup and was coming to her rescue. Pat waited until he'd slammed on the brakes before she ran to the driver's side. With the engine still running, he flung open the door and jumped to the ground. A grimace of pain tightened the grim set of his mouth. His expression was murderous.

"You'd better run, you bastard!" he yelled angrily at Lester, who was making a beeline for his truck. "I'll beat you to a pulp!"

"Let him go, Clint!" Pat cried, throwing her arms around his waist. "Please, just let him go without a fight!"

His hands gripped her shoulders. "Did he lay a hand on you?"

"No, he didn't! *Honest!* He was only here a few minutes!"

Lester's truck door slammed, and the engine sputtered and then fired up. He was floorboarding the gas pedal as he backed up, his wheels spinning in the gravel. Clint's fingers tightened, making Pat wince. "Get the hell out of here and don't come back!" he yelled. His lowered tone vibrated with frustration as he spoke to her. "Dammit, you shouldn't have interfered, Pat. If I'd beaten the bastard up, he would think twice about coming back."

"Hey, Clint! You're real brave, hidin' behind a woman's skirts," Lester taunted through the open window of his pickup. "Lucky for you she didn't let you fight me after I warned her I'd have you walkin' on crutches."

He shouted an obscenity and restated it by waving his arm out the window, his middle finger protruding, as he gunned the engine and hightailed it toward the highway.

"What a coward!" Pat said disgustedly.

"Just who the hell were you protecting, anyway? Him or me?" Clint demanded, unwinding her arms from around him. He looked and sounded furious at her.

"Certainly not him. In a fair fight, I knew he wouldn't have a chance against you, but I was afraid if you cornered him, he would take unfair advantage—"

"Finish your sentence," he bit out and completed it for her, "of the fact that I'm a damned cripple."

"You're not a cripple!" she protested. "Don't call yourself that! Please don't be insulted by the way I acted. He bragged about kicking your injured leg, and I couldn't stand the thought of him hurting you!"

He *was* deeply insulted, and her plea for understanding didn't soften the blow to his pride. "You weren't covering up for him when you said he hadn't roughed you up?"

"No. I would never lie to you. About anything. Clint, I'm so sorry."

Her apology wasn't accepted. That was clear from his body language as he climbed into the driver's seat. Pat backed out of the way, and he closed the car door with a force that could have shattered the window of a less sturdy vehicle.

When he returned fifteen minutes later, she had a speech all prepared, but he didn't even come inside the store. He got into the van and left to go and pick up a party.

"Darn it!" Pat exclaimed in frustration.

The rest of the afternoon he hardly said a dozen words to her, and every time she thought she might have a chance to talk to him, a customer dropped in or the phone rang. It was the last straw when he made his final trip of the day, got into his automobile and drove off to his cabin without so much as a terse "See you tomorrow."

I'm just not putting up with this! Pat decided indignantly. If she had to go to his cabin, then she would.

Chapter Twelve

Pat marched across the clearing, noting that the front door of the cabin stood open. "Clint, it's Pat," she called out, tromping up the steps. "I've come to have my say, whether you want to hear it or not!"

The rest of her loud announcement had taken her across the porch to the doorway. She blinked in surprise. He was standing at the sink, naked to the waist. "Oh, I thought you'd be out on the back porch," she said, trying her best not to gawk appreciatively at his deep-chested upper torso with its growth of dark body hair. "I know you don't want me to come here, but it's your own fault for giving me the silent treatment."

He turned around toward the sink without answering, treating her to a view of his back. Whatever he was doing with his hands caused a rippling in the muscles.

"Are you washing dishes?" she asked, stepping over the threshold.

"No," he said shortly.

When no further explanation was forthcoming and also no order to vacate the premises, Pat boldly walked into the kitchen and watched him wringing out a bath towel he'd saturated in a sinkful of steamy water. "A hot compress for your leg?"

"For my shoulder." The correction was curt. "I fell and nearly knocked over one of your trees on my way home last night." He'd shaken out the towel and draped it over the ball of his right shoulder.

"And you've been lifting canoes all day?"

"It hasn't bothered me much."

Sympathy had eroded all Pat's righteous indignation. "I have some ointment at my house. I could go and get it and massage your shoulder. That might soothe the pain."

He shook his head in brusque refusal of her offer. "Heat and ice will do the trick."

"Shall I make you an ice pack?"

She'd taken a step toward the refrigerator. Clint stopped her, grabbing her arm. "I can do it myself."

Pat sighed. "You're still mad at me, aren't you?"

"Yes, I'm mad." He released her arm and turned away from her, jerking the towel from his shoulder and dropping it back into the sink.

"What can I do to make it right, Clint?" she implored, touching his back. A tremor ran though his muscles before he leaned forward, pulling away from her hand.

"Not a damned thing," he said harshly. "Look, didn't you say something about going grocery shopping? I didn't buy motor oil for the van."

She dropped her hand. "I'm leaving now."

Pat paused at the door and glanced back. He hadn't moved. His whole body was tense as though he was willing her to go with every muscle. She had to swallow a huge lump in her throat to speak her parting words: "Don't worry. I won't forget the motor oil."

Her quick light footsteps seemed to leave an echo in the cabin, prolonging the sweet torture of her presence long moments after she'd gone.

I can't handle this, Clint thought. He'd never uttered those words of defeat in his mind once during the worst of his pain and depression in the weeks following his accident. He hadn't even thought them at the lowest ebb of his life when he was a nine-year-old grief-stricken kid. The message rising from the tough, hard core of him had always been *I can take this, dammit.*

His problem in dealing with Pat was that she undermined his toughness and awoke tender emotions. The only part of him capable of hardness when he was near her seemed to be his easily-aroused body. He hadn't operated on a hair trigger since he was in his teens and early twenties. Right this minute Clint was aroused, and the physical frustration added its own urgency to the powerful longings that threatened to get the best of him.

He wanted her with a hunger that was more than physical. A selfish hunger. Pat would be good for him, but he wasn't a good-enough man for her. The struggle to control himself around her was proof in itself of his inadequacy. Being disabled was something he couldn't help, but there was no excuse for not showing some strength of character.

It was a bitter pill to swallow, but Clint wasn't at all sure he could manage the rest of his promised two weeks. The combination of being sexually turned on and eaten up with jealousy of Wells while he was constantly battling the knowledge that he *could* win out over Wells and have Pat for himself might prove to be too much for him.

When he reached the breaking point, he would just have to pack up and go.

"Would you like a cola?" Clint asked. He'd come inside and gone to the back of the store to the coolers. Pat had been counting out change to some customers, who'd just left.

"Yes, I would." She tried not to sound eager and

pleased. He'd been almost friendly this morning for the first time in five days, and she didn't want to do or say anything wrong.

To her delight he brought the two colas to the table and glanced questioningly at her. She'd stayed behind the counter, unsure whether he meant to go immediately outside again. "Can you take a break?" he inquired.

"I could probably be tempted."

He popped open the two cans and sat down. "Homer hasn't been by lately. He's not ailing, is he?"

"No, he's been busy in his vegetable garden." Pat dropped down into Homer's rocking chair and reached for her cola.

"I was afraid the old fellow was a goner last Friday."

"He sure scared me, too. If he'd had a heart attack and died, I would never have forgiven myself."

"It wouldn't have been your fault. The same thing could have happened if Homer had just been visiting instead of tending store for you."

"I hired Lester, so I would have been responsible," Pat insisted. "That reminds me. I had a phone call earlier from a woman named Pearl Fox. She asked to speak to Lester. Evidently he'd led her to believe he was employed here. She said several times, sounding more and more angry, 'Lester *hasn't* been working for you all this week?' Something tells me I got him into hot water with her, whoever she is."

"That no-good bum. He hasn't shown up again, has he?"

"No, I think I've seen the last of Lester. Oh, darn!" she exclaimed, hopping up to go and answer the phone, which had begun ringing. "Tyler's." Pat spoke briskly into the receiver, determined to keep the call short and resume her visit with Clint.

"Miss Tyler?" A child's voice pitched just above a whisper came over the line.

"Mandy?"

"Yes, ma'am. My daddy doesn't know that I'm calling you. He has your number written on the front of the phone book."

"Where's Mrs. Grambly?"

"She went out to the mailbox to get the mail."

The little girl had seized her chance to make a phone call. "So what's up, Mandy?"

"Would you please invite my daddy to bring Jerry and me to your store to see your kittens? I asked him to bring us, but he said we have to have an invitation."

"I'll ask him to bring you soon. Okay?"

"Could we come this afternoon?"

"The kittens are only a week old, Mandy. They're tiny." And cute and cuddly. Pat could imagine the little girl's pleasure in seeing them and petting them. "Tell you what. I'll call your daddy later and suggest it."

"I *told* Jerry you would! Mrs. Grambly just came in the door. I've got to hang up, Miss Tyler. Bye."

Smiling with amusement, Pat cradled the phone. She filled Clint in while she was returning to her chair. "That was Mandy Wells, Jeremy's little girl, calling without anyone's permission to wheedle an invitation to see Mama Cat's kittens. She waited until the housekeeper had stepped outside the house."

"Wells hires a housekeeper full-time?"

"Combination housekeeper, sitter and cook. It's nice for his kids that he can afford that."

"I'll say it's nice." He lifted his cola and drank the rest of it, his throat muscles working, then set the can down and stood.

The break, all too short for Pat, was evidently over.

After he'd gone outside, she made the call to Jeremy and ended up expanding the invitation to include an informal supper with the offer to heat up frozen pizza. He accepted, for the same reason, Pat knew, that he'd asked her out on their three previous dates—loneliness.

She'd learned a new definition of the word. It wasn't a

generalized longing for human company, but a longing to be with Clint. Tonight she would still be lonely and feel incomplete, laughing and talking with Jeremy and his two children, as much as she liked all three of them. Jeremy would be in the same boat, missing Susan.

Which meant she and Jeremy had more in common now than ever before.

Clint was running behind schedule transporting his last party of the day back to the store. He'd had to wait at Rush for forty-five minutes because the group of six college-age guys had arrived ahead of him and gone off hiking. Since it was the final trip, he hadn't really minded. He'd found a quiet spot along the bank of the Buffalo, a short distance from the takeout site, and had sat soaking in the beauty and peacefulness.

I'm going to miss this, he'd thought.

Aside from the main reason he hated to leave the Ozarks—leaving Pat, he hated the thought of leaving the location itself. In a short time, he'd gotten used to breathing the fresh pine-scented air, gotten used to country highways and glimpses of wildlife. He even liked hearing the rural accents of the locals, enjoyed their humor and friendliness and down-to-earth bluntness. If things were different, if Jeremy Wells weren't in the picture—Clint could put roots down here.

He'd not only fallen like a ton of bricks for Pat, but for the spot where she'd grown up in the vicinity of the Buffalo River.

Her canoe-rental business suited him fine, too. He saw a lot of potential for making it more profitable if her means of transporting parties weren't so limited by having just the one shuttle van. That could easily be remedied by repairing the broken-down bus. If Clint stayed, he would tackle putting the bus back into service himself. He would clean up the junk around the place and paint the store. He would suggest some ways of modernizing the running of the operation.

But he *wasn't* going to stay, because Jeremy Wells, who had a college degree in business and ran his own gas station, could do much more to help Pat make Tyler's profitable than Clint could. Wells could assign his mechanic to overhauling the bus. He could give her the benefit of book knowledge and practical experience. He could bankroll capital improvements, in the event that he and Pat decided she would continue running Tyler's after she became Mrs. Jeremy Wells.

The biggest favor Clint could do for Pat was to remove himself as an obstacle between her and a secure future. Over and over, he kept coming to that same disheartening conclusion.

Approaching the intersection of Highway 635 and the more heavily traveled Highway 14, Clint braked to check for traffic. A bright red four-wheel-drive pickup with oversize wheels passed, coming from the direction of Yellville. It brought admiring comments from his passengers, but his attention was fixed on a sporty van traveling at a safe distance behind the pickup.

"Friends of yours?" the guy riding in the passenger seat inquired when Jeremy Wells tooted his horn and waved as he drove past, headed toward Tyler's. His children's waving hands were visible, too.

"Friends of Pat's," Clint answered, feeling as if he'd just been kicked in the gut.

True to her promise to Wells's little girl, Pat had obviously called Wells during the afternoon and invited father and children to pay a visit and see the kittens. She'd thought the last party would have left by now, that Clint would have gone to his cabin and the coast would be clear.

"Hey, man, you can go," a voice called impatiently from the back.

"Keep your pants on, buddy," he snapped. "It's a little late to get in a hurry."

Clint wouldn't have been able to catch up with Wells's van if he'd wanted to, and he definitely didn't want to. He drove slowly, hoping that when he arrived at the store, Pat would have had time to greet Wells and his kids and take them inside. Clint planned to park the shuttle van, get into his automobile, head back out to the highway and go somewhere.

Anywhere.

Call him a coward, but seeing Pat and Wells together at this point was just more than he could endure.

It was a silent ride until the store came into sight. "Hey, look, that cool red pickup came here, too," one of Clint's passengers observed.

"Let's go inside and meet the dude who owns it," suggested the fellow sitting up front by Clint. "I'd like to ask him what kind of gas mileage he gets."

"Naw, we'd better shove off."

Clint paid little attention to the debate. "You guys be sure to get all your things and have a safe trip home," he said as he pulled up and stopped.

"Sorry about holding you up, Clint."

The apology prompted a chorus of others that he didn't have time to listen to. "No hard feelings," he muttered, swinging his door open.

He'd taken several steps, heading toward his vehicle, when Wells's son appeared from nowhere, an eager expression on his face. "Hi, Mr. Adams. I was hoping I'd get to see you."

"Hi, Jerry. How're you doing?" Clint didn't slow down.

"Okay." The boy hurried to keep up. "My dad brought Mandy to see Miss Tyler's kittens. We're having supper with her later at her house. You were right. She is kinda nice. I'd like her if she wasn't dating my dad."

"Your dad's one more lucky guy, in my opinion. I'd give anything to be in his shoes."

"Then why don't you date her yourself? She might like

you better than my dad. He wasn't ever in the marines, like you were.''

"Clint!" Pat's voice called his name from the doorway of the store. "Hold it a minute, would you, please?" He stopped and waited while she walked quickly to him.

"What is it?" he asked, sensing that she was upset about something.

"Bill Lamberts, the man who worked as my driver last year, is inside. He just arrived today from Florida." She gestured toward the bright red pickup.

Clint sucked in a deep breath. "He wants his same job back?"

Pat nodded.

"Was he reliable and hardworking?"

"Pretty much." She sighed. "He can start work tomorrow."

"Hire him," Clint said harshly.

"You could stay on in the cabin for your extra week without paying rent. I owe you that much." Her words were more a plea than an offer.

He shook his head. "I'll be taking off in the morning."

"So soon? At least stay until Monday."

"There's nothing to keep me here. And the sooner I'm gone, the better. For you. For me." He glanced at Jerry Wells, who was listening solemnly to the adults' conversation. "For everybody concerned."

She bit down hard on her quivering bottom lip. "I don't even know how to contact you in Illinois. Will you give me an address or a phone number?"

Clint knew the answer should be no, but he couldn't get it out. "Let me think about it," he said.

"Maybe I can get it from you later tonight?"

Her real question was *Could I see you tonight?* Once again he couldn't force out the refusal he should have spoken. "Maybe."

From the way her face lighted up with hopefulness, he

might have said *Probably.* "You could join the four of us for supper. I'm heating up frozen pizza—"

"No, thanks."

"It probably tastes pretty good, Mr. Adams," Jerry added.

"I wouldn't be good company tonight," Clint said to the boy. "Plus I have some packing to do. You go inside with Miss Tyler, now."

"Yes, sir."

"I'll talk to you later," Pat said. "Come on, Jerry."

"Bye, Mr. Adams."

"You take it easy, Jerry."

Clint spared a glance for the boy, but his eyes were on Pat as she walked away from him. He was memorizing a hundred details that were already stored away in his memory to bring him bittersweet pleasure in the days and months ahead. Her springy stride, the rich gloss of her ponytail, the set of her shoulders, the slim curve of her hips and pert roundness of her rear.

Just like that first day he'd seen her, at Jeremy Wells's gas station, he wanted to follow her, catch up with her and bask in the sunshine of her presence and personality. That day, too, Wells had been inside waiting for her. Wells, the family man, the successful businessman, the upright citizen, the all-around decent, likable guy who would make Pat a great husband. Right from the beginning, Clint hadn't been in the running.

That hadn't kept him from...loving her.

He didn't dare stick around and see her tonight because he didn't trust himself not to tell her he was crazy in love with her. That he wanted her to marry *him,* not Wells.

Clint would be on the highway within an hour, driving north. It was the coward's way, but the only way he could deal with saying goodbye.

"You aren't eating," Jeremy commented, eyeing Pat's piece of pizza on her plate. She'd taken only a couple of bites of it.

"I'm not very hungry," she replied honestly.

"Are you worried that the new driver you hired won't work out?"

"No, I think Bill Lamberts will work out fine."

Jerry helped himself to another slice of pizza. "I think Miss Tyler is sad because Mr. Adams is leaving tomorrow morning, Dad. She wanted him to stay another week."

Pat met Jeremy's questioning gaze and nodded. "Actually, I would have liked him to stay a lot longer."

"I see," he said, his expression and his voice thoughtful.

"Mr. Adams likes Miss Tyler." Jerry addressed his words to his father again. "He told me he'd sure like to be in your shoes."

"Is that so?"

"When did he say that?" Pat asked, her eager tone betraying her.

"Today. Before you came out."

"Mr. Adams just volunteered that information to you?" Jeremy inquired.

"You didn't have much time to carry on a conversation," Pat said. She'd been watching for Clint and had hurried out when she saw that he wasn't coming inside the store.

Jerry finished chewing his mouthful of pizza. "Just time enough to tell him Dad had brought Mandy to see the kittens and we were having supper with you." He slid a reluctant glance at her and at his dad before he continued. "And that he was right about you being nice. And I would probably like you a lot if Dad wasn't dating you."

"His reply was that he'd like to be in my shoes."

Jerry nodded and hesitated, showing the same air of reluctance.

"And you said," Jeremy prompted.

"You won't be mad?"

"It depends on how much you insulted me." The retort

was mild, and a signal passed between father and son, easing the latter's concerns.

"I asked Mr. Adams why he didn't date Miss Tyler himself since she might like him...more than you." He shrugged in apology. "Dad, you went to college instead of going into the marines."

"And also married your mom and had a couple of kids. Not very exciting stuff, compared to driving tanks and fighting in Desert Storm, is it, son?"

Mandy had been quiet long enough, munching on her pizza and looking from one to the other. "I'm glad you married Mom and had us, Daddy," she spoke up in stout support.

"So is your brother, pumpkin." Jeremy reached over and squeezed his son's shoulder.

"What was Mr. Adams's answer to your question about why he didn't date me, Jerry?" Pat asked.

"He didn't have a chance to answer me. You called his name."

She knew what his answer would have been. *Your dad is a better man for Miss Tyler than I am.* But he was so wrong. Jeremy was a fine father. He would make some lucky woman a devoted husband when he remarried. But Clint was the best man for Pat; the man she wanted to be her husband, her partner for life.

Tonight she was going to tell him so.

"I'm glad to see you got your appetite back, Pat," Jeremy remarked in a gently knowing tone. She'd wolfed down the rest of her piece of pizza and was reaching for another. "Hearing about Jerry's conversation with Adams cheered you up considerably."

Pat blushed as she met his gaze. "I hope my appetite's back for good."

"I hope so, too." He helped himself to pizza.

After the meal, both the children were excused to go into the living room and turn on the TV. Jeremy and Pat had a chance to talk more openly while he helped her clear the kitchen table, where they'd had supper.

"I deserve to lose out, the way I've been dragging my heels," he said.

"You didn't lose out," she protested. "There was never any spark between us. Eventually we would have honestly faced up to that fact."

"There is a 'spark' between you and Adams, I take it."

"More like a bonfire. But he's fought it because he hasn't wanted to mess up my chances of marrying you. He sees you as a better catch. At least, I'm hoping that's the real reason."

"How successfully has he fought?"

Pat smiled a dreamy smile. "One night he completely lost the battle." One wonderful night. If she had her way, he would lose a second struggle tonight and make love to her again.

"I imagine that being discharged from the military for a physical disability must have been a big blow to his self-esteem. He's probably feeling down on himself."

"He's referred to himself as a cripple. And pointed out that you were college educated and owned your own business."

"Whereas he might not know at this point how he's going to supplement whatever disability income he'll be receiving. That's rough on any man with pride who isn't an ex-marine."

"Whatever field of work he went into, Clint would soon be in a supervisory position. He sizes up people almost instantly and commands respect. He's intelligent, conscientious, hardworking, decisive."

"Have you expressed all that confidence and admiration to him?"

"No, not in words. But I will now." They'd finished stacking the plates in the sink, and Pat had wiped the table with a wet sponge. She tossed it into the soapy water and dried her hands on a dish towel. "Darn, I wish we'd had this talk at least a week ago. I needed a male perspective. Thanks, Jeremy.''

"Any time." He wrapped an arm around her shoulders and gave her a brotherly hug. "Adams is a lucky guy. I hope things turn out the way you want and the two of you are as happy as—" He broke off.

"As you and Susan were." She finished his sentence for him, her voice soft with her empathy. "I want you to promise me that you'll keep on dating. Call Terri Baker up and ask her out."

"I only saw her that one time. She probably wouldn't remember who I was."

"I'll bet she remembers you."

"If she does, it's because I acted like an idiot that day. I gawked at her and got tongue-tied. And afterward I felt so damned guilty."

"As though you'd been unfaithful to Susan because you were attracted to Terri."

"Yes. Look, don't you worry about me. I'll be fine." He gave her another hug, and Pat hugged him back.

In the living room Mandy and Jerry were engrossed in a movie. "Why are we leaving so early?" the little girl protested in response to her father's announcement that it was time for them to go home.

Jerry provided the answer. "Because we have to leave before Mr. Adams can visit Miss Tyler tonight."

Or vice versa, Pat thought.

"Why?" Mandy persisted.

"Because they want privacy, pumpkin." Jeremy scooped her up into his arms, and she giggled happily, her disappointment forgotten.

Pat accompanied them outside onto the porch and waved goodbye. She would have felt sad if tonight were to be the last occasion when she would enjoy the company of father and son and daughter, all of whom she'd grown very fond of, but there would be other occasions in the future, hopefully with the addition of Clint and some nice woman Jeremy was dating.

But she was counting her chickens, Pat reminded herself, as the taillights of Jeremy's van disappeared from sight. Before she built her hopes up any higher, she needed to hear from Clint's lips what he'd meant by saying he would like to be in Jeremy's shoes.

"What's the hell's going on, woman?" Lester roared at Pearl as he jumped out of his pickup truck. She stood in the doorway of her trailer, his shaving kit in her hands. By the steps sat his battered old suitcase, bulging with his clothes, judging from the fact that the sleeve of one of his plaid shirts that had been on a hanger that morning dangled out. His few other possessions littered the area around the suitcase, among them his twelve-gauge shotgun, his guitar with several broken strings, his Stetson hat and the dress cowboy boots she'd given him for Christmas.

"I'm throwing you out on your butt, you no-good, lying, lazy bum! I ain't supportin' you no more! That's what's going on!" she screamed at the top of her lungs, throwing the kit at him. Lester caught it. "Today I called that Tyler's outfit over by Buffalo Point you're supposed to be working for! You got *fired* last Friday, Lester!"

"I oughta smack you hard! Callin' and checkin' up on me!" he yelled, balling up his right hand in a fist.

She reached inside the trailer and brought out a baseball bat, which she hefted at him. "It might be the last time you ever smack anybody, buster, because I'll brain you! And I wasn't callin' to check up on you! Stupid me, I actually believed you could hold down a job! But you're through pullin' the wool over my eyes. Pick up your trash and go find you another female sucker to move in with!"

"Pearl—"

The trailer door closed with a loud bang, cutting him off. Furious, Lester slammed his kit on the ground, charged up the steps and pounded the metal door with his fists. "Open up, Pearl! Dammit, woman, you can't treat me like this! It ain't right!''

''You'd better be out of this trailer park in five minutes! I've called the sheriff!'' she shouted at him through the barrier.

A window slid open in the neighboring trailer behind him. ''If you keep up the ruckus and I have to come out there and shut you up, I'm gonna break that guitar over your head,'' growled a man's deep voice.

Lester yelled a foul oath, but he hurriedly jammed the Stetson on his head and threw his worldly goods into the back of his pickup. He didn't doubt that Pearl had called the sheriff, and the dude next door was a bodybuilder.

Sure enough, less than a mile from the trailer park, he and a sheriff's deputy in a cruiser passed one another. Lester stepped harder on the gas pedal once the deputy was out of sight.

''Witch!'' he shouted, banging the steering wheel with his fist. But venting his anger and resentment didn't help to solve his immediate problems. Where was he supposed to sleep tonight? And what was he going to use for money to buy himself some supper? He was flat broke. He'd spent the twenty bucks he'd borrowed from Pearl's purse last night.

Lester was out on the streets, homeless and penniless, and it was all Pearl's fault and the fault of that Tyler woman who'd fired him after she'd agreed to keep him on as her driver for a week's trial period. By rights, she owed him the rest of that week's pay. What he ought to do is go and collect it tonight.

Yes, that was what he ought to do. Go and collect the money that was coming to him.

Should she sit out on the porch in the swing and wait a few minutes to give Clint a chance to come to her? No, she was too eager, too anxious to sit or wait, Pat decided.

Minutes later, flashlight in hand, she set out in the darkness, accompanied by Rowdy. With every step, her optimism seemed to dwindle, and doubts crowded in. "What if this is all wishful thinking on my part, Rowdy? What if he doesn't love me back?" she implored her pet. He whined in response, and the plaintive sound was not reassuring.

"I guess I should have waited at my house instead of barging in on him. Actually, he never committed himself to seeing me tonight. When he didn't point-blank refuse, I chose to think he was going along with the idea. He said things like 'I'll think about it' and 'Maybe.'"

Rowdy whined again.

"Please try to give me a little moral support!" Pat pleaded. "Especially since I didn't spritz on any cologne again. That bottle's going to last me a hundred years, at this rate. And I'm not wearing lipstick. I should have taken the time to put on that clingy pink blouse Edna gave me—for good luck, if nothing else."

It was pitch-black in the woods and the darkness had a dreary quality that the beam of the flashlight failed to dispel. Pat peered into the solid wall of tree trunks, straining for a glimpse of light shining from Clint's cabin. "Surely he hasn't gone to bed this early, Rowdy. You think the electricity went off? Wouldn't that be a weird coincidence?"

The sound he made was more a sigh than a whine.

The path opened out into the clearing. Her heart thumping heavily with the anxiety weighing her down, Pat shone her flashlight on the cabin steps and then on the porch as she tramped toward the dark building. The porch was bare. He'd removed the chair, probably returned it to its original place on the back porch. "Clint?" she called. Her voice came out small and unsure.

Silence.

She called out again when she'd reached the steps. "Clint? Please answer if you're there! It's Pat!" After noisily climbing the steps, she crossed the porch and rapped her knuckles hard on the rough surface of the solid wooden door.

No response.

He wasn't there.

"It's early, Rowdy. Maybe he went out to eat." She aimed the beam of light at the spot beside the cabin where the Suburban would have been parked. It was empty. "He'll be back. What do you think? Should we stay here and be a reception committee? Clint probably locked the door, or we could check to see if the electricity's off. If not, I could turn on some lights and make the place more cheerful, couldn't I?"

Pat tested the doorknob. It turned. The door wasn't locked. She pushed it ajar, felt for the light switches. Flipping them, she blinked at the sudden bright light on the porch and in the living area of the cabin. "Nope. Electricity's on. Seems like he would have left the porch light on, doesn't it?"

Her big dog had come up on the porch beside her. Whining, he nudged the door with his nose and made it swing open wider. Pat gazed at the table in front of the sofa. The several magazines and paperback book that had been on the table were gone. Glancing around, she didn't see a single sign of occupancy.

A huge mass of dread had formed in Pat's stomach. "That pizza's giving me indigestion, Rowdy. Maybe Clint has an antacid. You think he'd mind..." On numb legs she crossed to the doorway of the bathroom. The flare of bright light when she flipped the switch revealed no shaving kit. No toothbrush. No toilet articles. "I might be out of luck," she whispered, opening the medicine cabinet. The metal shelves were empty.

Dear God, he was gone. He'd left without saying goodbye.

"No," Pat murmured, the heavy mass inside her ballooning up into her chest like a fast-spreading tumor that fed on anguish and denial. She gulped air into her constricted lungs as she walked slowly to the bedroom.

The covers on the bed were spread neatly. No duffel bag or suitcase in sight anywhere. No single item of clothing hanging on the wooden pegs on the wall.

All the windows were closed, adding to the atmosphere of...vacancy.

"*No,* Clint!" The cry of despair was torn from Pat. "We were supposed to *see* each other tonight!" Tears welled up and flowed down her face, relieving none of the terrible loss. Sobs convulsed her body. Blindly she stumbled over and fell facedown on the bed where he'd slept. But the only scent embedded in the rough weave of the bedspread was the pungent blend of bleach and laundry detergent.

Lester switched off his headlights and coasted up to the store. A light over the door dimly illuminated the front of the building. His stomach growled with hunger as he eased the pickup door open. In addition to the money in the cash register, he intended to help himself to chips and candy bars and cookies to substitute for the supper he hadn't had.

It wasn't like he was stealing. He was just taking what was due him in loose cash and merchandise.

Too bad he couldn't stock up on cigarettes and chewing tobacco. He was almost out of both. Trust a woman not to sell the things a man really enjoyed, Lester reflected sourly, shaking a cigarette out of his last pack and lighting it up with some difficulty. He needed a drink bad to steady his hands.

"There better be some cash in that register," he muttered, taking a deep drag and reaching for his shotgun. It probably wasn't loaded, but carrying it made him feel braver.

Lester tried the door. Naturally it was locked. He tried the several casement windows. They didn't budge. The Tyler witch hadn't left him any choice. It would serve her right to have to replace a busted windowpane. Cursing, he used the butt end of his shotgun to shatter the glass of one pane. A swell of anger made him shatter a couple more, simply out of meanness.

For all his caution in reaching inside to unlock the window, it was just Lester's luck to cut his arm on a jagged edge. He yelped in pain. Climbing in, he bumped his head, knocking the damned Stetson off. He uttered a string of oaths as the hat fell to the ground. On his way out, he would have to remember to pick it up. Not only had it cost a pretty penny, but Lester's name was written on the inside band of the crown.

Finally Lester was standing upright inside the store, able to see the interior in the dim light shining in from outside. Making his way toward the cash register, he took a deep drag on his cigarette, holding it with his thumb and forefinger since it had burned down to a stub by this time—too short a stub for a deep drag. The fiery tip of the tobacco reached his fingertips and singed them during the second before he let out a curse and flicked the unfiltered butt. It sailed through the air and landed on a stack of paper sheets on the counter, where it glowed like an ember.

"Serve the witch right if I burned down her friggin' store," Lester muttered, sucking his burned fingers.

A loud meow from the room at the back of the store scared the wits out of him, causing him to jump. "Shut up!" he yelled, but the cat kept meowing and it was joined by a chorus of weaker meows. Lester had always hated cats. His nerves were in no condition for him to put up with the racket those cats were making. "If you don't shut up, I'll come back there and shoot you!" he shouted. The fact that it was probably an idle threat infuriated him that much more. Aiming the gun toward the rear of the store, he pulled the trigger, expecting nothing more than a click.

The loud blast of the gunshot deafened him and the kicking force nearly jerked his arm out of its socket. The smell of gunpowder filled the air, mingling with the smell of charred paper. "Damned gun was loaded," he muttered, suddenly panicky. In the distance he could hear a dog barking. An image of Pat Tyler's big dog flashed in his mind as he raced behind the counter to the cash register.

The drawer was pulled out an inch or so. Lester jerked it open and stared. Empty. Not even a lousy roll of quarters!

The barking had gotten louder. A woman's voice shouted something. Straining to hear, he was aware of a crackling sound and realized that the top of the counter had burst into flames. The stack of papers had caught fire without him noticing, and the fire had spread to the other odds and ends on the counter.

There wasn't time to stop and play fireman. He had to get the hell out of here before he got caught red-handed!

Lester ran for the window and scrambled through the opening. Once he was outside, he could make out what the woman was shouting over the deep, throaty barking. "Rowdy!" He recognized the name of Pat Tyler's huge dog, and recognized her voice as he dashed for his pickup. He'd almost reached it when he stumbled and fell.

So help him, he didn't deliberately discharge the shotgun, but its loud blast created an explosion of sound waves. With Pat Tyler's scream echoing in his head, Lester picked himself up off the ground, jumped into his pickup and hightailed it as fast as he could toward the highway.

It was an accident. He hadn't shot her on purpose.

He hadn't meant to burn down her store.

None of this was his fault.

Chapter Thirteen

Clint dragged himself out of bed at 5:00 a.m. He'd been awakened by the sound of automobile doors slamming and male voices. The small motel in the Bull Shoals area north of Yellville catered to fishermen who wanted reasonably-priced lodging. From the noises outside, he was the sole paying guest who wasn't up and dressed and headed for a fishing spot.

He hadn't slept worth a damn. For all the rest he'd gotten, he might as well have kept driving north instead of stopping and spending the night.

A hot shower didn't do much to wash away Clint's fatigue or boost his spirits. His reflection in the mirror was grim and disheartened as he lathered up his face to shave.

He was doing the right thing, but it sure felt lousy. The rest of his life without Pat seemed like a drawn-out, miserable existence.

By five-twenty Clint was lugging his duffel bag out to his vehicle, the only one remaining by this time. Fifteen

minutes later he stopped at a restaurant that was doing a
brisk early-morning breakfast business. All he wanted was
coffee, but he intended to eat some breakfast anyway.

Nine-tenths of the customers were men, he saw when he
entered. The tables were all occupied, but there was a space
at the counter. Clint took it and was soon sipping a mug
of coffee a heavyset waitress served him.

She'd just set his order of pancakes in front of him when
a man who was obviously a local came in. Several people,
including the waitress, Annie, greeted him by name, calling
him Wayne. From the good-natured banter, Clint learned
that Wayne's car had been stolen by an escaped convict
during the past year and later recovered and returned to
him. Obviously the incident was his claim to fame in a low-
crime region of Arkansas.

"Heard on the radio this morning that somebody broke
into a store over by Buffalo Point last night and set it on
fire," Wayne remarked, sitting down at the counter a few
chairs away from Clint. "One of them canoe-rental
places."

Clint's fork clattered on his plate as he laid it down.
"Which one?" he asked.

"Lemme think. Taylor's? It started with a *T*."

"Tyler's."

"That's the name."

Clint was already on his feet and pulling out his wallet
to pay for his partially-eaten breakfast. "Was anyone hurt?
Did the store burn down?"

Wayne couldn't answer the questions put to him. He'd
already volunteered everything he knew. "You can call the
sheriff's office," he suggested as Clint was headed out the
door.

"Mister, you left a twenty," the waitress called.

"Keep the change."

If he'd thrown down a hundred-dollar bill, Clint wouldn't
have waited. The only thing important to him was making
sure that Pat was all right. If she'd gotten hurt, he would

never forgive himself for not having been there to protect her.

Clint broke the speed limit, but the distance he'd traveled less than twenty-four hours ago seemed to have doubled or tripled. Finally the first Tyler's sign came into view and a mile farther on, the second sign with the arrow pointing down the road to the store. He took the turn as fast as he dared and accelerated, his wheels spurting gravel.

In his mind he'd been imagining the charred remains of the store. When it came into sight, familiar and shabby with no apparent damage to the exterior, his relief was enormous. At least it hadn't burned down. Parked outside were Wells's van and Homer's pickup, along with Lamberts's flashy four-by-four and Pat's old shuttle van. Were Wells and Homer inside with Pat? Or were they here on her behalf, assessing the damage and discussing emergency measures for operating her business for her on a temporary basis? The worst Clint had allowed himself to imagine was that Pat might be hospitalized.

He couldn't bear to think of a world without her.

For a moment he didn't believe his eyes when she appeared in the doorway of the store, a smile breaking across her face. Clint slammed on the brakes, jarring his neck, and drove at a safer pace, more grateful than he'd ever been in his life. *She was okay.* Joy exploded inside him as she walked with her bouncy stride to meet him, radiating her zest for life and happiness to see him.

He killed the engine, flung open the door and slid to the ground all in one motion. By then she was there and went into his arms. He picked her up and held her tight against him.

"You came back!" she exclaimed, hugging him around the neck.

"Are you all right?"

"Now I am. Last night I wanted to die when I discovered you were gone. I love you so much, Clint."

"I love you, too." The words he'd never spoken before

in his life came out easily. There was no taking them back—now or ever.

"I'm so *happy!*" she whispered.

"You're not getting much of a bargain in me. I'm an ex-marine with a high-school education." His bum leg no longer seemed a big liability.

"Oh, yes, I am getting a bargain. You're a hardworking guy with all the qualifications I need in a business partner. But most important, you're the man I always hoped would come along someday. I'd about given up and was ready to settle for less. You make me feel sexy and pretty—the way I've never felt before."

"You *are* sexy and pretty. And sweet and natural and outgoing. I was crazy about you within the first five minutes I met you."

"Really?" She drew back to look into his face. "Oh, Clint, that's so romantic it gives me goose bumps."

He kissed her on the lips, tenderness and possessiveness welling up in his chest. She kissed him back, and hunger and desire kicked in.

"Kinda early in the day fer that passionate kind of kissin', ain't it?" Homer drawled. "'Specially with an audience."

Reluctantly Clint ended the kiss and glanced up to see the old man standing about ten yards away. With him were Jeremy Wells and a short, powerfully-built fellow in his twenties. Clint assumed he was Bill Lamberts. All three men were grinning. Pat had looked over and seen them, but she was still slow about loosening her arms, as Clint put her down. He turned her around, clasping her waist and keeping her in front of him.

"Glad you're back, Clint," Jeremy said. He looked and sounded sincere. "Pat, I'll leave you in Clint's capable hands. Literally," he added, smiling.

"Thanks, Jeremy, for coming out and checking on me."

"Don't mention it. I'm glad the damage from the fire was minor and that you didn't get shot."

"Shot?" Clint questioned, his tone fierce. "The bastard who broke into your store shot at you?"

Pat covered his hands with hers, and he realized he'd tightened his hold on her. "I'll tell you all about it later," she promised.

"I'm off," Jeremy said and with a farewell salute, started for his van. Suddenly he stopped. His grin was mischievous. "It may be premature to bring up wedding plans, Pat, but don't forget you already have a flower girl lined up."

She glanced up at Clint, giving him a glimpse of her flushed cheeks. "It is a little premature since the subject of getting married hasn't come up."

Clint squeezed her waist. "It will, though."

Pat twisted around to smile up into his face, her own aglow with happiness.

"Seems like a sure bet to me," Jeremy said. "This time I really am going."

Homer cleared his throat to draw attention to himself. He was beaming and grinning from ear to ear. "Reckon I'd better have Edna air out my suit I wear to funerals and weddin's. This is mighty excitin' news for everybody but Bill, here. He's wonderin' whether he's gonna have to find him another job."

"Clint and Bill haven't met." Pat had obviously just come to that realization. She moved to Clint's side so that he could shake hands with the younger man, who stepped forward.

"No hard feelings, Pat," Lamberts said. "I can probably get on with another outfitter. I came to you first."

"I appreciate that, Bill. It's really Clint's decision as to whether we'll need you." She looked questioningly at Clint.

There wasn't any need to deliberate. "There's a lot to be done around here. It would free me up if Bill stayed on. Once I get the bus running, you'll have it and the van. You can use him and me both as drivers."

"Makes sense to me." She smiled at Lamberts. "You're still on the payroll."

"Good deal." Bill walked away.

Homer had stood by, watching and listening. "Something tells me business is about to pick up around here," he declared in a pleased voice, adjusting the straps of his overalls. "Well, it's mighty nice visitin' with you folks, but I'd better go see how many weeds sprouted up in my vegetable patch." He ambled toward his pickup.

"Bye, Homer."

Clint added his gruff farewell. "Don't be a stranger, Homer."

Pat linked her arm in Clint's and led him inside the store, filling him in on the details of last night's break-in. "A gunshot woke me up about eleven-thirty. I'd fallen asleep in your cabin. Old Rowdy went charging down the hill toward the store, barking like crazy. I ran after him, trying to call him back. I was afraid he would get shot. I saw an old pickup parked in front of the store."

Clint was in a cold sweat by this point in the story. "I hope you stopped and ran to your house and called the sheriff."

"No, I'd caught up with Rowdy and was holding on to his collar, but he was in his guard-dog mode. A man came running out of the store. Another gunshot went off. It scared the dickens out of me, and I screamed bloody murder. The pickup drove off. I ran on to the store and saw the blaze inside. My first thought was rescuing poor Mama Cat and her kittens, but I didn't have my keys to unlock the back door. So I hauled a hose through the open window and put out the fire. And then went and called the sheriff. Look, what a mess." She gestured at the front counter, which had partially burned. "The cash register is ruined."

"You needed a new cash register anyway. And I can rebuild that counter today. What I *couldn't* do is bring you back to life. Dammit, you might have been *killed!*" He wrapped his arms around her and held her close.

She hugged him tight around the waist. "Now I'm twice as glad I wasn't. Guess who the thief was."

"He's been caught?"

"The dummy left his hat with his name written on the inside band, in big block letters. Lester Madden. The sheriff arrested him and put him in jail."

Clint couldn't keep from voicing the punishment he would like to mete out personally.

"Where did you go last night?" Pat asked and followed up with more questions regarding the sequence of events that had brought him back to Tyler's. "So, if Lester hadn't broken in or if he had and you didn't hear anything about it, you would have kept traveling north?"

"Not because I wanted to."

She was silent, absorbing the answer that was still *yes*. "Then I guess Lester saved me a whole lot of trouble in tracking you down."

"Tracking me down?"

"With Jeremy's help."

"Wells was going to help you locate me?"

"He's a good friend. I hope someday he can find someone to love again. Maybe..." Her voice drifted off.

"Maybe what?"

"You remember I mentioned Terri Baker the night we made love? The girl all the boys always flipped over? Well, she may be back in town. I *could* call her and try to play matchmaker, but the truth is, I don't want you to meet her."

"Does she wear her hair in a ponytail?" Clint asked tenderly, threading his fingers through her glossy hair.

"Are you kidding? Not Terri. She has this gorgeous, naturally-curly auburn-colored hair."

"Does she have blue eyes that sparkle?"

"No, she has jade green eyes."

"Does she walk like she's bouncing on air?"

"She walks like a Miss America contestant, which is what she was."

"Then you don't have anything to worry about. Terri Baker can't hold a candle to you—not in my eyes."

Clint lifted her up against him. Pat framed his face in her hands and gazed into his eyes. He thought his heart would burst with his love for her when the anxiousness in her expression faded into belief, which gave way to female confidence. She pressed her lips to his and suggested, "Let's go take your things to my house."

He kissed her with passion and warned, "It won't be a quick trip, baby."

She smiled a seductive smile. "I was counting on that."

*   *   *   *   *

We have a magnificent new set of linked books
starting next month, all by favourite
Special Edition™ writer **Marie Ferrarella**.
Don't miss any of the
BABY OF THE MONTH CLUB books.

BABY'S FIRST CHRISTMAS

is the novel that starts everything
and here's a sneak preview...

Chapter One

"What do you mean, you don't have it?"

Sullivan Travis's voice thundered off the small [of]fice's glass walls, filtering out into the stark white [re]ception area.

The young woman looked up at him, torn between [be]ing annoyed and being intimidated. They didn't get [m]any irate people at the sperm bank. At least, none [sin]ce she'd been there, but there was a guard on duty [ju]st in case.

[M]artha Riley cleared her voice and tried to sound [of]ficial. "It's been used, Mr. Travis." What had he [th]ought they would do with his "donation"? After all, [he] had been paid for his contribution. It was the [in]stitute's property now, not his.

"Great, just great." He blew out a breath, momentarily stumped. *Now what?*

Sullivan ran his hand through his hair as he sighed. A rebel from the moment he formed his first words, Derek Travis had been one of a kind. He had been the epitome of the prodigal son, except that he had never returned home to make amends.

This latest stunt defied description. It was outrageous, even for Derek. Sullivan had still been reeling from his brother's sudden death when he had come across the letter from the sperm bank among Derek's possessions. He'd stared at it for several minutes, stunned. What made it all the more bewildering was that the letter hadn't been addressed to Derek. It had been addressed to *him*, care of Derek.

Derek had sold his connection to the future, his potential offspring, for what amounted to a few dollars. Sullivan assumed he'd done it to buy art supplies. Getting back at his father was only an added bonus, and he had put Sullivan's name to it, compounding the embarrassment.

The technician touched his arm hesitantly. "Are you all right? I mean, that *is* why you donated the sperm, isn't it? So it could be used?"

Sullivan thought of saying that *he* hadn't donated any part of himself, that it was his brother who had done it and then signed *his* name to the form.

"That's just it. I've changed my mind. I want to buy it back." He paused significantly. "At any cost."

The woman keyed in something on the computer. "According to my records, your..."

Raising her eyes to his, Martha blushed, then flustered, began again. "It was implanted March twenty-fifth." Her fingers slipped from the keyboard. "I'm afraid that it really is too late."

Sullivan looked at the technician. "All right, who was the recipient?"

The woman shook her head. "I'm afraid I really can't tell you that. It's against our confidentiality policy."

He could appreciate her dilemma, but he had a larger one to consider. "I realize that there are rules and regulations—"

She looked at him apologetically. Sullivan took out his wallet, his eyes on hers.

Her eyes were glued to the hundred dollar bill Sullivan carefully laid out on her desk.

She chewed on her lower lip. "It would mean my job if I showed you."

He added a second hundred to the first, carefully flattening a curled edge. "I'm not asking you to show me the name," he assured her. His eyes shifted to the computer. "You could, however, pull up the right screen, and then perhaps..."

"Drop your pencil on the floor," he finally suggested. "If it rolled under the desk, it might take you a few seconds to locate it."

The woman stared at the bills, tempted. Debating. The debate was summarily terminated when a third bill joined the first two.

Within moments he had a name, an address and a telephone number, as well as a sick feeling in the pit of his stomach. Marlene Bailey, whoever she was, was now carrying his brother's child.

"Thank you, Ms.—" Sullivan glanced down at the nameplate on the woman's desk "—Riley. You've been a great help."

With that he walked out of the office. He heard her sigh of relief in the background.

Too many people could be bought, he thought, as he hurried out of the building. The fact saddened him even though it did make his life easier. There was no honor left in the world, no principles. But then that was a given.

What was also a given, he decided as he got into his car, was that he intended to have Ms. Marlene Bailey sign over custody of her unborn child. The child would be a Travis, entitled to everything that went with the name.

He wondered just how much Marlene Bailey would hold out for before caving in.

* * *

Don't miss
Baby's First Christmas
A Silhouette Special Edition® by Marie Ferrarella
Available in December 1997

WANTED
FOR THE NEW YEAR:

Three gorgeous men ready to marry

New Year's Resolution: Husband

Usher in the New Year with three of the sexiest,
most eligible mates-to-be brought to you by
three of Silhouette's bestselling authors—

Anne Stuart

Rebecca Brandewyne

Carla Neggers

Available: December 1997

Price: £4.99

COMING NEXT MONTH

BABY'S FIRST CHRISTMAS Marie Ferrarella

The Baby of the Month Club

Marlene Bailey's baby was due at Christmas, and everything was going really well until Sullivan Travis turned up. He said that her baby was also his late brother's child and he wanted custody! But did he want Marlene, too?

HOLLY AND MISTLETOE Susan Mallery

Hometown Heartbreakers

Jordan Haynes needed someone to stay with him until he was back on his feet again and, as he'd injured himself rescuing her cat, Holly Garrett got the job. Together over the Christmas holidays...and beyond?

BAREFOOT BRIDE Diana Whitney

Parenthood

Reed Morgan found a bedraggled bride beside the road and his kids wanted to keep her. It was a mystery where she'd come from and no one was more in the dark than the lady herself, but she knew she wanted to stay!

PLEASE TAKE CARE OF WILLIE Tracy Sinclair

Cupid's Little Helpers

Alexandra Reynolds stepped into the breach when young Willie's mother just disappeared. That brought Willie's uncle, rugged Chase Mainwaring, into her life. When someone tried to kidnap Willie, Chase was a tower of strength and Alex realised he had a wonderfully broad pair of shoulders!

THE SHERIFF'S PROPOSAL Karen Rose Smith

Meg Dawson thought her whirlwind romance with Logan MacDonald would never lead to anything permanent—but then she discovered she was pregnant!

THE MOTHER OF HIS SON Janis Reams Hudson

For years Luke Ryan had wondered what had happened to drive Bethany Martin from his arms, but he'd never stopped loving her. Now she was back...and she'd brought her fifteen-year-old son with her!

COMING NEXT MONTH FROM

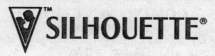

Intrigue
Danger, deception and desire

A MAN OF SECRETS Amanda Stevens
BABY IN MY ARMS Madeline Harper
PROTECT ME, LOVE Alice Orr
SUNRISE VOWS Carla Cassidy

Desire
*Provocative, sensual love stories for the
woman of today*

MONTANA CHRISTMAS Jackie Merritt
A BRIDE FOR CRIMSON FALLS Cindy Gerard
LOVE-CHILD Metsy Hingle
GABRIEL'S BRIDE Suzannah Davis
CHRISTMAS ELOPEMENT Anne Eames
JINGLE BELL BABY Kate Little

Sensation
*A thrilling mix of passion, adventure
and drama*

A BRIDE FOR SAINT NICK Carole Buck
SECOND FATHER Sally Tyler Hayes
FRISCO'S KID Suzanne Brockmann
THE ONE WHO ALMOST GOT AWAY Alicia Scott

WINTER WARMERS

How would you like to win a year's supply of Silhouette® books? Well you can and they're FREE! Simply complete the competition below and send it to us by 31st May 1998. The first five correct entries picked after the closing date will each win a year's subscription to the Silhouette series of their choice. What could be easier?

THERMAL SOCKS	RAINCOAT	RADIATOR
TIGHTS	WOOLY HAT	CARDIGAN
BLANKET	SCARF	LOG FIRE
WELLINGTONS	GLOVES	JUMPER

T	H	E	R	M	A	L	S	O	C	K	S
I	Q	S	R	E	P	M	U	J	I	N	O
G	A	S	T	I	S	N	O	I	O	E	E
H	T	G	R	A	D	I	A	T	O	R	L
T	A	C	A	R	D	I	G	A	N	A	T
S	H	F	G	O	L	N	Q	S	W	I	E
J	Y	H	J	K	I	Y	R	C	A	N	K
H	L	F	N	L	W	E	T	A	N	C	N
B	O	V	L	O	G	F	I	R	E	O	A
D	O	E	A	D	F	G	J	F	K	A	L
C	W	A	E	G	L	O	V	E	S	T	B

C7K

Please turn over for details of how to enter ⇨

HOW TO ENTER

There is a list of twelve words overleaf all of which
are used to keep you warm and dry when it's cold
and wet. Each of these words, is hidden
somewhere in the grid for you to find. They may
appear forwards, backwards or diagonally. As you
find each one, draw a line through it. When you
have found all twelve, don't forget to fill in the
coupon below, pop this page into an envelope and
post it today—you don't even need a stamp! Hurry
competition ends 31st May 1998.

Silhouette Winter Warmers Competition
FREEPOST CN81, Croydon, Surrey, CR9 3WZ
EIRE readers send competition to PO Box 4546, Dublin 24.

Please tick the series you would like to receive
if you are one of the lucky winners

Sensation™ ❏ Intrigue™ ❏ Desire™ ❏
Special Edition™ ❏

Are you a Reader Service™ Subscriber?   Yes ❏   No ❏

Name ....
                              (BLOCK CAPITALS PLEASE)
Address ....

....

....Postcode ....

(I am over 18 years of age)   C7K

One application per household. Competition open to residents of the
UK and Ireland only. You may be mailed with offers from other
reputable companies as a result of this application. If you would prefer
not to receive such offers, please tick box. ❏

Silhouette® is used under licence by
Harlequin Mills & Boon Limited.

**The prequel to *Rising Tides*—where the
foundations of the Gerritsen family
are carefully crafted.**

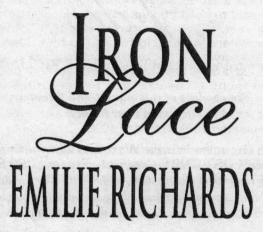

IRON *Lace*

EMILIE RICHARDS

Behind the iron lace gates of wealthy New Orleans,
and beneath the veneer of her society name, lingers
truths that Aurore Gerritsen has hidden for a lifetime—truths that threaten to change forever the
lives of her unsuspecting family. Now, as Aurore
faces her own mortality, she needs to reveal the
secrets that have haunted her for so many years.

"...vividly drawn characters...brilliantly complex work"
—Affaire de Coeur

MIRA® **AVAILABLE NOW IN PAPERBACK**

Get swept away by

RISING
Tides

by award-winning author EMILIE RICHARDS

The reading of a woman's will threatens to destroy her family.

In this explosive sequel to the critically acclaimed Iron Lace, family, friends and strangers gather for the reading of Aurore Gerritsen's will. The threat of an approaching hurricane becomes a minor incident as each bequest reveals yet another dark family secret.

Valid only in the UK & Ireland against purchases made in retail outlets and not in conjunction with any Reader Service or other offer.

50ᵖ OFF
COUPON
VALID UNTIL: 31.1.1998

EMILIE RICHARDS' *RISING TIDES*

To the Customer: This coupon can be used in part payment for a copy of Emilie Richards' RISING TIDES. Only one coupon can be used against each copy purchased. Valid only in the UK & Ireland against purchases made in retail outlets and not in conjunction with any Reader Service or other offer. Please do not attempt to redeem this coupon against any other product as refusal to accept may cause embarrassment and delay at the checkout.

To the Retailer: Harlequin Mills & Boon will redeem this coupon at face value provided only that it has been taken in part payment for a copy of Emilie Richards' RISING TIDES. The company reserves the right to refuse payment against misredeemed coupons. Please submit coupons to: Harlequin Mills & Boon Ltd. NCH Dept 730, Corby, Northants NN17 1NN.

9 904170 190503

0472 00172